LIES JANE AUSTEN
TOLD ME

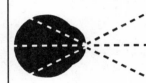

This Large Print Book carries the
Seal of Approval of N.A.V.H.

PROPER ROMANCE

LIES JANE AUSTEN TOLD ME

JULIE WRIGHT

THORNDIKE PRESS
A part of Gale, a Cengage Company

Farmington Hills, Mich • San Francisco • New York • Waterville, Maine
Meriden, Conn • Mason, Ohio • Chicago

Copyright © 2017 by Julie Wright.
Proper Romance® is a registered trademark.
Thorndike Press, a part of Gale, a Cengage Company.

LIBRARY OF CONGRESS CIP DATA ON FILE.
CATALOGUING IN PUBLICATION FOR THIS BOOK
IS AVAILABLE FROM THE LIBRARY OF CONGRESS

ISBN-13: 978-1-4328-6423-1 (hardcover alk. paper)

Published in 2019 by arrangement with Deseret Book Company/Shadow Mountain

Printed in the United States of America
1 2 3 4 5 6 7 23 22 21 20 19

For Jane Austen
For being with me through
heartbreak and true love.
For never leaving me while I
forged my own path
through the wildlands of romance.
And for giving me Mr. Darcy.
I owe you big-time for that one.

CHAPTER ONE

"It is a truth universally acknowledged,
that a single man in possession of a good
fortune, must be in want of a wife."
— JANE AUSTEN, *Pride and Prejudice*

Jane Austen is a horrific liar.

I used to believe that Jane, *my* Jane, could never be wrong about anything. She was the quintessential authority on all things to do with love, romance, and matrimony. Her complete works were the guidelines and rules I lived my romantic life by, beginning with my first introduction to the Regency period when I was fifteen years old and my best friend's mother invited us to join her in watching the movie *Emma* — the version with Gwyneth Paltrow in it.

How could I not love an author who wrote a book and named it after me? It didn't hurt that I shared a lot of the same features as Gwyneth Paltrow: pale blonde hair, pale skin, pale blue eyes.

But as I moved into my midtwenties and no men ever acted as gallantly as Mr. Knightley or Mr. Darcy, where no one ever called my blue eyes "fine" or tucked a wayward strand of my hair behind my ear, I came to a startling and wretched revelation.

Jane never found love.

Sure, she'd been engaged to the lucky Harris Bigg-Wither for all of one night until she recalled her acceptance the next day. She must have at least liked poor Harris on some level or she never would have said yes in the first place, but she couldn't have loved him or that *yes* wouldn't have been chased down by such an immediate *no.* And no matter how much we, as her adoring fans, wished for her to have felt real love with Tom Lefroy, how much of that is just wishful thinking on our part? How much of that is us refusing to accept that Jane never had the happily ever after she made us believe we could have?

Experience from my collegiate years taught me that it was far better to take advice from people who had walked the walk instead of just talked the talk. Jane died an unmarried woman, which in her day was something disastrous. In my current modern-day America, married or unmarried didn't matter much. But to be un-loved . . . *that* was disastrous. And I'd spent so much of my time being unloved that I knew something had to change if I wanted a different ending from the one my once-hero author had. I had to stop believing her.

The bad thing, the secret I carried with me all through my liberal education and feminist discussions with my friends as I worked my way to the executive levels in my company, was that I loved *love*. I wanted to be loved and to give love and to fight and make up and smile across the room at the one my heart raced for — smile because he was mine. I wanted it too much and was disappointed too often. Jane and I had to split up.

Breaking up with Jane was far worse than breaking up with any boyfriend. I felt as jilted by that lady author from two hundred years ago as I'd ever felt in love. The revela-tion of Austen's deceit allowed me to turn my focus to work instead of romance. Which was why I was spending the end of a Friday before a holiday weekend in the office instead of chasing ridiculous, romantic dreams.

"What are you still doing here?" Debbie asked me as she glanced out the glass windows of my office to where the marketing department gathered at the sofas for the meeting. A few of my coworkers cast curious glances in our direction — likely wanting to know the answer to Debbie's question.

"I should think it's obvious. We have a meeting before everyone goes home."

She growled her frustration and shook her frizzy blonde head. "Yes. *We* have a meeting. As in everyone in marketing *except* our CMO — that's you, Ms. Pierce. *You* are not invited to this meeting because it means you would end up missing something far more important. You were supposed to be gone hours ago."

I opened my top left drawer to grab my iPad, where I'd already jotted down the notes I wanted to review for the launch of the company's new gym in La Jolla. For the last thirty years, Kinetics had been one of the fastest-growing gyms in the nation. We had at least one location in every state throughout the West and Midwest; in California, we had twenty-two gyms lining the entire coast. Between dealing with getting new memberships, we also needed to advertise the gift store and restaurant located within each establishment since those areas were open to the public without requiring a gym membership.

I had no intention of letting anything fall through the cracks.

I purposely avoided Debbie's eye. "There will be other weekends."

"Emma, honey, when a hot, rich man invites you to join him for the weekend at his parents' estate, you know he's not looking at it as just *any* weekend. You only meet the parents when it's serious."

A few more curious glances were cast in our direction from the marketing team. I wanted to drop the blinds in my windows to keep the gawkers from staring, but when I'd been hired, I'd vowed to have complete transparency. That meant the blinds stayed up. Always.

"Blake understands. He knows this move up in the company means a lot to me. He's supportive of me making my own future."

"Even when you could be making a future *together*?"

I hedged the conversation about Blake inviting me home by narrowing my eyes and folding my arms over my chest. "What exactly did you tell the team that makes them stare at me as if I'm about to do a magic show?"

She finally stopped looking accusatory and had the good sense to look guilty. "I might have told them you'd be leaving early today and that you'd be coming back with a ring on your hand."

"Debbie!"

"What? It might have been true if you'd actually gone! You're such a fraidycat!"

"Since when has being a responsible executive manager been described as a fraidycat?"

"Since it became synonymous with commitment dodging. Blake is a nice guy. He's well connected, he's hot, and he's rich. What are you doing here when you could be there?"

Her points speared me with the precision of honesty. "I haven't been here very long. I want to prove myself," I finally said.

She sat on my desk. I hated when she did that. "Taking a Friday off is not going to impress the other execs. None of them are even here today. You being here will get you fired for making them look bad." She laughed like she'd made a great joke.

"I just want them to take me seriously. The problem with being twenty-six, blonde, and female is that no one considers you the boss; they think you're the one doing the Starbucks run."

"Oh, please. No one sees you as anything but a really creative leader. And because you gave up a weekend with your guy, you're going to be a *single* creative leader. How is it you read all those romances and watch all those romantic movies with women in corsets and yet reject your own matrimonial opportunity?"

I frowned. It was like she knew I had planned on spending the night having a *Pride and Prejudice* marathon at my best friend's apartment instead of meeting my boyfriend's parents. Breaking up with Jane's ideology did not mean I had to break up with her entertainment. Especially when Darcy in a wet shirt was part of that entertainment.

I knew Debbie was convinced Blake was going to propose, but I blew it off. Silvia, my best friend, had also made several hints that maybe Blake was getting serious, but I always laughed at her. What if both my friends were right?

"He's never mentioned anything about a ring. You're being melodramatic."

"You said yourself he's the sort of guy who likes big surprises. He probably has something crazy romantic planned." Her eyes widened along with her smile. "Oh! You could totally turn this around. You should meet him halfway on that!"

I scooted her off my desk to grab the magazines I needed for the meeting. "You're not making sense."

"If you surprised him by showing up anyway, he'll know that you care and that you can be spontaneous."

"I can be spontaneous."

She turned away from me but not before I caught the eye-roll of incredulity.

"I can!"

She whirled on me, a wicked gleam in her eye. "Prove it!" She tugged the magazines and iPad from my grip. "Go meet up with Blake. You can be there before bedtime, enjoy your weekend, get engaged, and trust that your marketing team knows what they're doing, unlike our last CMO, who never believed we were capable of anything and who spent more time with the advertising models than he did the marketing proposals."

I made an attempt to get my stuff back, but when she danced out of my reach, I gave up. Wrestling with her for everything would only end up with electronics smashed on the hardwood floor.

What if she was right? What if Blake intended to propose? Was I so determined to prove myself as a career woman that I was giving up having a normal life? But going to his parents' house, as if a daring romantic gesture on my part would guarantee me the happy ending, was just what Jane Austen would have wanted me to do. And Jane and I weren't on speaking terms.

"Unless you don't really love him?" Debbie's voice softened as if she hadn't considered the idea before that very moment.

My head shot up. "Of course I love him. He's amazing. He's funny and sweet and charming." I left out the hot and rich part since they were not only self-evident but also trivial. Trivial didn't matter long-term. And something I prided myself on were my long-term goals. Blake was a long-term goal, wasn't he? Jane be hanged. Blake mattered to me. A lot. "Fine. I'll go."

Debbie grinned.

"But not before I walk you through my notes and ideas for the store launch."

Though the grin didn't disappear, it faltered slightly. She probably hoped my leaving meant I'd cancel the meeting.

A few hours later, I was packed and in the backseat of a hired vehicle idling in front of a cobbled driveway caged off by the immense wrought-iron gate of Blake's family estate in San Diego. Traffic had been murder, and while I'd been stuck on the freeway, the sun had yawned its way to bed. The long drive had been painfully filled with screamo music, stale cigarette smoke, and a driver who wanted to argue politics with the victims he managed to get in his backseat. I planned on leaving a scathing review online.

I was grateful to escape and had no intentions of using a hired vehicle service again in the near future if I could help it.

The gate stood slightly ajar, enough space for a single person to squiggle through but certainly not enough for a car. If I wanted to really surprise Blake, it would be a mistake to ring him up and have him open the gates wider. I sucked in a deep breath for courage.

No matter what I told Debbie, spontaneity was something I read about in books, not something I actively participated in. I imagined his face lighting up with delight when he saw me, him taking me into his arms, and us losing ourselves in toe-curling, heart-stopping-and-pounding-all-at-once kisses.

Kissing Blake never disappointed me. And tonight of all nights, he would drown me in his kiss, and I would forget my ambitions at work and my fear of not being wanted. Debbie was right. Why else would he have invited me to his parents' estate if not to make our situation more permanent?

How many times had my best friend, Silvia, tried telling me the same thing, that

Blake loved me, that I was worthy of the love of a beautiful, well-connected, charming man?

I touched my fingertips to the big *H* — for the family's last name, Hampton — that graced the middle of the iron gate. Before I could talk myself out of it, I slipped inside the grounds. My carry-on bag didn't slide through so easily and ended up getting scraped and scratched as I forced it through the narrow opening.

Rounding the bend in the cobbled drive, my bag thumping behind me on its wheels, I actually gasped. The green, manicured expanse that led to the house could have been its own park. The driveway circled an elegant fountain, and the portico and central turrets had a decidedly Tuscan design. The smell of flowers dripped off every molecule of oxygen I breathed. The grounds reminded me of how I imagined Pemberley when I read *Pride and Prejudice* for the first time. A giggle bubbled up from me, along with the thought, "and of this place, I might have been mistress!"

Blake talked about his home, his childhood, his brother, his life, but I'd never comprehended the vastness of it until that moment. My father had provided well for me growing up, but the Hamptons lived a whole new level of comfortable. What kind of people had a mile-long driveway?

Celebrities and one percenters.

I knew Blake had a dog named Chester, so for a moment I worried a Doberman or pit bull might greet me with snarls and snapping jaws, but the entire place seemed deserted.

I took another deep breath and slowly exhaled once I reached the doorstep and pushed the doorbell. What if his mother answered? Was I ready to meet the parents? And if his brother answered? Was I ready to meet the brother Blake referred to as a saint? After considering it for several long moments, I realized that, yes, I was ready to meet the parents, the brother, the dog. Not having a mother or siblings of my own made the prospect of meeting someone else's a little terrifying, but I loved Blake. I could do this.

I frowned. It would help my readiness a lot if someone actually answered the door. I rang again, listening to the elegant chimes of "Ode to Joy" echo through the house. I knocked for good measure.

Through the intercom, Blake's voice fuzzed. "Emma?"

Startled that he knew it was me even though he hadn't opened the door, I answered, "Yeah, it's me working on my spontaneity. Surprise!"

"I'll be right down." The fuzz of the intercom cut off, leaving me to decipher his clipped tone.

He didn't sound happy to hear from me at all.

When the door opened, he stood in dress pants and a nice button-up shirt, his hair perfect. He would have been breathtakingly handsome if his expression wasn't so bewildered. I didn't miss the fact that he didn't open the door wide enough to actually invite me inside. Alarm bells clamored in my head.

"What are you doing here?" he asked.

It was the same question Debbie had asked me at work not many hours before. At least for her I had a good answer. For him, I suddenly didn't know what I was doing. "You invited me." My gaze slid past his shoulder to the interior of the house behind him. Was it my imagination or did he tighten the door against him to form a barrier?

He glanced to the circular driveway behind me. "Where's your car?"

"I hired a car so we could drive back together on Sunday."

"Oh."

"Blake?"

19

"Yeah?"

I tried at a smile, anything to lighten the awkwardness between us. "Are you going to leave me standing on the porch all night, or do I get to come in?"

He paled visibly but recovered himself enough to say, "Right. Sure. Of course." He led me inside the house, but instead of taking me toward the open and inviting entryway that led to what appeared to be a comfortable living room with floor-to-ceiling windows overlooking the grounds behind the house, he skirted me down a side hallway toward a kitchen.

No one impeded our movement. Not a mom, not a dad, not a brother, not a butler, not even Chester the dog. For all the lights glowing out from the windows, no one was there to use all that wasted electricity. No one except Blake and me.

Except that didn't feel exactly right either.

"So is everything okay?" he asked once we were in the kitchen, which was bigger than my entire apartment.

"I don't know," I said. "*Is* everything okay?"

"I think so. If everything is good with you, then it's all good with me." He took my hand and gave me one of his confident, breezy smiles — the kind that made women sigh even with me standing right there next to him while they did it. That smile still made me sigh. He kissed my palm, but instead of making my stomach flip, the action made me flinch.

"Where is everyone?" I asked as he pressed several more kisses to my palm and feathered a few others up my wrist.

"Everyone?" he asked.

And then I clued in to why my stomach bubbled in acidic anxiety and why I felt I was doing a tactical meeting for the other executives without having prepared first. I tugged my hand from his. "Everyone, Blake. Your family. Mom. Dad. Brother. Your dog."

"Palm Springs. They go every Fourth of July. Chester goes with them." He reached for my hand again, but I dodged his reach.

"So . . . what, exactly, are *you* doing here?"

He shrugged. "I don't know. Now that you're here, I'll get a room ready so you can get some sleep. I know you've had a lot going on at your office. You deserve to be treated like you're special."

No, I wanted to say. *I deserve to be treated like I'm intelligent.* "Before I got here. What were you doing then?"

"I was just kicking back, relaxing."

I rolled my fingers around my suitcase handle. "In your infamous impress-the-ladies-slim-fit-button-up blue shirt?"

"I wear it for business, too. You know that. I haven't had time to change."

His glance slid behind me but snapped back to my face fast enough to be suspicious. I also turned to look but found nothing. At least nothing I could see. "You got here yesterday. So, who else is here?"

He dropped all pretension and immediately went to excuses. "It's just dinner, Em. No big deal."

My breath left me as if I'd taken a punch to the stomach. I translated his words in my head before asking, "What's No Big Deal's name?"

He groaned and scrubbed his hand through his hair. "Trish. And it's just dinner. Like I said."

"Just dinner, while your parents are gone as if you were a delinquent sixteen-year-old? I thought they were the whole reason you invited me home with you this weekend, and they weren't even going to be here? If they go to Palm Springs every July Fourth, you knew they wouldn't be here. I thought we were meeting them. That *I* was meeting them."

He furrowed his brow and then shook his head as if his brain finally synced with mine. "You thought I invited you to meet my parents?" He laughed. It wasn't a cruel laugh, but more of a bewildered, "what in the world is this girl thinking?" laugh.

"So you don't want me to meet your parents?" I stepped away from him, not sure why that information hurt more than knowing there was another woman somewhere in a house so big you could play the most epic game of hide-and-seek ever.

"Baby." He reached for me, but I gave him my best back-off look.

"What kind of setup is this?" I asked.

"It isn't a setup. You said you couldn't make it this weekend."

"So because I couldn't make it, you decided it was okay to invite a stand-in?" I felt a little hysterical and blindsided over my new revelations. I was looking for a future; he was looking for a hookup. I began backing away in earnest. "What a nightmare. I can't believe I actually thought . . ."

"What? What did you think?" His tone proved he really wanted to know, that he really was confused.

Somehow in all of the confusions and clue ins, we had ended up winding back to the front door. "I thought you were going to propose this weekend." I hadn't meant to say the words out loud, but once they were out, there was no way to call them back.

Shame burned hot through me.

"Married?" He laughed. This time, it did sound a little cruel, a little mean-spirited. Laughter was its own language. Whole conversations could be had in various expressions of mirth. "Me? Now? I just settled into a career. I'm not ready to be settled into a person. I don't even think I'm the marrying type. You can ask anyone, and they'll tell you I'm not."

I knew that about him, had known from the beginning. All his friends said as much. I would have said as much even as recently as a month ago. So why had I imagined myself to be so amazing that he'd change for me?

He must have seen the emotions rage across my face because he immediately stopped looking amused and actually had the nerve to look concerned. "C'mon, Emma, don't act all victimized. We apparently have different ideas regarding our relationship. There's no need to get hysterical about it. This isn't some manifestation of your mother's abandonment."

His eyes widened at the same time I felt my own stretch to abnormal proportions. We were both, apparently, saying things neither of us meant to say out loud. I turned and jerked my suitcase behind me so that the wheels clacked on the Tuscan-styled tiles.

He muttered something I didn't quite catch before he decided to follow me. I yanked open the door as he said, "Where do you think you're going?"

"Home."

"It's night already. You can't go home. You don't have a car. Look, you can stay here."

"Stay? While you're entertaining Trish-No-Big-Deal? That sounds incredibly crowded, even for this house."

"But you can't leave tonight. It's crazy."

I whirled on him. "No. What's crazy is you thinking I'm going to stay. The fact that I respect myself enough not to pretend that none of this matters has nothing to do with my mother and everything to do with you."

He shook his head and gave one of his iconic smirks — the kind I'd always swooned for in the past. "Not just me, baby. You. This is you, too. You can't claim to be so totally committed to the idea of us when coming here this weekend was your second choice after *work.* You're so hung up on your mother not being there for you emotionally that you have no idea how to be there for anyone else."

I sputtered, my face hot with anger and humiliation. "Oh. Right. Nice. Which of us dared to commit to a long-term relation-ship this weekend?"

He scratched his neck. "Well, that's obvi-ous. You actually want to get married be-cause you're afraid of being alone. I'll never be that needy."

I found myself suddenly not as needy as he thought I was. That was when my palm connected with his cheek in a way that would leave a handprint on his great-grandchildren.

CHAPTER TWO

"It is always incomprehensible to a man that a woman should ever refuse an offer of marriage. A man always imagines a woman to be ready for anybody who asks her."
— JANE AUSTEN, *Emma*

I cradled my hand against my stomach with a cry of pain and felt some satisfaction that he held his hand over his cheek and his cry of pain seemed louder than mine. I'd never slapped someone hard enough to hurt myself before. I'd never slapped anyone at all before. I whirled around, out the door, and down the driveway. I was past the fountain when I realized he hadn't followed me.

That rotten, no-good, womanizing, self-absorbed playboy didn't even have the decency to follow me? What? Couldn't he take getting slapped by a girl? I looked at my palm — red from the intense contact. An ache throbbed from my palm into the wrist Blake had been kissing not too long ago.

How dumb was I to think this relationship was anything solid? But then . . . he'd never given me reason to think otherwise. He listened when I talked, opened my doors, acted respectful most of the time, and was quick to be tamed when he tried stepping over those boundaries. There had been no clues to inform me that I'd end up clacking down a rich man's driveway in the middle of the night after being deluded by my now ex-boyfriend.

I'd covered over half the distance to the gate when it opened all the way and a car passed through. I tried to hurry my step, to reach the gate before it could swing closed, but it shut before I could reach it. The nondescript silver car passed me on the driveway, flipped a U-turn, and came back my way.

I didn't stop for the car or look in the direction of the driver's side window that was opening with a soft purr. I kept my head straight and high and my feet walking.

The car's driver watched me before making a comment. He paced me in the car, the tires grinding tiny pebbles into the cobblestones. "I'm guessing you're my brother's latest mistake."

Mistake? Did Blake's sainted brother just refer to me as a mistake?

"Hey. Can you stop so we can talk for a minute?"

Nope. Go talk to your brother. Blake was probably getting all kissed better by Trish-No-Big-Deal. The thought made me grip the handle of my suitcase so tightly my fingers cramped.

"Please stop and talk to me. I can't have you running off telling people what a meathead my brother is. I don't want the press dragging my father's good name through the mud."

"Good name?" I asked, finally stopping and glancing over at him. I only faltered for a second at the surprise of seeing someone who claimed to be Blake's brother but who looked nothing like him. Blake was the tall, dark, and handsome type. This guy might have been tall — it was hard to tell with him in the car. He might even have been handsome, but I wasn't in the emotional state to make any such determination. He definitely wasn't dark. He had sandy-colored hair and eyes the color of snow in the shade — a sort of pale blue that startled me only because I'd never seen anyone else with eyes as pale as my own. I shook myself back into the conversation. "The stock in your *good name* took a nosedive just now, so I'm not really interested in talking about it."

"What did he do?" the man asked.

I stared at him without responding.

"Come on. Please tell me. Let me try to make it right. What do I owe you for your troubles?"

I glared at him and leaned closer to the car. "Owe me? As in paying for my silence?"

He had the decency to flush through several shades of red. "I didn't mean it that way."

"I don't actually care how you meant it." I shoved away from his car and stomped forward again. He sighed and inched the vehicle alongside me and my suitcase.

How was it that a perfect stranger was trying to help me when the man who claimed to care for me remained inside the palatial house behind me? Were he and No-Big-Deal laughing at me? Was he telling her about my childhood and how it led to paranoid insecurities that made me clingy and undesirable? The stupidity of my situation coupled with Blake's callous behavior quickened my pace. To have his brother following me down the driveway like a bouncer kicking me off the property made everything so much more ridiculous, so much worse. Was Blake's whole family like this? What good name could they possibly be protecting when they all acted like the world belonged to them and all people existed to serve them?

"What I meant was," the guy said, "can I give you some money to pay for a cab?"

I thought about the driver who brought me to San Diego. I didn't have the energy for a repeat of that experience. I could call Silvia, though it would mean waiting around for hours while she navigated the congested freeway system. "I'm taking the train home," I said. I'd never taken the Pacific Surfliner from San Diego to LA, but I knew people who did. Silvia could pick me up at the train station.

"How are you going to get there?"

I pointed at my feet. "I would've thought it was obvious."

"Do you have any idea how far the train station is from here?" He made a noise of frustration. "Look, I'll drive you at least that far."

I tossed a scowl over my shoulder at him, knowing he was right about the distance. How long would it take me to walk? All night. Or near enough that the point remained moot. I would have to hire a driver.

"Seriously, I'm not letting you walk. It wouldn't be right. Will you just get in the car?"

"I don't even know you. Why would I get in your car?" My heel caught on one of the protruding stones and tripped me. I managed to keep my feet under me even if I failed in keeping my pride unscathed.

"You know my brother," he countered.

When I laughed with all the derision I could muster, he mumbled something that sounded like he realized he was winning my case for me.

"Okay, so knowing my brother doesn't actually recommend me to anyone, but you should really get in the car because I *am* driving you to the station."

I whirled on him. "Does that usually work for you? Bossing people around? I'm not getting in your car just because you commanded it."

"But you will get in eventually."

"You are an arrogant —"

He interrupted me. "What I am is more stubborn than even you seem to be, and I can promise you I'm not opening the gate to let you off my property unless you allow me to take you to wherever you're going, so eventually, yes, if you want to leave, you will get in my car."

I slowly turned my head to the massive gate — firmly closed. No way would I guess the security code, and no way could I climb the narrow iron spires of the fence.

The desire to out-stubborn him almost overpowered my good sense. But the fact of the matter was that I wanted to get home. I wanted to have a good cry and maybe head to Silvia's house and let Mr. Darcy make it all better for me. My heart should never have wandered from Mr. Darcy in the first place. If I'd stayed loyal to him, none of this would have ever happened. The sooner I ended up away from this place, the better. But hiring a driver or calling Silvia would require me to wait for someone to pick me up, and the station in Sorrento Valley was a good twenty miles from the Hampton family estate.

I got in the stupid car, tugged on the stupid seat belt, and, just in case the brother was worse than the original, wrapped my fingers around the stupid pepper spray shaped like a tube of lipstick I kept in my purse for emergencies.

He opened the gate and drove me off his family's property. He tried a few times to engage me in conversation but gave up when my answers were one syllable. Between the few sneak peeks we took out of the corners of our eyes at each other, the quiet settled between us. His phone ringing like a blade slicing through our silence startled me so much he was lucky I didn't accidentally spritz him with my pepper spray.

He argued in low tones into his phone for several minutes, his words short and clipped and angry. The call ended with one word: "Fine." I'd never heard so much fury put into one word before.

"I'm really sorry about this, but we need to make a slight detour. I'm really sorry." He added the second apology as I was about to object, and something about the ex-hausted, beaten way he said it made me swallow my protests.

After the car made enough turns to make me wonder if we were driving in circles, we ended up at a Wendy's in a ghetto neighbor-hood. He took us up to the drive-thru window and ordered a chicken salad combo and a burger kid's meal — choosing apple slices and milk instead of fries and a kid-sized soda. I declined when he asked if he could get me anything.

When he drove us to an apartment build-ing that appeared to be filled with people who were more likely squatters than tenants, I realized my total folly. I'd trusted Blake to take me to meet his parents and got burned. I trusted his brother — who I didn't have a name for and couldn't even verify that he *was* Blake's brother — to take me to the train station and ended up in a slum where my body would likely be discarded in a Dumpster full of rotting vegetation.

Every bad decision had brought me to this moment. I gripped the pepper spray tighter and raised an eyebrow at the guy who had put the car in park, waiting for him to drag me, kicking and screaming, into the building that probably housed more dirty needles than it did actual people.

"I'll only be a moment," he said. "Stay here."

He gathered the bags of food, got out of the car, looked up at one of the top-floor windows, and headed up the street-blackened and litter-strewn front steps.

Stay here? Was that really a good idea? Was getting out and taking my chances that the street urchins with their pants slung low on their hips would let me pass with my suitcase unscathed a worse idea?

I decided to stay.

I locked the doors for good measure.

And then felt like a total stereotyping

hypocrite for assuming teens with gauges in their ears and safety pins in their eyebrows weren't just like everyone else. With my bachelor's in design and my master's in marketing, I'd had my share of a liberal-arts education. Tattoos weren't indicative of deviant behavior, just freedom of artistic speech on a skin canvas.

Blake's brother took a long time. I watched the minutes tick by on my phone while trying to focus on emails from work. Debbie had sent me the notes from the meeting I'd missed, but my brain wouldn't engage well enough to concentrate. What was taking him so long?

I checked the schedule for the train and found that if I left in the next twenty minutes from my exact location, I would arrive just in time to catch the last train to LA.

Two minutes. I would give him two more minutes to come back, or I was going in after him.

Six minutes and twenty-eight seconds later, I clutched my pepper spray like it was a cross and the gauged and safety-pinned kids were the unholy undead and all but leaped from the car.

I relocked the doors and took the apartment building steps three at a time before shoving open the glass door on its rusted hinges and tumbling inside.

Only then did it occur to me that I had no idea where Blake's brother had gone. Up the stairs? Down the hall? I peeked down the hall and took a step in that direction when something — either a small rodent or a large cockroach — darted across the floor. I couldn't force myself that direction. Besides, Blake's brother had looked up toward the top of the building.

I went up, taking care to glance back every now and again to make sure the teens with gauges hadn't followed. Other worries plagued me as I gripped the pepper spray and kept my distance from the greasy, blackened banister. What if the building had another set of stairs and the brother came down while I went up? What if I chose the wrong floor and he passed me that way? What would he do when he found me gone? Leave? Call the police? How long would I have to wait for a driver to come get me if he left me here?

The worries were all unfounded.

I heard a familiar, deep timbre. He was yelling. Another someone, a female, yelled back. A small child cried. I followed the sounds of the domestic violence dispute while reaching in my purse for my phone.

The police might get a call after all.

"Don't tell me you can't afford it! I know you can!" the woman yelled. "You got more money than the Kardashians."

I turned from the stairwell in time to see a woman who might have been blonde under the clumped greasy strands and who might have been pretty if she wasn't so thin. She looked like a hunched, quivering, raging stick. She flicked her hand at Blake's brother's expensive green button-up shirt — one that looked startlingly similar to Blake's infamous impress-the-ladies blue shirt.

The child, a little girl who was a miniature of her mother, cowered behind Blake's brother's legs, her shoulders shaking with sobs. She clutched her kid's meal bag in her hands.

"Giving you money doesn't help you, Denise. It makes it worse. You think I can't see the tracks on your arms? You think I don't see the shaking in your hands? Why don't you let me take April for the night until you calm down? She'll be safe with me —"

"I'm her mother!" The woman reached out and snatched the child's arm so suddenly the little girl didn't have time to get out of the way. The woman dragged her daughter to her side. "She's safe with me!" she screamed in Blake's brother's face.

I saw spit actually fly out and land on his cheek. To his credit, he didn't even flinch. April sobbed louder and harder and struggled to break her mother's iron grip.

"She's crying. Let me take her." Blake's brother tried again.

The woman rolled her eyes, and that was when she saw me hovering at the edges of her pandemonium. "What do you want?" she shouted at me.

Unlike the guy who was my ride and the only sane presence in my current circumstances, I totally flinched. "Hey," I said, trying to sound cheerful and confident. "I just came to see if you all needed help."

Blake's brother gave me a look so wide-eyed it might have been shouting, *What are you doing here?*

I ignored him as much as possible and looked down at the child, whose hand was turning purple due to her mother's tourniquet grip. "Hi, April. It's nice to meet you. Did you get a toy in your kid's meal?"

She stopped crying, probably because the whole situation was too much for her and her brain had simply shut down. I knew mine wanted to.

How many minutes did we have in order to catch the train?

Twelve?

I continued, not knowing what else to do. "I love kid's-meal toys. They're my favorite." Disarmed by my presence, the woman let go of her daughter. I took advantage of the situation. "Want to show me what you got?"

April realized her shot at freedom and fled before her mother could latch on again. I bent low so she could show me what was in her bag, though now that she was up close, she seemed pretty hesitant to get any closer. She made no move to open her bag. So I opened mine instead. My purse was at least interesting enough she didn't start crying again, but not interesting enough to keep the other adults from resuming their fight.

"Is she child services?" the woman asked. "Someone from the state who calls herself Stephanie has stopped by three times. She keeps leaving a card under my door. You called her, didn't you? Is this Stephanie?" She said the name with dripping venom.

"No. She's —"

"Oh, I get it. She's stamped with the Hampton seal of approval. Her daddy probably owns a senator or two."

"Knock it off," he growled.

I showed April my lip gloss — an organic, all-natural, super expensive — as far as lip glosses go — gift from the owner of Sun Kissed, a company whose products Kinetics had just decided to carry in our retail stores. April rolled it over her lips and smacked them together with a berry-colored pucker.

The fight broiled and brewed beside us while I frantically showed her pictures on my phone of the hike I'd gone on during the weekend and from a formal event at work where everyone was in elegant evening wear. She liked the evening gown pictures better than the ones of waterfalls.

She never said a word, but the other two said plenty. She leaned into me, and I put a protective arm around her shoulders as if my arm could block the words from reaching her ears. Seven minutes. We had seven minutes left to leave. When would I have to intervene to get us out of here? Five minutes? Three?

He finally handed over some indiscernible amount of money, insisting she use it on rent and groceries and nothing else.

"Quit acting like you're doing me such a favor, Lucas. You totally owe me after you left me for your mansion and swimming pool." She said all this with a sneer that seemed dangerously close to triumph.

I felt triumphant, too, because I now knew what the guy's name was.

"April!" The woman called to the child like a cruel master would call for his dog.

The little girl jolted and hurried to her mother's side.

She still had my lip gloss, and I made no move to retrieve it. Every little girl needed something in her life to help her feel better. If berry lip gloss worked, then so be it.

Lucas hugged April, his face over her shoulder a projection of pain that pinged my heart. His pain looked hauntingly familiar. "I love you, kid. You have my number. Call me if you need anything. Okay?"

She nodded just before her mother jerked her over the threshold and slammed the door on us.

As we walked back down the several flights of stairs, it occurred to me that an entire brawl had happened in the hallway and no one else had opened a door to investigate the situation.

Once we were in the car, which still had all its hubcaps in spite of my prejudices of the gauged teens, and driving toward the Amtrak station, Lucas shot me a look of gratitude. "Thank you for sidetracking April for a few moments. That was really nice of you. She's been through a lot. Any kindness is appreciated."

"It's no problem. She seems like a sweet kid."

"Yeah. A sweet kid." A slow breath of

supreme irritation hissed through his teeth, but it didn't seem directed at me. His fingers tightened on the steering wheel, and his eyes stayed on the road.

It took all my effort not to blurt out the question that confused me most, the one that demanded to know why he would let his daughter live like that when he was a Hampton. But it wasn't my business. After being confronted with the reality of Blake Hampton and discovering that loyalty wasn't something he held in high esteem, was it really a surprise to find Lucas's little April caught in the cross fire of disillusionment and abandonment?

Yes. Abandonment.

No matter how Blake denied the comparison between my mother and his own actions, there were similarities.

Selfish similarities.

And from both brothers.

I pressed myself against the door and wished for the ride to the station to end. I was done with the Hampton family and their commitment issues. I was glad that Lucas acted like his voice box had been broken because talking to him would have been a huge imposition when I was busy reveling in how much I disliked him. Even if he had rescued me from walking, I'd seen too much of him and his family that could not be unseen.

At the Amtrak station, his jaw worked — tightening and flexing like he might have been grinding his teeth to powder. He finally said, "I should at least walk you inside so I know you're safe." He swung his legs out of the car and shut the door before I could protest. I scrambled out to save us both from the awkward position of him trying to open my door for me.

Once my ticket was in my hand and he felt assured of my security, he gave a single nod of his head. "I'm sorry about my brother." He turned to go.

"Lucas?"

He looked over his shoulder and waited for me to speak.

"Thank you . . . for helping me." I owed him that much. No matter what else, he'd done me a favor with no real reason.

He nodded again and was gone.

I let out my own deep breath between my teeth. "Well, that was interesting," I said to no one in particular.

I sat to wait for my train and noticed a smudged little old man staring at me. The gray stubble on his chin bristled when he flashed me a smile that showed a gap big enough to have once housed three teeth.

"Will you marry me?" he asked.

I laughed. What else could be done? "Thank you, but no," I said.

His hopeful expression turned to a solemn nod of understanding. "I'm not very pretty. I thought it might be a long shot to get you to say yes."

So, not *every* man expected to have his proposal of marriage accepted, not that I knew many men making offers of that nature. Apparently, it took some pretty humble circumstances for a man to let go of his ego long enough to want to commit. I bought my smudged suitor a bag of chips from the vending machine and boarded the train. At least now I could tell Silvia and Debbie I'd gotten my marriage proposal.

CHAPTER THREE

"I could easily forgive *his* pride, if he had
not mortified mine."
— JANE AUSTEN, *Pride and Prejudice*

"He didn't say that!" Silvia gasped as she
flipped the popcorn bag from the microwave
to the counter to keep her fingers from being singed.

Like the good friend she had always been
to me, Silvia picked me up from the train
station and brought me back to her apartment, where we would make good on our
original plan to watch the A&E version of
Pride and Prejudice. She listened with all
the horror and righteous anger of a woman
scorned that my predicament deserved as I
unfolded the entire story to her in magnificent, humiliating glory.

"He not only never apologized for having
some other woman over for dinner, but yes,
he really did say I was needy and desperate

and then blamed it all on my insecurities that came from my mother's abandonment."

Pity washed over her face at his cruel words. "I am so sorry he brought your mother into it. That was a low blow." She pried open the popcorn bag with two fingers, the steam exhaling from the opening as if relieved to escape. "An unforgivable low blow." She swept back her red hair and dumped the bag's contents into a glass bowl.

Silvia fixed her hazel eyes on me, or rather she fixed her *one* eye on me since she only had one. She'd lost her left eye to cancer when she'd been five years old and never looked back, but only because she *couldn't*. That was her favorite joke. She thought she was hilarious. I thought so, too. Most people had no idea my best friend was a cyclops. Her glass eye usually followed the real one faithfully, but not always. Today was a day where the glass didn't take orders from anyone. It rolled the other way as if tired of our conversation and eager to participate in something new.

My phone buzzed with an incoming text.

Blake. "I'm sorry about tonight. Let's talk. I can explain. Call me."

I read it aloud to Silvia, who crossed the

kitchen and tried to take my phone from my hands. "Uh-uh! I can see you caving. Don't even think about it. Did you forget everything you just told me?"

I pulled the phone away from her reach. "He said he could explain . . ." I trailed off, recognizing the neediness in my words.

"He also called you desperate and stabbed at your mom-wound — which is totally off-limits — *and* he didn't even follow you or do anything to make sure you arrived home safely. For all he knows, you were abducted by a serial killer and are now doing the dead man's float in the Pacific Ocean."

I scowled at her. "But what if this is one of those times where a simple explanation fixes everything? What if this is the moment when I would discover my own happiness if I just listened to what he has to say?" I shouldn't have gone there. That was a knee-jerk Jane Austen response. I needed to remember my decision to break up with Jane.

"Em, love, maybe tonight isn't a good night for Colin Firth. Maybe tonight, we should just talk and stay firmly grounded in reality."

"After everything I've been through, you really want to take Colin away from me?"

"If it'll keep you from running back to the

48

heartbreaking womanizer, then, yes, I do." She held the glass bowl out to me. "I'm even willing to give you a pedicure while we talk to make up for it."

This was a sacrifice indeed considering Silvia hated feet in every way imaginable. She even hated baby feet, which was weird because baby toes were the cutest. If feet stayed properly shod with shoes, she was fine, but as soon as they were bared, she started to dry heave. Oddly enough, she was okay with toes peeking out of sandals or even brazenly announcing themselves to the world from atop flip-flops.

I shook my head, declining the olive branch of a pedicure, and hugged the bowl to my chest. Tears suddenly blurred my view.

"Oh, no, honey, don't cry." Silvia cooed the words as if talking to a baby bird. "Blake is not worth crying over. Come here." She wrapped her arms around me and held me, even with a glass bowl between us, even though I was likely getting snot all over the shoulder of her T-shirt.

"I knew better," I blubbered. "I knew he didn't want anything serious or permanent from the beginning. He was just so wonderful and funny and easy to be around that I forgot I wasn't supposed to fall in love."

"Do you love him?"

I searched my feelings before nodding. How else could I describe the ache in every nerve ending, the sad in every breath?

"I think it's bad luck to salt popcorn with tears." She pulled the bowl from my grip and led me to the living room couch. "And he's *not* wonderful," she said as she settled me into the cushions and placed a lap blanket over me. She turned to the TV stand to find her remote and fiddle with the controls of the various machines. "Wonderful guys don't invite other women to their childhood homes while their parents are away."

"But how much of that is my fault?" My shirtsleeve did double duty as a mop as I dragged it over my face. "I chose work instead of him. Maybe if I'd just —"

"Don't you dare!" She whirled on me. "Don't you dare make this your fault. Not everything that happens in this world is your fault. Sometimes people do horrible things and make horrible choices, but they do it without any prompting from you."

The whimsical piano tones of *Pride and Prejudice*'s opening credits filled the room. Apparently, I'd earned Colin Firth after all. I nodded at her as if agreeing. Placated by the gesture, Silvia sat next to me on the couch and settled the popcorn between us.

I forced my eyes to stay open and focused on the screen because if they closed, I would see him, see Blake as he smiled down at me with such affection, such acceptance. I tried not to think about how, when we talked, his eyes stayed fixed on mine as if he cared about every word that fell from my lips. I tried not to think about the way he'd encouraged me to pursue the CMO position at Kinetics, the way he insisted my youth and gender brought a fresh perspective, the way he helped me pull together a portfolio by letting me test my advertising campaign ideas and marketing strategies on him, or the way he had kissed me dizzy when I told him the job was mine.

I tried not to think about how my insides felt frozen and cramped with the ache of knowing I had never loved anyone the way I'd loved him. And now . . . now it was all over. Though I'd nodded my agreement with Silvia, the thoughts that came unbidden into my mind were the ones that listed all the ways I could have tried harder to be the kind of girlfriend Blake Hampton would want to bring home to meet his parents.

Blake called several times that night.

He left a message with each call, his voice sounding genuinely distressed at my absence. Where was that distress when I'd been right in front of him?

The first message consisted of panic over my safety laced with insults. "Em. You're being crazy stubborn right now. I'm really worried about you. Call me and let me know you got home safely. I don't even know where you are. I'm really worried. You should've just stayed here instead of being so obstinate and unreasonable. Please call me to tell me you're okay. I mean as soon as you get this. I need to know you're okay."

The second message consisted of something closer to an actual apology. Closer, but not quite. "I should never have let you leave. You could be lying in a ditch bleeding out right now, and I can't do anything to help because you didn't bother to tell me where you were going. I sent Trish home immediately after you left. It really was just dinner. She's just a girl from my office who, when I mentioned I had a killer recipe for grilled halibut, said she'd be interested in trying it out. You hate fish and didn't plan on coming down this weekend anyway. If you would've stayed, you would know all this. It wasn't a big deal."

If he had started with the third message and worked his way up from there, I would have definitely caved and called him back.

"Emma, baby, I am so sorry. I know you're mad. You have a right to be mad. You didn't know what was going on, and it was probably pretty startling — especially when you were just trying to be sweet by surprising me. I should never have let you leave, and I'm really sorry. I was just kind of shocked and then the accusation in your eyes put me on the defensive. Luc came home and told me he took care of you. I'm glad you're safe."

I let Silvia listen to each message as they came, and when I showed signs of giving in to the last message, she took my phone away and slipped it in her pocket as if putting both it and me into a time-out. "Did you forget what he said to you *before* he apologized?" she asked.

"No, but he *did* apologize — sort of."

"He let you leave in the middle of the night."

"It wasn't the middle of the night. And he worried about it after." I looked back to where the screen was paused on George Wickham's face — a visual warning to foolish girls everywhere.

"He didn't worry enough to go after you or do anything beyond a fairly limp attempt at contacting you. He didn't even really apologize until after he talked to his brother.

It's like he had something to prove, like he didn't want his brother showing him up. Promise me you'll stay strong and not go running back to that guy just because he gave a crummy excuse of sorry. If he'd started with sorry, I might believe him. But he started with calling you stubborn and desperate and threw in obstinate and unreasonable. He's a complete creep. You remember that."

Silvia was right, of course. No matter how sorry Blake insisted he was, the fact remained that he was there grilling halibut for an eager female coworker. He hadn't gone down to San Diego out of some familial obligation. He'd gone because the house would be empty. And who wouldn't want to spend the weekend alone in a sprawling estate when given a choice? But he hadn't gone alone. He chose to go there with her instead of staying behind with me while I spent the extra day at work.

And it wasn't like he couldn't have delayed a day. All he would have needed to do was wait until after the Friday meeting, and I would have been his for the weekend.

But he'd insisted on his own time frame, even knowing I had the meeting.

He'd chosen that, whatever that was, instead of us in the same way he'd insisted

I'd chosen work instead of us.

Silvia stared at me until I gave the required promise. Once I did so vocally, she turned back to the screen and hit the play button.

My phone buzzed twice more from her pocket, and she finally grunted, yanked it out, and pressed the off button until the swooshing chimes sounded. Satisfied, she turned back to the movie. "You can have it back in the morning after you've slept and had time to shake off some of your emotional energy."

She didn't give it back the next morning, declaring I wasn't ready yet.

My phone finally found its way back to my possession Sunday night when I'd managed to wipe my eyes dry, pull myself off Silvia's couch, and stand on my own feet to face my life.

The two-day time-out from both my phone and my life reminded me of a few things: I deserved to be with someone who loved me, not with someone who ditched me to grill fish for someone else. A single apology didn't guarantee he wouldn't do it again. Also, his apologies didn't start until after his brother Lucas got home. That meant his brother had been the puppeteer working the strings of Blake's remorse.

I was a professional woman with intelligence and skills, and my opinion of myself did not depend on what a guy thought of me . . . or on what my mother thought of me. It only mattered what I thought of me.

Silvia, my self-appointed therapist, seemed proud I had come through the event with such clarity and internal peace.

I was simply glad I'd come through it at all. I was also glad I could throw myself back into work until I was ready to put myself out into the dating world again. *If* I was ever ready to put myself out into the dating world again.

I went home, deleted Blake's messages in case I felt the urge to wallow in breakup events, and went to sleep.

Monday morning began in muddle-headed confusion that progressively worsened as I made my way to work. The freeway was a snarl of traffic that inched forward rather than flowed. The column of smoke ahead left no question as to the cause of the delays. As I crept closer to the source of the black smoke, flames became visible. The four lanes narrowed to two, and the gawkers gawked, making the procession even slower. I didn't join in the gawking. I'd been camping often enough with my father to have seen my fair share of campfires. Flame was flame. Nothing about a burning car was all that interesting except for the oddity of its location.

So I kept my eyes forward and my hands on the wheel.

Then the burning car exploded.

Like *genuinely* exploded. The flash of flame and heat seared through my car window, and it felt like it left a brand across my cheek. The shock made me jerk the wheel and bump into the car next to me.

The following mayhem of the fender bender was not appreciated by the police department, the fire department, or the miles of traffic behind me and the guy I hit.

I didn't appreciate it either. My thirty-minute traffic delay suddenly became a three-hour traffic delay. I texted Jared, the CEO at Kinetics and the only actual boss I reported to, and filled out the report for the police.

Instead of being early, I showed up at the office frazzled, harried, and sorry I ever left Silvia's couch in the first place. As soon as Debbie saw me, she leaped up from her desk and followed me into my office. She looked harried as well, and I made a mental note to ask her about that as soon as I unloaded all the baggage filling my own mind.

"Do you know what I hate more than

anything?" I asked as I dropped my things on my desk and rummaged through the stack of notes left from Friday's meeting.

"The fact that Jared outsourced East Coast marketing?"

"No. I hate cars exploding on the five. Wait, what?" I frowned, realizing Debbie had managed to unload her news before I'd a chance to get rid of mine.

"Seriously? A car exploded on the five?" She looked interested in the information as if the news she'd shared hadn't been its own atomic blast.

"Yes, explosions happened. Apparently you had your own here at the office? What's this about Jared?"

Debbie sat on my desk, but my irritation over the infraction was buried by the panic her words caused me. "Yeah, he's bringing the new guy in this morning. He thinks we can't market to Easterners unless we understand Easterners. Like we can't understand them if we've never lived in New York."

"I've been to New York," I said as if that mattered. Jared was all about being "at one" with the inner workings of people and places. If he wanted a New York native, a tourist would not be an acceptable substitute. I slumped in my chair and stared at Debbie. "Are you serious? He's really bringing in someone else?"

Debbie nodded, her face solemn, her blonde frizz bouncing with the motion.

"I bet he wouldn't do this if I was a man," I grumbled.

Debbie lifted her right shoulder in a noncommittal gesture. "I think he might," she said. "He did it to the CFO when we hit ten million. He said he wanted a consultant to help us navigate the bigger seas we found ourselves in, or something like that. It isn't personal. And it isn't forever. It's just a consultant — I may have exaggerated the whole outsource part. The new guy'll be gone in six months."

"I'm pretty new. Who's to say he'll keep me and not this consultant?"

"Whoa." Debbie's hands went up, trying to placate me. "No one said anything about your job being on the line. I didn't tell you to make you feel insecure about your position here. I told you so you had a heads-up when the new guy got here. I'm not worried about anyone being displaced, and you shouldn't be either. This is just how Jared operates. What you should be worried about is someone coming in and messing up the really great workflow mojo we've got going on. This last little while has been kind of amazing since you took over, and I hate that someone is going to come tangle it up again just after you got all the snarls out of our department."

I took several calming breaths. "You're right. Sorry for freaking out. My weekend has made me paranoid. This has just been a busy morning, what with cars exploding and cars crashing and hostile office takeovers."

"This isn't a hostile takeover," Debbie said with a grin that disappeared. She looked at me as if seeing me for the first time that morning. "Wait. What happened on your weekend? He proposed, right?"

She didn't ask about the car crash or anything else. The words she fixed on were all about the weekend.

I held up my bare hand, wriggled my fingers, and shook my head. "Guess again."

Trudy sauntered into my office at that exact moment with a Starbucks in hand and a grin wide enough to split her face into two separate pieces.

I dropped my hand immediately and folded my arms to tuck the offensive bare finger away from prying eyes.

She took a sip of her Starbucks before making demands. "So! Let me see it!"

Debbie's eyes widened, and she gave a nearly imperceptible shake of her head as if somehow that would stop the inevitable train wreck. "Not now, Trudy. Emma and I have a lot to discuss regarding the new La Jolla location and the East Coast plans — especially since the consultant will be here any time."

"Don't give me that!" Trudy gave a short bark of a laugh. "It takes two seconds to see a ring and for me to gush over sparkly happiness."

"There is no ring." The flat words actually hurt exiting my mouth.

"What?" Trudy scrunched her face in confusion. Her chin-length, gold-red hair stuck to her lipstick as she pursed her lips. "Oh! I see. You guys are going ring shopping to pick it out together. That's so romantic. And smart. I still hate the ring Greg picked out for me." She held out her left hand so we could see for ourselves.

The ring didn't look bad enough to merit the word *hate* or the depressed sigh that escaped her as she folded her fingers back up as if ashamed by their presence.

"No." Debbie looked from me to Trudy as if unsure how to make it all go away. "That's not exactly how things went down."

"Okay." I dropped the notes on my desk and took a deep breath. "Let's get this over with all at once, shall we?"

I marched out of my office and rang the

marketing bell. "Impromptu town meeting, guys. Designers, content team, programmers — I need everyone here at the couches," I called out.

Heads poked out of offices and cubicles, and, seeing that a meeting really was gathering at the couches, my staff came out to participate. My boss did not come out of his office, and while I was annoyed that he ignored my call to a town meeting, I was glad he'd been gone all day Friday and had missed the gossip chain regarding my upcoming faux engagement. His presence for my announcement would have made a terribly awkward situation a million times worse.

They all assembled, many of them beaming at me as if they were in on a secret — the good kind — not the less-than-great kind I intended to share with them.

A couple of low whispers of congratulations found their way to my ears, and I saw a couple of expectant smiles. Part of me wanted to die right there. But I was the leader. This was my team. The fact that they all liked me well enough to want my happiness consoled me. I wouldn't have made such a big deal about it except that announcing it all at once would be easier than dealing with the whispers behind hands for several days until everyone knew.

Gossip was a monster that never went away unless you chopped its head off.

I took a big breath, enough that every spare place in my lungs filled to capacity. If only I could do the same thing with my heart.

"Everyone, I know you all think that I went away for the weekend to meet my boyfriend's family and for him to put a ring on it . . ."

Several people chuckled at that.

"But" — I lifted my hand to display the bare ring finger — "the truth is that I am not engag—"

The word strangled in my throat as I looked up and saw Jared enter the room with another person.

The other person was none other than Lucas Hampton.

Blake's brother.

"You're not what?" Jeremy asked from where he leaned against the wall. He didn't have a view of my empty hand since several others stood in his way.

Lucas smiled when he recognized me standing there. That smile oozed confidence, a natural sort of pride. He felt no unease at all. I could have forgiven him for being up to this second meeting. I *could* have except his presence made me want to dissolve through the floor. And not because he'd done anything wrong, but because he happened to come in at that moment when *I* had to do something. With Lucas's eyes locked on my own, I had to tap out of the pride battle and admit he'd won.

And all of that with three words.

"I'm not engaged."

CHAPTER FOUR

"We neither of us perform to strangers."
— JANE AUSTEN, *Pride and Prejudice*

The silence after my announcement thundered around me.

I didn't blink or look away from Lucas Hampton. And if he was surprised to see me standing there announcing to my team that his brother had played the part of a noncommittal louse in my weekend drama and that I held the role of pathetic, jilted female, he didn't show it because he didn't blink or look away either.

No one said anything for four seconds. I know because I counted. Four seconds is an incredibly long time to stand in such a position. Long enough for heat to crawl over my body as if trying to cover up my ache with something else.

I broke the silence with a smile and a clap of my hands. "It's no big deal. I'm super fine with how it all went down. I just wanted you to know so we could all get back to work. That's it, guys — no harm, no foul. Back to work! We've got memberships to market!"

As if they had all been in a hypnotist's trance and had been awakened by the clap, conversations started. Jeremy from the social media department offered to kill Blake for me, and several people agreed to help hide the body. Others told me he didn't deserve me. I only smiled. What else could I do? Crying would have been ridiculous, and taking them up on offers of murdering Blake in front of his brother would have been inappropriate enough to send someone complaining to HR.

So I smiled, shook my head, pretended like it was no big deal, and died a little more each second.

The town square of couches emptied until it was me, Debbie, Jared, and Lucas Hampton standing there. I sent mental waves of gratitude in Debbie's direction for not abandoning me to handle this on my own. Since she was the supervisor over the content team, she had a right to be present, and I had never appreciated a show of solidarity more. The other supervisors went back to work as I'd told them, which was too bad. A few more bodies in this uncomfortable mix would have been nice.

"Emma . . ." Jared started and then hesitated as if unsure what more could be said. His loose, blousy linen shirt, khaki pants, and bare feet made him look like he was doing a photo shoot for beachwear. He hated shoes and seldom wore them. Bare feet in an office was definitely quirky, but the CMO announcing a nonengagement could also be considered quirky. I wasn't in a position to be critical.

"That was quite a way to introduce yourself to the newest member of the Kinetics family," Jared said, motioning with his left hand, the one holding the ever-present kombucha bottle, toward the new consultant.

I turned my smile all the way up to glaringly-bright-and-perky and stuck out my hand. "Well, Jared, no introductions are actually necessary. Lucas Hampton and I are already acquainted. Hello, Lucas."

Lucas took my hand and gave it a strange sort of jiggle while pressing my palm too tightly to be comfortable. He held on an extra second too long, making the whole handshake exchange awkward.

"Yes. Miss . . ." He paused, clearly not knowing my last name. "Emma and I have already had the pleasure."

Pleasure. Well, that was one way to put it. Our brief acquaintance was anything but pleasant.

However, Jared looked pleased to see we already knew each other, as if perhaps that made him psychic or extra clever in bringing us together to work. He drummed his toes like other people might drum their fingers. I figured it was a skill set acquired by people who went sans shoes as a lifestyle choice. "Brilliant. Perfect. Just brilliant."

Jared used those words quite often. I believed in my heart he was always talking about himself when he used them, like affirmations or something.

Jared took a swig of his kombucha — a fermented tea he insisted would solve all my life problems but which I refused to drink because it tasted like sweaty socks — and clapped Lucas on the back. "Lucas here is going to be advising us as we acquire more properties on the East Coast. Turns out he grew up in New York and has some great ideas for launching that branch of the company into something astronomic." Jared beamed. Lucas smiled. I frowned.

"Aren't the Hamptons California stock? Did they send you away to boarding school or something?"

"Not exactly." Lucas's smile shifted in a

way that felt like I'd intruded into matters that weren't my business, so I dropped the subject. Maybe the Hamptons did send their kids away to school. Who knew what rich people did?

Jared saved the dwindling conversation by bringing everything back to business. "I'd like the two of you to spend the day together, eat your meals together. Use the company credit card for that, Emma. Get to know one another on a more personal level, and then, once you feel like you've made enough of a connection that you can be in sync, start brainstorming. Synergy matters, you know." He gestured wildly with his empty hand, making his shirt billow like sails.

"All that in one day? Want us to build Rome while we're at it?" Lucas hid his absolute incredulity behind a pleasant tone and a smile that didn't seem to stop so much as shift with the conversation as if his lips were an unspoken part of the discussion.

"You already know each other," Jared explained. "Finding synergy shouldn't be any real stretch for two like-minded individuals."

Calling us like-minded seemed to be a pretty intense assumption on Jared's part, but he plowed ahead figuring we'd make it work.

"Do you want all the supervisors involved today also?" Debbie asked.

"No. I need your focus on the La Jolla store."

"Shouldn't I focus on the La Jolla store as well?" I asked.

He waved off my question. "No. You've already laid the groundwork. Your team can handle the rest. I want you focusing on stores we haven't even thought about yet. Today is a day of collaboration and exploration. It'll help you get over the fiancé that didn't happen — which is a good thing in my opinion. It's tough to plan a wedding and an empire at the same time." He sauntered off towards the hallway that led to his office. "Find a workspace for Lucas, Emma, will you?" And with that, he was gone, his bare feet making little slap noises with each step against the stone floor.

Debbie tossed me a pained look, and she didn't even know how bad things really were for me. She had no idea the blood relative of Blake Hampton stood with us or that he'd been there for my greatest humiliation ever. "I really do need to get the ad sheets in for La Jolla before going home tonight. Are you going to be okay getting everything settled?"

I was one of the executive team. I should have been okay, right? Though nothing felt okay, I assured her everything lived in the neighborhood of "under control." She left, leaving Lucas and me standing at the couches.

Refusing to let things become even more awkward than they already were, I gave him my best restaurant hostess grin and said, "Let's get you a working office before we build Rome, shall we?" I led him to the office next to mine. It was meant for the personal secretary Jared had approved in the budget for me but hadn't hired yet, so the space was cramped and didn't have a window. But it was the only office available.

Placing a Hampton in a cubicle seemed wrong, like putting a prince in coach on an airplane. And though I felt like the Hampton family could stand to be brought down a peg, the one following me around the Kinetics offices was also the one who had rescued me and seen me to safety the other night.

No matter what else I thought of him, he had been fair and just and gentlemanly to me. I did have other opinions of him after the whole episode with the little girl, and even more opinions now that I knew he'd been hired as a consultant. I didn't need a consultant. What could Jared have been thinking? Was he trying to replace me already? And why would a Hampton want such a regular, everyday kind of career? The family had their own businesses and foundations. Why would Lucas Hampton have any desire to work the corporate circuit of California?

Voicing my questions would make me look paranoid, so I stayed silent as Lucas peeked into his office and then straightened again. "It's kind of a surprise to see you here this morning."

"Yes. A surprise," I agreed.

We both hesitated as if waiting for the other to talk when I finally gave a cheery, "I'll let you get settled before we get to business. So set up anything you have to set up" — I gave a meaningful nod to the messenger bag over his shoulder — "and come to my office when you're ready. I'm right next door."

This make-him-prepare-his-new-office tactic was the only way to give me a few minutes alone to think through the bizarre and cruel twist of circumstances that had landed me in my current predicament.

I left before he could ask questions, make further comments, or stall my escape in any way. Once in my office, I shut the door and leaned against it. The focused deep breathing the office yoga instructor taught me was not working. Why wasn't it working? She promised deep breathing exercises would exorcise all my anxiety demons. I'd have insisted on a refund except training with the office yoga instructor was a perk of working for Kinetics.

This is what happens when you don't tip the perk people well enough.

The knock behind me vibrated through the glass and into my shoulders, startling me. Huddling behind a glass door made for a terrible hiding place. I spun and found myself face-to-face with Lucas Hampton.

I opened my door. "Yes?"

"All done."

"Already?"

He shrugged. "I didn't have much to put away."

I briefly wondered if that "not much" included a photo of his daughter on his desk. I decided that it probably didn't, because any photos would raise questions he probably didn't want to answer. Considering how much he'd allowed me to witness, it surprised me that he hadn't asked for me to sign a gag order regarding the whole affair. But maybe he feared calling attention to the elephant wearing a tutu pirouetting between us. I shook the thought from my head and forced myself to behave professionally. "Right. You wouldn't, yet, would you? And you can't even log onto the network since I'm sure IT hasn't had time to get you into the system."

"Emma?"

"Hm?"

"This doesn't have to be awkward."

I barked out a laugh. "It's not awkward. I mean, yeah, three days ago, your brother did some fishy cheating and you drove me to a building that will likely melt into sludge due to its criminal history of meth cooking. And just now you heard me announce to my office that your brother didn't propose, which would lead you to believe that I was *expecting* him to propose, which is totally pathetic. What could possibly be awkward about any of that?"

Good job, Emma. Way to keep it classy.

He leaned against the doorframe. "Fishy cheating?"

"He grilled halibut for her." Why did that confession make my eyes burn with tears? I blinked fast and hard to ditch the evidence of my weakness.

"She wasn't there when I got back to the house."

I sucked in a breath that felt like lead.

74

"This all falls into the realm of sharing too much information. What Blake does or doesn't do, or who's staying at his house or not, is not my business anymore. It's fine."

"He's really sorry."

Jeremy headed toward us with a stack of ad sheets in his hand, but upon seeing me standing in my doorway, gripping the door as if it held me up, he did a U-turn in the hall and headed toward Erik's office instead, likely wanting someone to sign off on them and not wanting to get involved in more drama than I'd already stirred up in the office.

"Sorry?" I meant, *Sorry, please repeat yourself because I had been distracted and not listening,* but it turns out I basically repeated what he was talking about anyway.

"Blake is shredded over losing you. He's so sorry. He called you. Did you get his messages?"

"Yes." Was the office too warm? Did our air-conditioning unit break? July was a terrible time for the air-conditioning to go out, especially when our servers were on-site, and, though we had backup servers off-site, overheating would be very bad for them. "He called. There were messages."

Leaving him in the hallway while I barricaded the doorway probably appeared odd to both him and Jeremy and anyone else who might wander by. Besides, someone might overhear the conversation and misinterpret things, or worse, get things exactly right. I stepped aside and said, "Why don't you come inside my office? We can sit down and get to work."

To me, "get to work" meant not talking about Blake anymore. Apparently it held a different meaning for Lucas.

"Did you listen to the messages?" he asked. His concern for his brother's faux broken heart would have been endearing if I didn't know the brother so well. Since I did, it only served to irritate me. No answer could dignify his brother's messages, so I gave none.

He sat in the overstuffed, Caribbean-blue guest chair that came with the office. The thing was incredibly comfortable, and I found I sat there far more often than in the executive, high-backed, leather number at my desk. I frowned at him taking my accustomed seat but resigned myself to the fact that I was the executive, which meant the executive chair belonged to me.

Did kings and queens look askance at their uncomfortable thrones and wish for a nice recliner with a cup holder?

Lucas leaned forward. "I didn't realize you

worked for Kinetics."

"I didn't realize you did either. New York, huh? Blake never mentioned living in New York." Saying Blake's name in front of Lucas shamed me to my toenails. What was this? Amateur night? Wasn't I trying to change the subject from Blake?

But Lucas flushed enough to make it seem like the embarrassment was all his. "We were both given different experiences growing up."

I laced my fingers together on top of my desk. "And seeing as how you're now our consultant, everything's working out for everybody. Let's hear what you can tell me about the East Coast market."

"Right. So where would you like to begin?"

Finally. Real work. I pulled out my iPad. "Let's talk locations. Demographics of income and age are important to consider. A retirement community has merit and is something we'll consider if we can find enough evidence to make a case for it, but our target market is twenty-five to forty. Most of our members have reached a certain level of affluence — enough that the extra they pay for a gym membership isn't a big deal, so neighborhood is important. Jared is all about location, location, location. Beachside is preferred in coastal communities, and —"

"Whoa. Slow down. I thought Jared wanted us to get to know each other first?"

I set the iPad on my desk. "Look, I'm going to be honest with you. Playing Twenty Questions doesn't make any sense to me. Synergy is something you either have or you don't have right from the beginning. Our beginning had the kind of 'off' one would expect to find in the smell of day-old fish accidentally left out on the counter. We had friction but no spark at our beginning, if that makes any sense. So let's not waste time with icebreakers and get on with what we're here to do — our jobs."

Lucas leaned back in my comfy Caribbean-blue chair while I sat straight-backed in my lame executive chair. He surveyed me long enough to make me want to fidget. I didn't fidget — I just really, really wanted to.

Being that blunt wasn't my style, but the whole experience with his brother taught me that boundaries were a good thing.

"I think we had lots of spark from the beginning."

"What?" Did he really just say that out loud?

If the room felt too hot before, it suddenly

became sunning-myself-on-a-rock-in-a-Death-Valley-summer too hot. And I couldn't help it. I looked at him from a different point of view. For a brief flash, the consideration of us *sparking* seemed interesting. What it might be like to date Lucas . . .

Oh, no. No. Not that. Hadn't I already dated a Hampton? Didn't I already know how that turned out? Hadn't I already witnessed Lucas Hampton's particular way of handling cast-offs? A meth head and an abandoned child were not the proper way to handle anything.

Making sure we kept our relationship strictly professional, I interjected a laugh. "Spark is definitely not what I would call the launch of our introduction."

But before I could explain the importance of professionalism and how he shouldn't even hint at things like actual *spark,* he interposed his own opinion. "What else would you call a situation where two people are thrown into adverse circumstances and work together to improve those circumstances as much as they can? Spark is seeing the light of something good in someone. I saw a lot of good in you. You involved yourself with my personal family drama in a way that really helped, where most people would have stayed out of it entirely and not considered it worth their trouble or even their notice. April even asked me about you when she called me yesterday. She told me you gave her lip gloss. The good I saw in you was definitely a spark of light."

So that was what *spark* meant to Lucas Hampton?

He didn't think of it in dating terms at all, which was good, weird but good, since I felt pretty sure he was in the minority. Who thought of spark as a light in humanity? I could get behind that definition even if the guy who'd given it to me had been involved in darkening the spark of a little girl's world.

Stop it, Emma. Stop judging. You don't know the situation there.

Sadly, reprimanding myself not to judge and actually not judging were two totally different things. But maybe the case with April had already gone to court and they'd awarded full custody to the meth mom and Lucas really didn't have a say in what happened to his daughter. I doubted that scenario, but maybe?

In spite of the fact that I told Lucas I had no desire to play get-to-know-you games just because my unorthodox boss thought it was a good idea, we ended up doing a version of Twenty Questions anyway.

It started so organically I almost didn't realize he'd led us into it until we were in the middle of questions and answers. "So who's in that picture? Your sister?" he asked, pointing to where the image of Silvia and me sat framed on my desk.

I looked at the picture and couldn't help but smile. "That's the ghost and the cyclops." When he furrowed his brow, I explained further. "My best friend from childhood. She calls me the ghost, and I call her the cyclops. I don't have any siblings. It's always just been Silvia and me."

"Sounds like there's a story there. Little girls don't normally come up with monster names for each other."

"Monster names for monster situations. Silvia only has one eye. She had cancer when she was five and lost it."

"Ouch."

I shrugged.

"What about the ghost part?" he asked.

I shrugged again. "I've always been winter pale." That wasn't the story, not really, but I'd already told the real story to one Hampton and then ended up taking a backseat to Trish the Fish. I still couldn't believe Blake blamed my anger over his infidelity on my mom's abandonment. What kind of person dredged up someone else's pain and used it as a weapon to cover their own guilt?

I would never let that happen again.

Fool me once, shame on you. Fool me twice, shame on everyone.

"I'd ask about your siblings, but I think I already know your pedigree," I said, shifting the focus to him. "So why don't you tell me which of those family members you'd put a picture of on your desk."

It was a low-blow question. I had no right to judge people for being terrible humans since I wasn't being a very good one myself. But that little girl's face haunted me. It felt too familiar, too close to home.

"My brother, naturally." He beamed at me but then frowned when he realized I wasn't beaming back.

"Naturally," I said, unable to hide the flat tone of disbelief.

"I know you're mad at him right now, but he really is a good guy. The best kind of brother a guy could ask for. He's pretty much the reason for my existence."

I exhaled a short burst of nervous laughter and hoped he didn't translate laughter the way I did. "Isn't that an exaggeration? Shouldn't your existence be credited to Mr. and Mrs. Hampton?"

"I mean, a lot of people made me the man I am today. But Blake . . . I don't know how to explain. Blake just made everything easier for me."

He twitched as if wanting to say something but was unsure of how to proceed. Then he blurted, "I think you should give him another chance. I've never seen him so wrecked over a breakup before. I think he really cares about you."

My office was definitely too hot. I jumped to my feet and waved my hands as if that would silence him. "Okay. I am glad you have a good relationship with your brother. That's really sweet, but can you do me a favor and keep the conversation off of my relationship with him. It's not open for discussion, debate, or debunking. Let's stick to work-related get-to-know-you questions, okay?"

He nodded, but the nod was reluctant. He clearly wanted to continue barraging me with all the good qualities of his brother.

Just my luck. Jared hired a cupid consultant when we needed an East Coast consultant. Well, we didn't really need an East Coast consultant since I could handle the task of fieldwork and research, but either way, cupid had to store his arrows in a locked cupboard while we were at work.

So we discussed our education, jobs we'd had, internships we'd hated, and companies we dreamed of working for if given the chance.

I hated the fact that by the time I had his résumé background, I really liked him in spite of my personal feelings about his personal life.

His professional life rocked, and with every word he uttered about his work taking the company Endurance to the global market, Jared's decision to bring him in made more and more sense.

And his personal life? That wasn't any of my business.

We pulled up Google maps and spent the rest of the day talking ideal locations in New York. Most of his ideas were beachfront and fabulous, and he seemed to know exactly where new development was taking place and where land was actually for sale.

I would have spent days tracking down all the potential sites, but we had over a dozen picked out before lunchtime.

And it shouldn't have mattered to me, but by the time we were gathering our things to head to lunch together, I realized how hard I had worked to prove myself competent and capable. I wanted him to like me. I wanted him to think well of me. I wanted him to return to Jared and tell him how lucky he was to have hired me. I wanted him to return to Blake and tell him what a fool he was to let me go.

As we walked downstairs to the Kinetics restaurant, and I sneaked glances at him out of the corner of my eye, I finally laughed and said, "Confession time."

He stopped right on the staircase. "Let's hear it."

"I've treated this day like I was on the job interview of my life. I'm not normally this intense when it comes to brainstorming ideas and problem-solving. I just realized it could be problematic if you thought I was always like this and I decided to come in tomorrow as my regular self."

He laughed. "Well, then . . . you know what C.S. Lewis says?"

I shook my head, confused how a literary quote from Narnia applied to my confession.

"He said that friendship is born at that moment when one person says to another: 'What! You too? I thought I was the only one.' "

I laughed. "Not really. Not you, too?"

"The job interview of my life. I've never been so panicked to please."

While we shared a good laugh at our own absurdity, I considered how I had always thought myself to be like Elizabeth and

Darcy. I was not someone who ever performed to strangers. Why bother when strangers usually turned out to be so disappointing? But apparently, I did perform, sometimes. And as much as I didn't want to like him, I had the feeling Lucas Hampton would not be disappointing.

CHAPTER FIVE

"When pain is over, the remembrance of
it often becomes a pleasure."
— JANE AUSTEN, *Persuasion*

We decided to eat lunch at the facility restaurant as if we were regular patrons of the gym so I could give him a tour of the place and show him all the perks of membership. Since he was now officially a member of the Kinetics family for six months, he had access to everything Kinetics had to offer. I'd save Jared's offer for lunch on the company credit card for a later date.

The facility we stood in was also the largest because it housed three floors of offices and meeting rooms that most of the other facilities lacked. Lucas already proved he'd done his homework on the company because of how much information he shared with me throughout the morning, but I could tell seeing it all up close and personal impressed him, which impressed me.

For a kid who grew up on an estate with access to everything the fine life had to offer, he shouldn't have been so easily awed. But he appreciated the architecture, the fact that we kept a chef on staff at every location, and the fact that the restaurant had an outer entrance so it could be frequented by anyone who liked healthy fine dining, Kinetics member or not. He nodded his approval at the way the smoothie and snack bar was located right outside the heavy workout areas and raved about the meditation rooms. Anyone would have thought he'd found a golden ticket to Wonka's factory when he saw the indoor rock-climbing wall and skydiving tunnel.

"As you've probably guessed," I continued, "we pride ourselves in being a full-service fitness experience, from your mental and emotional state to your eating and exercise. We even have leisure covered for people who just want to have a nice meal at a nice restaurant where they don't have to compromise their health for the convenience of dining out. The rock-climbing wall and skydiving tunnel — you should really try that one — offer more for the thrill seekers. Our personal trainers are the very best. We aren't just another gym membership; we are an entire experience package."

He grinned at me.

"What?"

"Did you even take a breath in that whole long speech?" he asked.

My cheeks warmed, and I shrugged. "Breathing is secondary when you're talking about exciting things."

"I was just wondering if we planned on actually eating sometime today. We've walked pretty much everywhere except to the restaurant. You keep talking about your chef, and my stomach is wishing you'd introduce me to him."

"Right. Food. Right. Sorry." I turned us around and headed back toward the stairs that would take us to the dining room.

"No elevator for you?"

"Maybe when my legs are broken."

He didn't say anything else, and neither did I, at least not until we were seated at a table with menus in our hands and napkins over our laps. Well, a napkin over my lap anyway. Lucas tucked his into his shirt.

"Really?" I asked as he smoothed the napkin over his chest.

"What?"

"Just surprised is all. Does your mother know you do that?"

"My mother was the one who taught me

how. She got tired of washing my shirts after every meal and told me I needed the full coverage of protection that napkins can provide."

In that one sentence, Lucas gave me a picture of his family I hadn't ever considered before. He made them sound normal — like everyone else. Blake had always spoken of them as if he were name-dropping. Lucas spoke of them like *family.*

His mother sounded like a real mom and not a jet-setting socialite running charity foundations and shaking hands with presidents. His mother sounded like a lady I might not be nervous to meet the way I had been the other day when I thought I actually was going to meet her.

Not that the chance to meet her had ever been a real possibility.

But with Lucas describing her as a mom with flexible ideas about laundry, I felt the loss in not getting to meet her. I studied moms the way I studied laughs. You could learn a lot about people based on the mothers they were or the mothers who raised them, the same way you could read whole conversations in various laughs. Blake's description of his mom fit Blake's personality. But Lucas's description fit Lucas's personality. And the woman described did not sound like the same person at all.

That fact interested me a great deal. There was so much about the brothers that was the same, down to certain mannerisms and style of dress, but not enough to really identify them as brothers. Even in looks, they were contradictory. The whole incongruity paired with their sameness both puzzled and fascinated me.

"So what's good?" he asked as he surveyed the menu.

"Everything."

"You have to say that because you're the marketing exec and it's bad business to trash-talk any aspect of it when your job is to promote it."

"Yes, but I also say it because it's true."

He folded his menu and leaned in, his face reflecting his disbelief. "So you've actually tried everything on the menu?"

I folded my menu as well. "You can't market what you don't understand."

"So what's your favorite?"

"They have a beet and avocado salad with a dressing that tastes like sunlight and happiness."

He narrowed his eyes and pursed his lips as if thinking. "A salad, huh?"

I smiled and lifted a shoulder. "Sunlight and happiness."

He smiled too. "Fine, but I'll take my sunlight with a side of branzino with capers."

Well, the brothers had fish in common. My mouth tightened, and he must have noticed because he shot me a quizzical look and said, "What? You don't like fish?"

"Not really, no."

His mouth fell open, and a small gasp escaped him. "Oh! I'm sorry. I forgot. My brother and the fish. I promise I wasn't trying to be insensitive."

I would have laughed at his oversensitive reaction while he declared himself insensitive except he hit the mark pretty closely.

"He really is sorry, Emma. And he —"

I held up my menu as the waiter approached. "I'll have the beet and avocado salad, fully dressed, please, Sam."

Sam took my menu and held out his hand for Lucas's as well. Best timing ever. I decided to double the tip I had originally planned. Waiter for the win and worth every penny.

He looked to Lucas to give his order as well, which Lucas did finally.

"Thank you, Sam," I said before the waiter hurried off to turn our orders over to the chef.

"So you know everyone here?" Lucas asked.

Success. He had dropped the conversation about Blake. How many more times would I have to end such conversations while Lucas worked with Kinetics? Six months would be the equivalent of forever if he kept this up. I gave a brief accounting of all the staff within the restaurant and topped it off with my explanation of, "People matter. They're worth getting to know."

"I'm sorry I doubted you. And sorry I doubted you knew the menu so well. Growing up, I used to eat at a dive of a place not far from my school. The owner was awesome about giving me free meals, and I ended up doing chores for him quite often to work the meals off — not that he ever really expected me to since he was a generous kind of guy. Anyway, I knew their menu so well I could recite it top to bottom. I loved that place."

Why would a Hampton need a restaurant owner to be generous? The idea made me pity the poor restaurant owner who was trying to eke out a living with his own business while giving a rich kid freebies. It seemed wrong that a kid from such a prosperous life should accept such generosity when he could afford to pay, but I was glad to hear that Lucas had worked off the generosity.

I groaned inwardly. Again with the judg-

93

ing. Hadn't Elizabeth Bennett and Emma Woodhouse taught me anything regarding making judgments about people? But the judging came easy when I had evidence of Lucas not acting honorably towards a certain little girl. How could the guy who took a complete stranger to safety be the same guy who left his child to suffer insecurity and pain?

We fell into a silence probably brought on from our mutual discomfort over his brother and my guilt for justifying my judging. He finally broke the silence, grasping at the only thing he knew enough about me to question.

"So you've been friends with the cyclops since you were children? How young?"

I set my water glass down and smiled. "Silvia and I have been friends since we were five."

"Five? What, kindergarten meeting or something?"

"Actually, no. She was my dad's best friend's daughter. My mom didn't really like any of my dad's friends so she never let him see them, but he could see who he wanted after she —" My breath caught in my throat. I bit back the words and swallowed them down.

Why had I almost said that? I didn't even

know this guy. Was I really so pathetically desperate for someone to understand me that I was willing to throw my entire history out to the wind like that?

I didn't even tell Blake about my mom until we'd been dating a month. And even then I really hadn't wanted to tell. I only felt obligated to share because Blake complained that I kept my personal details to myself too much for a girl who'd been dating the same guy for so long.

But with Lucas, I found myself wanting to tell him things. His blue eyes had tiny creases at the corners that made it seem he smiled a lot but not in any silly way. He had the look of someone who knew what compassion was, who understood how to smile through pain, who totally got the concept of empathy.

This kindness vibe he gave off contradicted the fact that we left a little girl alone with a demon-lady in the scariest apartment housing I'd ever seen. I really was an amateur if I could look into those blue eyes and feel such trust.

But I couldn't help my feelings. He exuded trustworthiness in a way I hadn't seen in any man since my father passed away.

"Your mom?" he said in a voice so soft and sincere and full of acceptance that I made a decision right then and there.

Maybe if I told him my story, shared that hurt and pain in a way he might understand, maybe he could draw a parallel to the girl we left in the ghetto apartment. It was worth putting my own emotions on the line if it might help him understand how completely abandonment could kill a child's soul.

Maybe sharing my story would help him want to help her.

My finger traced the rim of my water glass in a slow circle as if spiraling me back to a time I didn't like thinking about. "My mom left us — my dad and me — when I was five. Once she was gone, there wasn't anything stopping my dad from turning to his friends, especially when he needed help with me."

My focus stayed fixed on the glass, but I didn't see it anymore. I only saw the dark walls of my bedroom as my younger self cried for a woman who would never come. "I wouldn't stop crying that first night or the second night or the night after that. I couldn't stop crying because no matter how hard I looked, I couldn't find my mom anywhere. My dad was panicked and exhausted and dealing with his own grief, so he bundled me up and went to his best friend's house. They also had a five-year-old girl. Her name was Silvia. Dad's friends told us to spend the night and pushed me into their daughter's room."

It was all too much to share. Too much too soon, but I didn't stop, and he didn't stop me. My voice continued as if I was telling the story as much to myself as to him. "I stood at her bedside, not knowing what to do. When she woke up and turned to me, we both screamed. She screamed because she thought a pale ghost had drifted into her room. I screamed because the child with the patched eye looked like some monster from a fairy tale. Once we stopped screaming, we decided to like each other, and she scooted over to let me sleep by her.

"Both of us had lost something huge that month. I lost a parent. She lost an eye. Through meeting each other, we got perspective, I guess. She still had one eye. I still had one parent. And now we had each other. We've been cheering each other on and cheering each other up ever since.

"But I never really got over it, you know. My mom not being around crippled me in so many ways. Children need their parents to be in their lives. Parents shouldn't disappear just because. They can't flit in and out at their own whims. They need to always be there and available because when they're not, the hole they leave behind is just too big to fill, you know?" I gave myself a shake and picked up my water glass, draining it until I was sucking the moisture out of the ice. Who knew hard truths could be so dehydrating?

The confession drained me the way I'd emptied the glass. I stared down into it as if it were Alice's rabbit hole and remembered the last moment with my mother: a fight that ended with her heaving the phone so hard it shattered the phone and slamming a door so hard it shattered my heart.

"Do you ever see her anymore?" Lucas asked, making me jump.

I'd almost forgotten he was there. Almost forgotten that I was in the middle of an object lesson and not a therapy session. "No. Never saw her again. Couldn't even find her. The police weren't interested once they realized she wasn't dead. Dad hired private investigators, but she disappeared in one magnificent magician's act. The clarity of the details makes me wonder how much of it I made up out of desperation and how much of it was just trauma that seared itself into my mind forever."

I finally allowed myself to lift my eyes to his and was surprised at the warmth I found there. He stared at me for several long

98

seconds, but neither the silence nor his gaze felt awkward. They felt natural . . . normal. How was such a thing possible? Did he not see the similarities between his little April and me? Did he not feel some bit of guilt over her loss that was so much like my own?

He cocked his head and said, "It seems we never forget the hard things. But it also seems like we shouldn't, you know? The things that make us stronger and more capable and more compassionate — those are the things we should be fighting to remember."

How different his response was from his brother's. Blake told me to forget my past, to let it go, to bury it like a dead pet and move on with my life. My regard for Lucas grew exponentially in that moment. It shouldn't have since he didn't seem to think of April at all even after what I'd shared. But he understood *me*. I felt his understanding, and my trust in him grew in spite of my mind screaming that he had wrongs to set right in his own life.

Our meals arrived with glorious perfect timing that kept the conversation from becoming too heavy to handle. Good thing, too.

Tragic events did not make good lunch companions.

After we started in on our food, the foolishness of what I shared with him settled over me. It hadn't accomplished anything. And the only way for me to speak more plainly would be to accuse him outright of neglect, which would be entirely unprofessional. The only thing I could do was own the mistaken conversation and move on.

"I'm really sorry," I said, looking up from the beet speared on my fork. "It was inappropriate of me to tell you all that when we've just met. I don't know what compelled me to do so."

His warm smile filled his face. "Maybe it's the bump on your head."

"What?" I reached up to where he pointed at the left side of my head and felt that, yes, there was a bump there. And touching it hurt like agony dipped in acid. "Oh. That was probably from the car accident this morning."

At his look of alarm, I laughed, glad to have something else to talk about. "The accident wasn't actually that big of a deal. A fender bender. And the bump didn't come from the accident. When the burning car on the freeway exploded next to me, my head must have hit the window."

"A car exploded?" He looked like he didn't believe me, but then seemed to change his mind. "You've had a busy morning."

"You have no idea. Is the bump really noticeable?"

He shook his head. "No. Not at all, really. I didn't notice it until you tucked your hair behind your ear." He cleared his throat, swallowed hard, and looked down at his plate as if embarrassed. Whether embarrassed for me and all my crazy sob stories or embarrassed for himself for being forced to hear all my crazy sob stories, I didn't know.

"I'm not really a train wreck," I said after a moment of silence. "Or a car wreck either. Or a car explosion. Today's just been really . . . overexciting."

"I guess. How did a car explode?" he asked.

"It was on fire. Traffic backed up forever. I happened to be the lucky girl next to the car when the fire hit the full gas tank. At least I guess that's what happened. No one ever really explained it to me."

Maybe it was because he felt my discomfort as deeply as I felt it, or maybe he sensed my growing panic over all I'd shared because he said, "Well, we have a lot in common."

"A car exploded by you, too?"

He laughed and put down his fork. "No. But I know how you feel. Really, I do. And I don't think you're a train wreck. I asked some very personal questions, and you were brave enough to answer honestly. Honest answers are pretty rare currency these days." He adjusted his fork on his plate. "I grew up in New York — as you know. We moved all over the East Coast, from house to house, room to room, homeless shelter to homeless shelter. We never stayed in any one place longer than a year. One day, I went to school and came back to the shelter to find that my mom had packed up and left."

I understood all his words, but when he put them together the way he did, I didn't understand at all. Did Lucas Hampton say he'd lived in homeless shelters? That his mother left him like mine had left me?

"But you're a Hampton." Food suddenly seemed less important than information.

He looked startled to hear me put his pedigree so bluntly. "Blake didn't tell you I was adopted?"

Adopted? How could he be adopted? And yet, his sandy-blond hair, his blue eyes, his politeness that came from genuine humanity instead of societal expectations — all these things stood as proof of his declaration. Adoption explained so much. "Blake apparently left a lot of things out of our conversations. How old were you when this all happened?"

"Thirteen. My mom, Caroline Hampton — my *real* mom, not the one who dumped me — found me at the homeless shelter while she was there on a crusade for her literacy foundation. She liked me and took me home with her."

"Is that even legal? It's not like you're a puppy she found on the side of the road." I shouldn't have said it out loud, but my greatest fault was saying the thoughts that came into my head out loud where anyone could hear them.

He didn't seem to mind. "It was a long time ago. Child services was a lot more relaxed in their rules and laws back then. I hadn't really been processed into the system yet, and the people at the shelter weren't sure what to do with me. Caroline Hampton promised to look after me until they could find my mom, and since she financed that entire place, she could've asked for ten kids and they probably would've given them to her."

His pain was so tangible it pinged my own.

"I'm sorry," I finally whispered. Here I was, trying to provide a hidden sermon for him on the dangers of neglecting a child when he'd grown up on neglect's battlefield. I felt like a monster.

"Like I said — we have something in common." He shrugged, cleared his throat, and tackled his beet salad with the enthusiasm of a man retreating from the current conversation.

"It's good she found you," I said, trying to find the sunshine in his cloudy skies. "Mrs. Hampton, I mean. Good that she was there, that she took you in."

His eyes met mine. "It really is. The Hamptons changed the entire world for me. Blake's immediate acceptance and friendship guaranteed his family as my own. I owe my brother everything I have, everything I am."

Those words settled between us, a prickling reminder to me that I had no interest or desire to get to know and like Lucas Hampton. He was Blake's brother. This lucky recollection kept me from the dangers of liking Lucas too much, of caring for the little boy abandoned at a homeless shelter, of wishing I could soothe the hurt so evident in his face as he shared his past pain.

It kept me from wishing that Lucas's understanding could soothe my own pain away. The conversation about my mother had placed a malignant lump in my heart, one that would be hard to shake off. I never should have mentioned her, never should have even thought about her. Remembering didn't make it any better. Not for me and clearly not for Lucas. That pain did nothing but slice the cut a little deeper, infect it a little more.

And remembering didn't change anything for April.

CHAPTER SIX

"Her own thoughts and reflections were
habitually her best companions."
— JANE AUSTEN, *Mansfield Park*

Lucas knocked on my office door before poking his head in at the end of the day. "Jared wants to see you, probably to determine if I'm worth what he's paying me. If I agree the beet and avocado salad was the best thing I've ever eaten, will you put in a good word for me?"

I laughed and agreed that he could count on me.

We had abandoned our serious conversations, leaving them at the table as if the busboy could clear them away. The rest of the day had been lighthearted and superficial and far less satisfying because it felt like something had been lost between us, which was ridiculous because he was my ex-boyfriend's brother and the unneeded consultant-slash-babysitter at my place of employment. He was also involved in a seriously dodgy situation involving an unfit mother and a sad little girl.

There was also the fact that we barely knew each other no matter what kinds of things we shared at the table.

I should have been grateful to have our conversations turn toward the shallow posturing. We discussed favorite books; he laughed when I told him that Jane Austen was a literary genius. He *laughed.* And I didn't even tell him the part about her being a liar because I had the sneaking suspicion he'd agree with me. I absolutely did not want him to agree with me. Jane was like family. I could pick on her, but no one else could.

He acted superior when he said Stephen King was the one true author genius and that everyone else was a slug by comparison. We discussed favorite movies where I valiantly defended the A&E version of *Pride and Prejudice* and gave the director serious props for staying true to the author's original intent. He declared the *Avengers* franchise to be the most reasonable fiscal decision Disney ever made. We debated between ice cream versus frozen yogurt, donuts versus brownies, and sleeping in versus watching sunrises.

Through all of that, we prepared several proposals for locations so Jared could pick his favorites and we could start acquiring the land and hiring the contractors. I wanted my team busy getting the New England communities excited for how their lives were about to change.

Working with Lucas, knowing the parallel of our lives, made me tolerate both his intrusion on my workspace and his many compliments of his brother, which he laced into almost every conversation. Lucas had no interest in taking my job, but merely doing his own. Working with him also made me more curious than ever how the little girl fit into this picture of a guy who had overcome the worst childhood ever to become a successful businessman and contributor to society.

But the puzzle had to be put on hold because I couldn't go home until Jared had been filled in regarding the work I'd done that day. Even when Jared was out of town, he liked me to text him the highs and lows in marketing. He was an attentive CEO even when he wasn't around in spite of what Debbie thought of the executive team.

"Come in!" Jared pointed to a chair opposite his desk when I showed up to report to him.

I took the chair closest to the door and refrained from rolling the tension out of my neck muscles in front of him while he finished up his phone call.

After he put his phone down, he folded his hands in front of him on the desk. "Before we start, I have something I need you and your team to be thinking about. Kinetics needs a foundation, a charitable opportunity to give back to the communities they exist in. The board is thinking kids and health, like healthy lunch options in the elementary schools or something like that. Some kind of initiative that will make us feel good about our good deeds and make us look good to the communities that are watching. Brainstorm that, and we'll meet back in a couple or three weeks, okay?"

I jotted a quick reminder for later and promised him that my team would have some ideas to present when we met again.

That pleased him, and he unfolded his fingers so he could drum them on his desk, a *tap-tap-tap* rhythm he did while thinking. The noise used to make me want to drown myself in the nearest basin of water to escape it, but I'd trained myself not to let the drumming make me anxious. Well, almost trained myself.

"So," he began. "Tell me how it went. Highs and lows. I want to hear it all."

I wasn't about to tell him the low of the day. There was too much wrapped into that low for both me and for Lucas. "He's certainly a find, Jared. You couldn't have procured anyone better for location development."

"When we were at NYU together, he had an incredible knowledge of the area. I knew he'd work well for us. So tell me . . . how do you like him?"

"I like him just fine. Like I said, he knows the lay of the land. He told me his family vacations all along New England, and the location he suggested for the Boston facility is so perfect I think I'll weep literal tears of regret if we don't end up with that property."

Jared waved his hand as if shooing away an inconsequential fly. "Yes, of course. I know all that, but how do you *like* him? On a personal level, I mean."

Was this junior high? Were we doing the whole "Who do you like" and "Do you *like*-like him" thing? Weren't we too old for that? "Jared, I don't really —"

"It's an important question because you'll be spending a lot of time together when I send you back East with him to procure the sites. And I don't want to deal with the drama if you hate each other and inadvertently sabotage Kinetics."

"What? Me? Back East? But —"

"Of course you. I want advertising efforts made before we ever dig the first shovel into the dirt. I need you to see it all, to experience the neighborhoods, taste the flavor of each community. I hired Lucas because he will help with all that."

I understood what he wanted. The concept of me traveling and being part of the initial survey of each location made sense in the most practical way possible. And I knew my job required travel. It was one of those sticking points that was a make-or-break deal for Kinetics. If I hadn't been willing to travel, they wouldn't have hired me.

So why did my heart flop against my ribs like a drunk bird trying to escape a cage at the thought of spending so much time alone with Lucas? No heart flopping could be allowed. This wasn't junior high. We were all adults, and we could all act like adults. I hardly knew the guy. Neither his commonalities with me nor his faults were so much as to interfere with our working relationship, so why was I being ridiculous?

Jared waited for my answer — the one he

asked me about traveling with Lucas, not the one I asked myself about being ridiculous.

I squared my shoulders and gave him my most competent, confident smile and said, "Of course I like him. Don't worry about a thing, Jared. He's a great member of our team, and I know we'll work just fine together."

Jared relaxed visibly. Had my opinion of Lucas given him anxiety? My opinion was certainly giving *me* anxiety.

"Good. A consultant only works if you're willing to consult with him. You've got to like each other for that to be possible."

Jared seemed to expect that we'd leave on the weekend. He didn't care about the launch of our new La Jolla store or all the work that still needed to be done there. He all but shoved me out of his office, saying, "We hire competent people so we don't have to babysit them while they do their jobs. Get packing. Katie will need to make the travel arrangements, so text her before going home so she has a heads-up. It's best she does it first thing in the morning. Good night, Emma. I'll see you tomorrow." And then he closed the door to his office, leaving me out in the hallway blustering with all the things he never gave me time to say.

If it surprised me that Lucas and I would be scouting locations together in person, it was nothing to Lucas's surprise the next morning when I broke the news to him that we were to be travel buddies and that we'd be flying out sooner rather than later.

He actually looked more concerned about it than I felt, which was insulting. I was a perfectly fine traveling companion, thank you very much.

"Katie already has us booked to leave Sunday evening so we're ready to hit the ground running bright and early Monday morning. The way I see it," I told him as I pushed my sleeves up to my elbows, "is that we have a lot to do before then."

He nodded his agreement, even if his face did have the ashen-gray color of someone who was sick over the news he'd received. I tried not to be offended by that.

Of course, my mind kept imagining all the reasons for his apprehension. I imagined Blake telling him stories about me and my insecurities. I imagined him thinking I was overly needy, which would be a natural response to someone who dumped their whole life story in his lap without provocation. Since he never made the parallel between April and me, he could only view my info dump as immaturity.

I really was an amateur. What kind of chump poured out her sad little childhood all over her ex-boyfriend's brother? How would he have made any kind of parallel between what April experienced and what I experienced? Why would I have imagined any of that made sense?

Even with all my self-admonition, sharing my past hadn't been totally fruitless. Hadn't I learned something about him as well?

The problem was that what I'd learned made me like him in a way I had never anticipated. We had too much in common for me not to feel something for him. He'd overcome too much for me not to admire his strengths.

But internal conflicts couldn't get in the way of external responsibilities, so I took Lucas on a tour of our facilities in other cities, starting with the not-yet-open La Jolla location. Having him in my car for a day trip would be good practice for us when we were let loose on the New England states.

I smiled at the guard checking the comings and goings of the workers during construction. He waved when he saw me and swept his hand over his graying hair as if trying to make himself presentable for me.

"Hello, Grady," I said.

He straightened at my use of his name.

114

"Hello, Emma. What brings you here today?"

"Just doing a tour is all." I pointed to Lucas. "This is Lucas Hampton. He'll be with the Kinetics family for the next little while, so if you ever see him alone, make sure to deny him access to anything he asks to see. He's absolutely not allowed on the premises unaccompanied."

Lucas startled at my words.

Grady smirked, and I laughed as I said, "Oh, fine, I guess he's okay. You can let him in if he can give you the secret password."

Lucas rolled his eyes at me and gave my arm a gentle shove. "Nice. Prank the new guy." He leaned close to my ear and whispered, "So what's the secret password?"

I had to think about that one for a second, which was hard with him so close to me. *Please* was too obvious. *Open sesame* was too grade school. Grady seemed to be waiting as well.

Finally, I said in a low, dramatic whisper, "Ms. Pierce is perfect."

Grady nodded as if I really had spoken magic words. "She's not wrong there."

Lucas hadn't moved away from where he whispered in my ear, and having his face so close to mine made me feel vulnerable.

"Ah, but she *is* wrong," Lucas said. His

eyes filled with humor and mischievousness and something else I couldn't read.

Vulnerability turned to outright insecurity at his words.

"Why am I wrong?" I asked, ready to give him a handprint to match his brother's.

Grady scowled. "Yeah, what makes her wrong?"

Lucas's eyes never left mine. "Because no one calls her Ms. Pierce."

"That's the point of a good password," I said, stepping back so I had breathing room. "It has to be something not many people know."

I sucked in a deep breath, took another step back, and refused to analyze my increased heart rate or suddenly sweaty palms.

Lucas also moved away and turned to the door, but Grady wouldn't step aside. At Lucas's questioning look, Grady shook his head. "Sorry. I didn't hear you use the magic words."

Lucas laughed, a hearty belly laugh that warmed me to hear. "Grady, my man, they are not paying you enough." His gaze slid my direction and back to Grady. "Ms. Pierce is perfect. Obviously."

Grady moved aside to allow us entrance.

We entered the building, and the smell of new carpet and fresh paint nearly bowled us over. Lucas said, "It's impressive."

"It is, isn't it?" I beamed at the entrance to the newest edition of the Kinetics empire.

"Well, the facility is nice too, but I mean you."

The smile slid off my face. "Me?" How could he say I was impressive when earlier, when I'd told him we were taking the East Coast tour together, he'd acted like I'd promised him liver and lima beans for dinner?

"You know everyone's name — from your marketing team to the receptionists to the wait staff to a random guard in an entirely different city."

I moved farther into the reception area, running my hand along the newly tiled counter. "Knowing the people I work with is not impressive."

"How many times have you actually worked with Grady the guard?" He followed behind me.

I shrugged. "A few."

"You act like you guys are best friends."

I rounded the corner and stood behind the counter. "He's a nice guy. Why shouldn't he be my best friend?"

He laughed at me. "Is Livvy nice enough to be your best friend as well?"

Livvy was one of the housekeeping staff at

the main office. I didn't even remember communicating with her when Lucas had been around. "Livvy is a sweetheart. She's everyone's best friend," I answered.

We faced each other on opposite sides of the counter. He placed both of his palms flat on the tile. "I've been in business long enough to know that it's rare for executive officers to remember the names of janitorial staff."

"That's just sad that you've worked with such monsters." I was making fun of him a little, but I felt like mockery was the only way to get him to stop staring at me as if he'd never seen me before. The truth was that his compliment flooded me with gratitude.

But it also unnerved me.

The only way I knew how to offset my discomfort was get back to business.

We discussed the various benefits of the facility and the ways we were marketing it to the La Jolla community. Every facility was built to be a unique representation of the community it served. Lucas showed me a few places where I'd missed opportunities to cater to La Jolla's distinctive tourist demographic, and while my initial response was one of resentment and a desire to reject his suggestions, once I got over myself, I found he was right.

I made notes and texted them to Debbie so she could get Jeremy working the ideas through social media. By the end of the day, our online traffic had risen dramatically and sign-ups for facility tours during opening week broke all our previous records.

I hated to admit it, especially to Jared, but Lucas was earning his keep. I had to give Lucas props when I called to report the highs of the day to Jared, but Jared took the compliments and gave them to himself for being smart enough to hire Lucas in the first place. He mumbled something about the other executives trying to tell him he didn't know how to run his own company and then hung up, smug and self-satisfied.

Whereas Jared patted his own back over the "synergy" between Lucas and me, Silvia glowered at me in suspicion. After work, she met me for pizza at Geppetto's, and she listened patiently while I told her all about Lucas and everything that had happened since leaving her couch several days before. The more I talked about all his great ideas and how funny it was that I knew more about him in a few days than I ever knew about Blake after months, the more her eyes narrowed.

"You cannot fall for your ex-boyfriend's

brother." Her interruption caught me off guard.

My smile slid downward into a frown before she hit the end of her sentence. "I'm not falling for him!" I took a bite of pizza even though I knew it ruined the effect of my glare. I needed to fill my mouth with something because I didn't like the shake in my voice on that last protest.

And the protest didn't even accomplish anything. Silvia obviously didn't believe me. "Since we've been seated, the only time you paused to not talk about this guy is when we ordered the food. You didn't even stop when the food actually showed up."

"Well, yeah. He's the guy Jared hired to basically do my job for me, and he's my ex-boyfriend's brother, and he's this crazy, confusing mix of really nice and hiding dark and scary things. He's a puzzle." Surely Silvia could understand needing to solve a puzzle. She was the only person I knew who had solved a mystery room in San Diego by herself in the allotted hour just because she wanted to see if she could.

Silvia wiped her hands on her napkin and stared at me with her one eye. "If you want to solve a puzzle, I'll buy you a jigsaw. It's not healthy for you to be so interested in him when there's no chance of a future with him. This guy is someone you should probably stay away from."

I laughed and pointed at her. "How do you propose I do that? I'm leaving for New York on Sunday with him."

She dropped her fork to her plate. Silvia was the sort of girl who ate pizza with a fork and knife while I remained a strictly hands-on pizza eater. "You're leaving the state with him? No. You can't leave the state with him."

"Tell that to Jared." I picked up the last slice of pizza from the metal plate and folded it in half to make it easier to eat. Silvia hated that I did that, insisting it was messy and uncivilized. I used to play the no-mom card when she complained about my untidy ways, but she finally got tired of it and insisted her mom had mothered us both well enough that she knew I knew better.

She was right. I did know better.

I just didn't care.

Besides, how could I enjoy the satisfaction of grossing her out by licking my saucy fingers if my fingers never got saucy to begin with? And Geppetto's pizza sauce was plate-licking-clean good. It may have been the lemon squeezed over the top of every pie. It may have been the fresh herbs crushed into the sauce. Whatever it was, Geppetto's was comfort food and comfort place all in one.

"I'm serious, Emma." Silvia looked serious, and since I'd let my mind wander to food, I had to remind myself what had her dark eyebrows bunched in two little knots above her nose. "You're on the rebound, hard-core. A guy could really take advantage of that. You could get really hurt."

Right. Lucas. Going out of town with him. I shook my head. "It's not like that. Lucas spends every day highlighting the angelic qualities of his brother. I usually have to shut him down several times when he gets carried away. He's not interested in me for him, he's interested in playing cupid with me for his brother. Besides, even if he had any interest in me at all — which he doesn't — he would never do anything to hurt his brother. As long as Blake keeps calling me, Lucas will be keeping a respectful distance. And even if it wasn't for his brother, Lucas isn't the kind of guy to pounce on wounded prey. He's one of those painfully nice boys."

"Blake keeps calling?" This information clearly confused her as much as it confused me. "Have you answered any of those calls?"

I pressed my lips together.

She sighed. "You have."

"It's rude to ignore people. And don't

worry, I didn't actually talk to him. I texted him that I was leaving town and couldn't talk until I got back."

Her lips quirked to the side in amusement. "Did you tell him you were leaving town with his brother?"

I growled. "You said I couldn't fall for his brother."

"And I'm absolutely right. You can't. But the situation has its humorous sides."

"Hilarious." I deadpanned.

The waitress refilled our water glasses and left the bill in a black folder on the table. Silvia grabbed it before I could.

"Hey," I argued, "we made a deal that I would buy all eat-out meals until you found a new and better-paying job."

She opened the black folder to look at the bill. The folder hid her face, but I caught the grin before she could cover it completely. "Then today is your lucky day."

I tugged the folder down so I could see her fully. "You got a new job?"

Her laugh, excited and filled with future possibilities, told me everything, but she said, "You are looking at Portal Pictures' newest, and undoubtedly their most amazing, film editor."

I squealed and jumped up from my seat. I pulled her out of her chair to give her a proper hug. "Not bad for a cyclops. Not bad at all! Portal Pictures?" I released her from the hug and gave her a scowl. "And you let me drone on and on about my own life without even hinting at it?"

"Good news can keep. Bad news needs venting before it can fester. But yeah, I'm pretty crazy excited right now. And granted, it's just assistant film editor. There's a whole team of people who have been there longer and have more experience than I have and who will be over me in the command chain, but it's really . . ."

We said at the same time, "A 'wish on a star' dream come true." Then we laughed and hugged again before taking our seats.

"So when do you start?" I asked, too excited to worry over my own life any further and too excited to even finish my last slice of pizza.

"Three weeks. I had to give notice for Mid-Scene Films before leaving them. So . . . kinda cool, huh?"

"Are you kidding? This is what you've worked so hard to accomplish, and you're years ahead of schedule. It won't be long until you get your real dream and get a job with Disney Studios. Girl, you are on your way! How did you hear about it?"

She picked up her fork and knife and cut

her pizza into bite-sized pieces. "It was actually Ben who told me the position was available and who told me I should apply."

"Ben? As in your boss, the editor from Mid-Scene Films?"

She nodded. "Pretty great of him, huh?"

I nodded. It *was* pretty great. It was downright stupendous for him to be willing to give her up so she could have bigger and better opportunities in the industry. "I am so excited for you! I can't believe I didn't even know you'd applied."

"I kept it to myself because it was such a long shot. I didn't want to hear my parents tell me to stop dreaming and you telling me that of course I would get the job when there was a very real chance that I wouldn't. Sometimes discouragement and encouragement create the same paralysis in me. It was easier to send in the application and resume and not think about it at all. It was a bridge jump. Had to be done."

When we'd been teenagers, Silvia wanted to go bungee jumping. I agreed to go with her as long as she didn't ask me to do it, too. But after she did it and the video looked so cool, I changed my mind and harnessed myself in for the jump. She told me I had to jump the second they clipped me in. I told her that maybe I needed a minute for her to either talk me into it or for me to talk myself out of it. But Silvia shook her head, not allowing me to hesitate. It was one of those moments when it was best to just jump without thought.

I jumped and screamed the whole way down. But the whole way back up, I laughed. From that moment on, the words *bridge jump* were our private code for doing something scary without overthinking it or seeking advice or approval.

It was the phrase that allowed us to forgive each other when we acted without telling each other first. Learning that we didn't have to tell each other everything, that there were bridges that needing jumping from in our lives, saved our friendship.

Before she could protest, I snatched up the little black folder. "I'm buying. You still have three weeks of being underpaid and likely another two or three weeks after that to collect a paycheck that isn't depressing. You can buy when you're solidly entrenched in the Portal Pictures payroll."

She tried to argue, but I had the bill and wasn't about to let it go.

"To think," I said, "*my* best friend is working at a major motion picture studio. Do you think you'll get to go to premieres? Oh! If you do, you had better let me be your plus-one! You need to hurry up and get employed by Disney. Isn't that who does the *Avengers* movies?"

I actually started daydreaming about presenting Lucas with an invitation to an *Avengers* premier before blowing out a long breath. Not only was it highly unlikely Silvia would be working on an *Avengers* movie anytime soon, but thinking about Lucas in any kind of daydream capacity was simply wrong.

Silvia cut into my thoughts with a laugh. "Don't you worry; I'll be at Disney soon. In the meantime, it'll be nice to work for a company that provides real tech, where I won't be expected to edit old-school by cutting up actual film and taping it back together."

"Aw, c'mon. Mid-Scene Films wasn't that bad."

She gave a satisfied smirk. "No. Not that bad. I'm grateful they gave me such a great start. I never would have landed this new job without that stepping-stone. Seriously. I owe Ben so much for his help."

She actually looked a little sad. I bumped her hand on the table. "You okay?"

She flashed all her teeth at me to prove she was happy, though the action looked more like a grimace than a smile. " 'Course

I'm okay. I just found the escalator to success, and it's going nowhere but up."

I tsked at her. "Escalator? You're so lazy. You don't even take the stairs in your dreamworld."

She acted like I'd said something disgusting. "Stairs do not belong in any dreamworld of mine."

I handed the folder to the waitress and leaned in toward Silvia. "That can be a new film for you. A horror film — *The Bad News Stairs.*"

Silvia shook her head at me. "Your puns are getting worse."

"I know. It's what happens when the vampire of corporate America sucks away all of my good ideas. Lucas laughs at my puns, by the way."

Silvia covered my hands with hers. "I'm serious, here. No flirting with Lucas."

"How are bad puns flirting?"

"They aren't, I just think you should beware of your reactions to a guy who has a kid and a psycho ex, especially when he's the brother to *your* psycho ex."

The waitress returned the folder to the table, and I made quick work of filling in the tip and signing so we could let someone else take our table. Geppetto's was busier than normal, and passing by those waiting to be seated made me feel guilty for lingering so long over the meal. But I'd needed that time with Silvia. To hear of her advancement in her career was the best news ever. And to get her perspective on Lucas was useful. She brought up the two points that continually plagued me.

Lucas and the kid.

Lucas and his brother.

But worse than those two points was the other, rather weightier, admonition she'd given me.

I was not allowed to fall for Lucas.

Of course, that wasn't even a possibility. Liking him as a person and as a professional and being able to appreciate his ideas and insight were not even close to the same thing as falling in love. Falling in love came to people who didn't have messy tie-ins or tie-ups. Lucas and I had both. I gave Silvia an extra-tight squeeze before she got into her car. I was proud of my cyclops friend for chasing her dreams, but more, I was grateful she acted as the voice of reason in my life.

Something happened inside me when Silvia shook me down for information regarding my feelings toward Lucas, something I'd never experienced before with Silvia.

I had wanted to lie.

I wanted to tell her that Lucas was ridiculous, that he had no good qualities at all, that he really was just the deadbeat dad I had accused him of being when Silvia and I had talked on the phone the night before, and that he was my competition at work.

Not that those things were really lies; I did believe those things about him.

But I also believed so many *other* things about him. I believed he was smart and interesting and funny and handsome. I believed his ice-blue eyes could melt me into a puddle of absurdity if I let them. As my mind battled between the many conflicting thoughts, I realized something important. I couldn't trust my own thoughts anymore. Silvia was right to warn me. I hoped I was smart enough to listen to that warning.

CHAPTER SEVEN

"Now they were as strangers; nay, worse
than strangers, for they could never
become acquainted."
— JANE AUSTEN, *Persuasion*

Lucas must have told Blake we were leaving
for New York because Blake's calls became
more frequent. He sent flowers to the office, which Lucas gave me a thumbs-up
over. He showed up at the office to take me
to lunch, which I got out of without too
much difficulty because I had meetings with
several radio stations regarding airtime for
our advertisements. Seeing him had sent
me into a tailspin. Ignoring his phone calls
and flowers was much easier than ignoring
him in person.

When I walked into the reception area and
saw Blake standing there, I wasn't sure
which of the three I wanted to do more:
run away, throw up, or pass out. I did none

of those things but instead offered a shaky smile and a shakier handshake.

His eyebrows went up at my proffered hand, and he moved past it altogether, encroaching into my personal space and enveloping me in an embrace that he had not received permission from me to give.

Lucas walked in at just that moment and halted, looking as though he'd been caught in a freeze ray.

I don't know why, but having Lucas witness my embrace with his brother made me feel wrong somehow . . . guilty. I yanked myself out and shook my head. "What are you doing here?" I wasn't sure who I addressed the question to.

The brothers shared a look, and with that look, Lucas stepped back, and Blake stepped forward. "I wanted to see you before you left, to talk to you — really talk to you."

As he moved toward me again, I backed up. "We don't really have anything to talk about."

"Baby . . . don't be like this. Aren't those months we've spent together worth a little time to fix the mess we're in now?"

I might have imagined it, but it seemed Lucas flinched when Blake called me *baby.* He lowered his head as if watching a particularly squeamish scene in a medical documentary.

Katie sat at the reception desk and watched my personal soap opera play out in front of her.

"Blake," I said, glancing between the brothers, uncertain of whom to direct my rejections to. "Blake," I said again, deciding on him. "I have a lot going on right now. As you know . . ." I shot daggers at Lucas for being the company mole. "I'm leaving town. And right now, I have a meeting I can't just drop because you feel the need to explain your fish fry to me."

"We were grilling."

Lucas's head snapped up, and his eyes widened as mine narrowed in confusion. "What?"

Even though Lucas shook his head at his brother, Blake said, "We weren't frying, we were grilling the fish."

"Seriously?" I said, looking at Lucas, who shrugged helplessly as if he couldn't find a defense for his brother's stupidity either.

"Blake . . ." Finding words to dignify the situation and wishing I could make Katie disappear so none of this ended up in the rumor mill actually made my brain hurt. "I will talk to you when I get back, but not until then, okay? Don't stop by my office again without my permission."

I left Blake in the reception area, but Lucas followed me to my office. He must have signaled Blake to stay put because Blake made no move to leave. "Let me handle the meetings," Lucas said. "You can go to lunch. You deserve a break . . . some time off to keep your work-life balance in check."

"Back off, Lucas. You're the marketing consultant for the East Coast, not the social coordinator of my personal life. Remember what you were hired for."

He squared his shoulders and tightened his mouth, apparently properly chastised. "I apologize, Ms. Pierce. I didn't mean to intrude in your personal affairs." He inclined his head as though paying respects to someone of actual rank and turned to leave.

His change in demeanor made me inwardly roll my eyes. How had I become the bad guy in this situation? "Lucas, wait." He stopped and turned back to me. "I'm sorry if I came off as overly harsh just now. Blake is a sore topic for me. I admire the way you defend him and care about him, I really do. But *if* he and I get back together, it will have to be at a time when I am mentally and emotionally prepared to make that happen. I can guarantee that time will definitely not be before this trip when I need to focus on my job."

His face went from sullen contrition to hopeful.

Apparently, no one had ever informed Lucas what *if* meant.

Lucas must have relayed my message to Blake because he all but vanished from my voice mail and only left a mere whisper of a text message every morning reminding me to have a good day, which was still more communication than I ever received from him while we were dating.

"He's a far more attentive ex-boyfriend than he ever was a boyfriend," I told Debbie during lunch on Friday. We'd gone down to the Kinetics restaurant for something quick enough to get us back to our desks in a timely manner but long enough to make us feel like we had a break.

"You need to scrape him off and let him know you've got someone new."

I laughed. "That might work if I actually had someone new."

"Oh, come on. Are you really playing dumb on this one? You have to know we've all noticed."

"Noticed what?"

"That consultant guy, Lucas, seems pretty attentive, too. You two are always together. Always talking. He spends more time in your office than he does in his own. Anything you'd like to share on that?" Her eyes glittered with a deep need to know and the excitement of possibly finding out.

I snorted. "Please be serious. We have to be together all the time because every single thing Jared wants us working on is stuff we have to do together."

"None of the other execs get invited to your exclusive office parties."

Sometimes, I really wished my friends had their own exciting love lives so they could quit imagining exciting love lives for everyone else. "That's because Lynette has already done the projections and budgets, so her part is done, and Chase is working his magic with La Jolla. He needs to focus on sales that can happen right now, not ones that can't happen because we don't even have ground to break, yet."

"But the guy is super hot. Like fever-dream hot. Those blue eyes? I totally thought they were contacts for the first week. You can't tell me you haven't paid attention to the way he looks. More importantly, don't tell me you're so blind you don't see the way he looks *at you* or smiles at you or agrees with everything you say."

I put up my hands to stop her overactive imagination from getting more vocal than it already had. "He's Blake's brother."

She squinted as if trying to see really tiny print. "No, he isn't." She shook her head as if dislodging the ridiculous thought out of her mind.

"Yes, he is."

I suddenly wasn't hungry and wiped my mouth with my napkin before placing it on the table next to my plate. "He's Lucas *Hampton*. Blake *Hampton's* brother. So if you see him acting overly attentive toward me, it's because he's on a mission to get his brother and me back together."

I stood, needing to get back to work and not needing to feel like the office-gossip topic. "I have a lot to do before I leave this weekend. I need the content for the La Jolla landing page finished and edited and in Erik's folder on the server so he can get the page live online. Let me know when it's done, okay?"

She didn't say anything while I gathered my things but grabbed my arm as I stepped away from the table. "Are you serious about Lucas? He's Blake's brother?"

I nodded. "Ice cream falling off the cone serious."

"What are the chances?"

I shrugged. "Right? Anyway, gotta go. Keep me updated on the landing page content."

She agreed she would and went back to her food. Debbie didn't like eating alone, but she would eat much faster and get to her work much sooner if I wasn't there to talk to. I really did need her to get her work to Erik and only felt a little bad for manipulating her by using her discomfort of sitting by herself against her.

Though, I would likely have stayed if she hadn't been using me for gossip fodder. Again. At least Katie had kept the whole argument in the reception area to herself.

Within the hour, Debbie reported the assigned task as completed and also reported that her content team had the billboard ads hammered out and to the design team.

Good.

Having everyone actually working instead of offering me love advice removed a huge source of frustration from my shoulders. Lucas still acted weird every time I mentioned our trip and tried to cement schedules so we knew what we were doing, but I figured his issues with leaving town with his brother's ex-girlfriend were his issues, not mine.

By the time the weekend rolled around and I said good-bye to my teams and reported highs and lows to Jared, where he commended himself again for hiring the new consultant and instructed me to take those consultations seriously, I found myself actually looking forward to getting out of town and away from the office for a few days.

I tried not to focus too intently on why I looked forward to getting away, tried not to think about what Debbie had said about the way Lucas looked at me *or* the way he looked. I wasn't that girl. I would take Silvia's warning seriously and keep my heart out of messy families. Besides, who cared how the consultant looked when Jared was looking at the consultant with those starry eyes.

When I boarded the plane on Sunday, I was surprised that Lucas hadn't shown up yet. I checked the flight itineraries Katie had forwarded me and saw that he was assigned to sit in the seat next to mine. He just wasn't there.

I sincerely hoped he wasn't the sort of guy who missed flights. We didn't have time for that kind of nonsense. But if he did, the trouble would fall to him and Katie to fix. Maybe this would show Jared I didn't need help and that the consultant wasn't so totally awesome after all. Maybe it would show *me* he wasn't perfect after all, and I could stop thinking about him.

"I'm not thinking about him," I mumbled to myself as I tucked my luggage in the overhead bin.

"Not thinking about who?"

"Lucas! You scared me!" I whisper-yelled and placed my hand on my chest to calm my heart. Feeling grumbly over his over-hearing the tail end of something I did not want him overhearing, I took my seat and buckled in.

Katie, bless her, had booked us first-class plane tickets so we had stretch-out room and comfortable seats. But the seat didn't make me any more comfortable when I was hyperaware of my traveling companion. Packing the night before had been emotion-ally exhausting. I would have consulted Sil-via on what to pack except she would read too much into the question. Or she'd read the question exactly right and give me lectures that were filled with good sense but that I knew I wouldn't follow anyway, so why bother bugging her about it?

My phone buzzed with new messages from Debbie and Erik.

"Doesn't that thing need to be off?" Lu-cas asked. His voice had a nervous edge to it.

I inspected him from the way he sat rigid in his seat to the way his seat belt was so tight he would likely cut off the blood supply to his legs. He had a book with him — the real kind with paper and ink and binding. There was not an electronic device to be found in his general area. I laughed. "You're afraid to fly." It wasn't a question.

"No, I'm not."

"Oh, okay, those white knuckles are an anemic reaction to your iron-poor breakfast, then?"

"I'm just saying that your cell phone could interfere with the plane's navigational instruments, and it's airline policy to keep it off. We're representing Kinetics right now and should follow all airline guidelines."

His intense sincerity cracked me up. "One, neither of us has any identifying tags that link us to the Kinetics name. Two, even if we did, we are not in any way shaming the company because you only have to keep your electronic devices off during takeoff. Furthermore, you can keep your device in airplane mode during the flight and still use all the apps you have. Three, they haven't even closed the cabin, yet. And four, I don't believe phones actually affect navigational instruments."

My phone buzzed with another text, startling him so much that if he hadn't been belted in so tightly, he would have leaped right out of his seat.

"But you don't know phones don't affect it. Why would you risk the life of every person on this plane just because you're a skeptic?"

This was seriously too good. Confident, self-assured Lucas Hampton was afraid to fly. "Don't rich people fly all the time?" I asked. "Shouldn't you be used to airplanes?"

"I don't fly much now that I'm on my own. And when I was younger, it was easier flying with the family. My mom always sat by me and talked me through it."

"Did she hold your hand, too?" I shouldn't have snickered, but I couldn't help it.

He didn't deny it but got defensive. "I was a kid."

"You weren't adopted until you were thirteen," I reminded him.

When he turned red, I knew I'd taken it too far. He huffed and turned his face forward, closing his eyes and leaning his head back against the seat.

My phone vibrated again, but he didn't jump this time. Instead his jaw flexed, and his nostrils flared. I glanced at the message from Jeremy updating me on the statistics of our Facebook ads, sighed at the thought of lost time, and turned my phone to airplane mode.

"You can open your eyes now. The big bad phone is turned off."

He peeked an eye open and closed it again. "That is not off."

"It is too."

"Your screen is still lit up."

I pried one of his eyes open so he could see the little plane icon on my phone. "It's in airplane mode, which is off enough."

The voice on the loudspeaker crackled instructions to prepare for takeoff. She specifically mentioned electronic devices could remain in airplane mode. It probably was a juvenile response to say "I told you so" to Lucas, so I poked his arm and lifted an eyebrow at him instead. The charades version of "I told you so" seemed less juvenile somehow.

He opened his hardback book — one that had to weigh five pounds and that he'd probably be done reading before the trip was through, which meant he'd either need to buy a new book or be bored on the way home — and began reading.

"If you had an electronic device, you could fit the entire Stephen King canon and several hundred other books besides, all on something that weighs half of what that book probably weighs." I wasn't making fun of him. Not really. I just wanted to show

143

him a more efficient way.

Sadly, unsolicited advice is never appreciated.

He turned his whole body away from me and snugged his book in closer as if to stop me from peeking over his shoulder.

"I'm sorry," I said and meant it. To prove it, I powered my phone all the way off. "See? I'm not even taking cavalier risks with the other passengers' lives."

At the sound of my phone chiming off, he turned his head to verify my honesty. "A lot of people are afraid of flying," he said tightly. "It's a rational response to getting into a confined space with a couple hundred strangers and then rocketing to near the stratosphere with nothing but a little wind and cumulous between you and the earth."

"Fair enough, but I bet if you studied airplane disasters, you'd cure yourself."

He twisted back in his seat so he could stare at me in total disbelief. "You really think watching planes fall from the sky in fiery streaks of human terror would make me feel better?"

"Yes," I answered and hurried to explain before he thought I was still teasing. "If you studied airplane disasters, you'd know that most of the time when something goes wrong, where a step is missed or executed poorly, the flight crew takes care of it. It's kind of like when we mess up at our jobs, which we're bound to do because we're real people, we figure out the error and how to fix it so the error doesn't hurt anything."

"You're forgetting that when *we* screw up, hundreds of people don't fall to their deaths."

"No, but we usually fix things before anyone even notices anything went wrong. Airplanes go up and down safely every day, hundreds — maybe even thousands — of times a day, and yet we hardly ever hear about planes going down or having issues. That's because the crew is prepared to handle stuff. Trust the crew. They got their jobs by doing what they do well. They troubleshoot better than anyone. They will get us safely back on the ground once we're up."

The plane backed out of the gate and began to taxi toward the runway. I felt Lucas tighten even more next to me. "Really," I said. "You're okay. I promise this plane will land on the other side of America, right where it needs to."

"I should have taken the train," he said.

I laughed. "Great plan. You'd arrive just as I left. Kind of defeats the purpose of the trip if you aren't there." The engines rumbled underneath the wings, and Lucas gripped the leather armrests hard enough to leave permanent indentations of his fingerprints.

The plane picked up speed, racing to catch the lift of wind that would take us to the clouds. Lucas's mouth moved with words I couldn't hear. The guy was truly terrified, which made me feel even worse for harassing him about his aerophobia. I probably caused more of his current panic by talking about things going wrong.

"Hey," I said. "Hey, we're safe. We're going to be fine. I promise you that this ride will be smooth and easy and trouble free."

"You cannot promise that," he said through lips so pale he appeared to have used a white lipstick on them.

"Sure I can. Pinky promise." I pried his pinky off the leather armrest and twined mine with his.

His eyes snapped open, and he twisted to gape at me. I met his stare with a smile and tightened my pinky grip on his in a way that I hoped was reassuring. "We're safe. We'll be safe. Pretty soon we'll be at JFK, and then we'll wish we were still on the plane because finding a cab to our hotel will be impossible." I was glad Katie booked us into JFK since every flight I'd ever had into La-

Guardia had been dicey. The landings were always terrible at LaGuardia.

The plane nosed into the air, and the friction of the wheels on the tarmac suddenly gave way to open sky. That moment when the wind and gravity fought each other for their right to hold me was the best feeling in the world to me. Lucas squeezed his eyes shut again, and his pinky formed a death grip on mine. His shallow breathing almost started to make me panic as well, but I glanced out my window and saw all the reminders of why I wasn't afraid to fly.

"Lucas, open your eyes."

"I will in a second," he managed to say between erratic puffs of breath.

I tugged the hand with the connected pinkies. "Look now, or you'll miss it."

He took several more shallow breaths, holding the last one, and then he pried one eye open. I covered our pinky-clasped hands with my other hand and said, "See out there? A whole world of wonderful."

Katie had timed our departure with the sunset over the Pacific Ocean. The clouds separated in a way that soaked in every drop of sunlight until it looked like their fluffy tops had been set on fire. I tightened my grip on our hands and grinned at him. "Isn't it beautiful?"

He tried at a smile, but it was shaky and fearful, so I kept talking. "The first time I flew in a plane, I was twelve. My dad took me to San Francisco, where he had a bunch of work to do. He was a salesman for hospital equipment. He couldn't find anyone to stay with me for the week he'd be gone so he took me with him. The minute the plane lost connection with the ground, I felt all the possibilities in the world. If humans could make planes fly and send people to the moon and machines even farther than the moon, then humans could do anything. And since I was human, I knew I could do wonderful things, too. It was a really empowering moment for me."

I glanced at him. He was still with me, still listening, still leaving his eyes open to the horizon of sky and sea outside my window. "So you shouldn't look at flying as something to fear, Lucas Hampton."

"No?" That one word still had a quake to it, but not as much as before.

"No. Flying is a way to get perspective. Down there on the ground, we drive into neighborhoods that don't make any sense, roads going everywhere except where you think you want them to go, but up here, those same roads have a defining pattern. They go exactly where they're supposed to go, maybe not where we wanted, but where they need to go. Flying is the great metaphor."

A laugh burbled out of him. I think it surprised him as much as it surprised me. "The great metaphor?"

"Sure. The one I just gave of seeing the pattern and how it all works like it's supposed to and more. I mean, everyone has problems, right?"

He nodded his agreement.

"Problems are hard to deal with if we can't see all the pieces clearly. We need to get above them and see all the pieces. We need perspective and a way to appreciate the complexity and beauty that can come from them."

"Beauty? From problems?" He was looking at me now and not out the window, but he had color in his lips again.

"Yes. Problems help us know what we're made of. They help us to recognize our strengths and to overcome our weaknesses. Have you ever flown above a storm?"

His lips paled again and his mouth tightened as he shook his head. *Flying* and *storm* were apparently words that didn't belong in the same sentence together while he was in the air.

Focus on me, buddy, I thought. *Stay with*

me here. "I saw a lightning storm up close and all around me once. The plane flew above it, but we had to go through it to get above it — another metaphor. The clouds were dark except when the light sliced through them and made me see spots for several moments afterward. But once we were through, the sun was setting just like it is now. The cloudy, gray day we'd endured was done. It was beautiful. It's all about perspective. And you can't tell me a little perspective isn't beautiful. Just look."

His eyes stayed fixed on mine.

"Well? Go ahead. Look outside."

He blinked and tore his gaze away to do as directed.

I was proud of him for daring to look out again.

"Perspective is beautiful," he said.

When I glanced back to beam at my new pupil and his ability to get over his fear of the sky outside the window, I realized he was looking at me again. He hurried to avert his gaze as if I'd caught him doing something wrong. He bravely looked out the window.

I laughed. "If you'd rather look at a person in order to stay grounded and feel calm, it's okay. You don't have to look out the window. I can't expect you to conquer your fears in under a half hour."

He swallowed hard. His Adam's apple bobbed into his tie knot, and his cheeks reddened. "I think it's better if I look out the window."

"Sure. You're right. But don't push yourself too hard to get over your fear of flying. I don't want you passing out on me and forcing me to resuscitate your terrified, stopped heart." I don't know why I said it, or worse, why I allowed myself to imagine a resuscitation scenario, but my own cheeks reddened at the thought of leaning down for mouth-to-mouth.

The seat belt light pinged over our heads, and I looked down, realizing that our hands were still locked in a pinky promise and that somehow our other hands had joined the tangle. Not wanting to seem like touching him had affected me, I gave his hands a squeeze and said, "I may not be Caroline Hampton, but I'm glad I was here to hold your hand during takeoff."

He startled and looked down at our hands as if he too hadn't realized what had happened. He barked out a nervous laugh, and we let go of each other at the same time.

"Sorry," he mumbled.

"It's not a problem," I said. Except that it was. I had liked holding his hands. I had liked sharing the little bit of my sunshine childhood with him in the same way I had felt relieved in sharing my rainy-day childhood with him.

Lucas Hampton disarmed me in a way that made me share everything. In many ways, he knew more about me than Blake ever did.

That was a problem indeed.

CHAPTER EIGHT

"Is not general incivility the very essence
of love?"
— JANE AUSTEN, *Pride and Prejudice*

We kept to mostly ourselves for the rest of
the plane ride. He read his Stephen King,
and I organized our schedules so our days
were filled entirely with work but our
evenings were free. Though I'd been to New
York several times, it was big enough I felt
confident I hadn't seen everything, and I'd
never been to Boston.

With all of that out of the way, I considered reading the new eBook I'd purchased
for the flight, but peeked over at Lucas and
decided not to risk sending him into a panic
attack.

Instead, I pulled out a very worn, very
torn, paperback from my bag. I kept it there
for emergencies when I was stuck with an
uncharged device or somewhere with no

Internet service and nothing to entertain me.

I snuggled into my seat, turned away from Lucas so he couldn't see the cover, and began reading.

A while later, Lucas's voice broke through the plight of the Bennett sisters having to deal with Mr. Collins. "Hm?" I asked, blinking away the images of the girls walking to Meryton to make the best of the time they were forced to spend with their odious cousin.

"You weren't kidding when you said she was your favorite," he said.

"And you weren't kidding when you said he was your favorite." I pointed to his Stephen King.

"Yes, but mine is still writing new books, still giving me new entertainment. Yours has been dead for, what — two hundred years?"

"Her breathing status doesn't change the fact that she is entertaining, that she understands the subtleties of humor and people and how they work together to make reading an enjoyable experience."

He smirked and went back to his own book.

I felt fury at his puffed-up sense of superiority. "Are you really going to snub me for my reading choices when *Pride and Prejudice* is considered a literary classic by scholars? Yours is still just commercial fiction."

I knew the look he gave me, the one that said he knew more about something than I did. I saw it a lot when we were choosing viable locations for Kinetics. Such a short amount of time with the guy and I could already read him almost as well as the worn-out paperback in my hands.

"May I remind you, dear lady, that the works of Jane Austen were 'just commercial fiction' during her lifetime and even for quite a while after her lifetime? Very few books qualify as classics while the author is alive. I guarantee the works of Stephen King will be considered classics someday, and college kids will be writing comparisons between the gothic of Shelley's *Frankenstein* and the gothic of King's *Salem's Lot.*"

"You're right," I said.

His eyes widened. "Did you just say I was right?"

"I'm not stupid enough to let my ego get in the way of facts. You're right. He will be studied. I've even read a lot of his books. Does it surprise you to know I've read *Salem's Lot*?"

He turned his body so he faced me, something he wouldn't have been able to do if we'd been flying coach, and rested his head against his seat. "I admit I'm a little surprised. Does it surprise you that I've read *Pride and Prejudice*?"

"Not really. You likely had to read it in college. Like I said — a literary classic."

His quirked-to-the-side lip was hard not to stare at, but I made myself focus on the intensity of his blue eyes.

"True," he said. "But does it surprise you to know that I read the rest of her books on my own just because I was curious?"

He had me on that one. "Yes. Yes, it does. Did you like them?"

"Kind of. Kind of not."

The plane intercom interrupted us with a reminder that we were preparing for landing and all tray tables needed to be stowed and seats needed to be in the upright position.

By that point, he'd begun breathing again like he was running from zombies. I instinctively took his hand again. It worked the first time, after all. I didn't allow myself to look too deeply into any other motive I might have had, like the incredibly attractive fact that he'd read the entire works of my beloved Jane.

Ugh.

No.

Not beloved. Jane and I were no longer

together. She'd let me down too many times before. I needed to remember that.

He didn't pull away when I took his hand, but instead hung on with a grip that felt like it might leave my hand numb for a week. But, at my request, he didn't close his eyes, either. New York at night was not a sight to be missed from this vantage point. Lucas stayed with me for it, his eyes fixed on the window and all it offered.

"That wasn't so bad, was it?" I asked as we tugged our luggage from the overhead bins when it was all over.

"No," he said. "Not bad at all." But he frowned as he whispered the words, which I interpreted as flying couldn't be improved in any way, shape, or form.

From there, we had to focus on hiring a cab and getting to our hotel. Since it was one in the morning, the congestion of cars and people had eased up, but since it was New York, it was still plenty busy. I felt an immense sense of gratitude when the front desk attendant at the Hilton on West 57th Street handed me my room key card and pointed in the direction of the elevators. Lucas seemed in as much a coma state as I was in as we silently dragged our bags behind us onto the elevators and up to our rooms. The elevator sped through the many floors, making me wonder if Lucas had a problem with elevators, too, but he seemed okay with the ear-popping ascent into the skyscraper hotel.

His room was next to mine. I saluted him as he waited for me to get inside before attempting to open his own door. It was nice for him to wait, to make sure of my safety. Also, it was strange having him right next door. Would he hear when I sang in the shower? Would he complain to the manager if my TV was too loud? Worse, was he the type of person to crank *his* TV too loud?

It was as I plugged in my laptop just before crawling into bed that I remembered the schedule. Lucas didn't know the schedule. How could I expect him to be prompt and available when and where I needed him if I'd never bothered to tell him where and when those places and times were?

I verbally scolded myself, but not too loud since I had no idea what Lucas could hear or not hear through the walls. The problem was that I'd handwritten the entire schedule since Lucas hadn't wanted me to use an electronic device on the plane. I couldn't email it to him unless I transcribed everything onto the computer, and I was much too tired to do that. The fastest option would be to have the front desk make me a copy.

I deliberated on whether I should change into respectable clothes or simply wear my yoga pants and the vintage Dr Pepper T-shirt I'd inherited from my father when he'd died. A quick glance in the mirror assured me I didn't look inappropriate, exactly, especially for the middle of the night when no one was likely to see me. I shrugged, stuffed my feet into my shoes, and headed down with my key card and handwritten notes.

The man behind the front desk helped me with the copies, and I was back in the elevator with schedules and addresses in no time.

I intended to hit the ground running the next day, but hard copies were definitely less convenient than digital ones.

Once on my floor again, I tiptoed to Lucas's room to slip the schedule under the door so it would be where he would see it in the morning.

"What are you doing?"

The voice from behind me startled me. I jumped and inadvertently gave myself a paper cut on my pinky finger.

I turned and saw Lucas surveying me as he leaned against the wall, a Dr Pepper bottle in hand. "I'm giving you your schedule. What are you doing? It's the middle of the night."

"Couldn't sleep. Needed a drink." He raised his bottle to me. "Hey, we match."

"We do." I nodded and tugged at the bottom of my oversized shirt and felt incredibly exposed.

He nodded, and I nodded some more, and we both stood stupidly in the hallway in the middle of the night when we both really needed some sleep. "Well, then, since you're here . . . this is for you." I handed him the paper, and only after he was in full possession of it did I realize that a smear of my blood from the paper cut darkened the corner.

"Oh! I'm sorry. Here, take this one."

He glanced at the stained schedule, laughed, and insisted he was fine. He ran his hand under his nose and inspected our schedule. "Nice. Tight, but not unreasonable, and I see you've given us our evenings free. Good job, boss."

He hadn't ever called me that before, and while it might be true on a technical level, I felt strange hearing it from him. A lot of people in marketing called me "boss." He was probably only parroting what he'd heard others call me. Instead of correcting him, I merely explained my reasons for the lax evenings. "If we don't take a little personal time each day, then we'll put too much on ourselves and be less likely to make good choices in situations where our clear heads would be vital. Besides, it's a shame to go somewhere new and not see any of it."

"Haven't you been here before?"

I shifted and tossed a glance at my door. "Yeah, a few times, but I haven't seen everything. You could live here and not see everything. But it's important to at least try. My father always taught me to take advantage of the opportunities life gives you at the time they are given because some opportunities only come around once." I smiled at him, thinking of the bridge-jumping experience. My father was one of the reasons I decided I had to at least try it. "Consider your free evenings to be a gift of opportunity. You're welcome."

"Your dad sounds like a great guy."

"He is — was . . . is." I frowned and shook my head. "Anyway, he worked hard to make up for other things I was missing. He took being my dad very seriously. He called raising me his best opportunity. I think he liked being my dad. 'You are my one shot at fatherhood, so I'm going to do it right,' he'd say. So, yeah. Great guy."

After another awkward pause, I hitched my thumb in the direction of my door. "Well, um, we've got a long day tomorrow."

"Right." He stepped aside so we could switch places and get to our respective rooms.

"Good night, Emma," he said.

"Good night, Lucas."

I opened my door, but before I could close it again, he said, "Emma?"

"Hm?"

"I'm glad you had a great dad."

I smiled. "Me too."

Once I was in my room and leaning against my closed door, I wrapped my arms around myself as if I could hug the shirt and in some weird way hug my father. I really missed him. He'd died of a heart attack while I'd been a senior in college, and, in the process, rendered me an orphan. The conversation about him with Lucas had been strange, to say the least — in an uncomfortably intimate way.

But telling him about my dad made sense given the circumstances. It likely stemmed from Lucas pointing out the shirt I was wearing.

Why did I keep justifying spilling my guts to this guy?

"Gah!" I shouted, then slapped both my

hands over my mouth. No way Lucas did not hear that noise. "Go to bed, Emma," I whispered to myself.

I did as I was told.

The next morning, everything seemed fine. Lucas was even ready and waiting downstairs several minutes before I arrived. We met with the real estate agent, who toured us through the Manhattan properties. As I took notes, Lucas murmured his opinions on the neighborhoods, the likelihood of significant client sign-ups, the proximity of public transportation, and nine million other things I would have spent weeks wandering the city to discover.

Halfway through the tour, as the agent was trying to sell us on a property that had looked great online but looked less impressive in real life, Lucas texted me, "I've squatted in nicer warehouses than this when I was a kid."

I held my laughter in check by biting my lip and feeling grateful I had set my phone to vibrate. I texted back, "The neighbor's doghouse was better than this. I'd say my own doghouse, but I didn't have a dog since my childhood was sadder than yours."

Lucas didn't have my self-control, and he laughed out loud. The agent frowned at him. "Nice," Lucas texted. "You got me in trouble."

The texts back and forth continued for the rest of the day, silent communications behind the agent's back that kept us entertained while we worked. We waged a who-had-a-sadder-childhood war that made stifling giggles harder as the day went along. I found that Lucas took my opinion as seriously as he expected me to take his. He didn't act competitive toward me in the way I felt toward him and that fact helped me relax. Relax and feel a little stupid that I'd allowed myself to view him as a work rival when he apparently had no such emotions.

At the end of the day, I forwarded all my notes to Jared, phone conferenced with him and several others about our options, and was instructed to return to two of the locations to take pictures and video for the team.

As much as Jared hated listening to the advice of the other executives he hired, he did care what they thought about how he ran his business.

An evening off felt well-earned, and when Lucas and I walked out to the taxi, it occurred to me that I didn't know what happened next. Did we take the shared cab back to the hotel and separate there to get dinner and see the sights on our own? Or did we separate now and each get our own taxis? Or did we stay together?

Lucas apparently had no such quandaries. "So, where are we exploring tonight?" he asked, obviously assuming we'd spend our time together.

The thought didn't bother me as much as it should have considering I'd just gotten off a call with Jared that praised every attribute Lucas had and probably several Lucas didn't have.

Manhattan in July had a miserable heat to it that made me desperate to get into the taxi, but I stopped to consider Lucas's question. "I don't really know. Tonight, I wanted to rest easy. We got in so late last night, and I'm kind of tired, so while I want to get a bite to eat, I don't want to be out doing actual exploring. But you don't have to stay with me, you know. I'm perfectly capable of maneuvering through the city on my own."

He bobbed his head before handing the cabbie some money and saying, "We'll walk. Thanks for waiting."

The cabbie took his fare and left.

I blinked. Did he really just send away my taxi when I'd already declared exhaustion?

He laughed at my expression and put his arm over my shoulder. The movement felt friendly, natural, not predatory or pretentious. It was almost like he didn't even realize he'd done it. "You were planning on tour by cab. How could any self-respecting native to the city allow such a thing? You can't see this city from a taxi window. You can only see it by pounding the pavement. Let's get some dinner and walk back to the hotel. It's a nice night."

Did he just call the sweat-dripping-ogre's-mouth-of-humidity a nice night?

But I went along with him. Compelled by curiosity and the fact that he had his arm over my shoulder. We ended up at a burger joint where he ordered us both the special, which consisted of concrete shakes, burgers, and fries. We ate our meals at a patio table on the street, with passing traffic and honking horns as our background music. "Ever been to the Shake Shack before?"

I shook my head and took a bite of my burger. I had to refrain from sighing out loud. Once I tasted it, I felt like I'd been missing out.

He watched me for a moment. "Tell me more about your dad," he said before biting into his own burger.

"Not much to tell, really. He was a salesman for hospital equipment. He liked Dr Pepper and The Smiths. And trains — whenever he had a chance to ride a train, he took it. He was funny. Loved dad jokes.

He spent his whole life making up for the crummy things that happened in mine."

"Nice."

"What about you?" I asked but then had to repeat myself because a large truck rumbled by, horn blaring.

"Which one do you want to know about?" he asked once he heard me.

I'd forgotten he had more than one option. I shrugged. "Whichever one you want to discuss."

"My biological father was never a part of my life. Honestly, there's no guarantee that the guy my mom claimed to be my dad is actually my dad. My stepdad I had before the Hamptons found me was a real winner. He took me with him on drug deals every now and again because he figured he'd look less suspicious to the police if he had a kid with him. He finally ended up in prison — big surprise, right?

"But I had people in my life who made it seem like the universe wanted to apologize to me for my childhood. The Hamptons made up for a lot. Allen Hampton loves basketball. He loves the game. Loves to play it with his kids, loves to watch it on TV, and he supports the Lakers with a devout attention usually reserved for religion or politics. And when his wife brought home a stray"

— Lucas pointed at himself — "he shrugged and said, 'Never leave the toilet seat up, kid. She'll throw you out the first time you do.' He's a pretty cool guy, even if he did make me paranoid about using the bathroom for a while."

"Good dads making up for other lousy parents for the win." I cringed internally, realizing how such a thing might sound considering he still hadn't explained his position as April's dad. Over the few days we'd been together, I found myself wanting to give him the benefit of the doubt, wanting to excuse him somehow, as if all the blame of April's situation could be shifted to Denise, the mother.

He smiled at me, and I had to look away to where the breeze blew an empty garbage bag across the street and into the gutter. The conversation turned to Blake as it did pretty much anytime Lucas felt like he could sneak his brother into the discussion.

Lucas was careful not to mention how Blake and I would be great together. Ever since I'd dressed him down in my office for butting into my business, he skirted those edges as if they were lined with land mines.

But Blake as a brother? That apparently qualified as safe territory. And Lucas eased his brother into the conversation so organically, I didn't realize we'd gone from talking about dads to talking about brothers.

"Allen Hampton was crazy intimidating when I first arrived on the scene. Having lived in homeless shelters for half my life and in spare rooms belonging to strangers the other half, I felt like a complete misfit when I showed up at that house carrying all my belongings in a black garbage bag. I think I would've been scared of him if it hadn't been for Blake. Blake took me in immediately, helped his mom empty out the room next to his, and moved me right in.

"Since the Hampton family loved basketball so much, Blake taught me how to play. He practiced with me every day after school to help me figure out how to work a backboard to my advantage. He got me to the point that, within a week, Allen Hampton claimed me as one of his own. It was kind of a shock when it happened. The first time he said, 'Good job, son! That's my boy!' I stopped right there and stared at him. That was the day I belonged somewhere and to someone. Blake made that happen for me."

I wanted to say that Blake was a cheating snake, but the fact remained that, up until recently, I had envisioned a future with Blake Hampton. I had called him my boyfriend with no small amount of pride, had kissed him good night, had texted him or called him for both good news and bad news moments. No argument could change those truths.

"He felt the same way about you." I told Lucas. "You would not believe how proud he is of his little brother."

Blake had never told me Lucas's name, at least not that I remembered, but he did talk a lot about his brother. Oddly though, he usually acted like he was in a competition with Lucas, as if Lucas was the good son no one could compare to. Lucas was the sensitive one, the one whose moral compass always pointed true north.

"He told me once your halo was so shiny he could see himself in it sometimes," I told Lucas. Blake really wasn't the devil even if I had mentally painted horns on his head every time I pictured him. He did speak well of his brother, even if the compliments had the bite of competition in them.

"Yeah, he likes that one. The halo one. Which is crazy because whenever we were playing ball in the house or wrestling and something got knocked over and broken, he always took the blame for it."

"That's hard to believe. Is this the same guy who never accepts responsibility when he's late for anything?"

Lucas laughed and leaned back. "He has his faults."

I leaned forward with my elbows on the table. "You don't have to convince me."

He laughed again, his blue eyes bright. "But we all do — have faults, I mean, don't we?"

I nodded my agreement. We held each other's gazes a little longer, then we both looked away. I couldn't say why he did, but I looked away because, even though we spoke of Blake, my thoughts were only on Lucas.

His past felt like a mirror of my own. His pain was so tangible and real to me. The connection between us felt like a gravitational pull that would make Silvia shake her head at me.

We meandered our way back to our hotel while he shared interesting tidbits about the West End and Midtown. By the time we'd made it back to the hotel, I wasn't tired anymore and wanted to stretch the time, but he inclined his head and said good night.

I was in my room, lounged out in my pajamas and brushing my teeth, when my phone vibrated with an incoming text. I read the name on my screen before opening the message. Lucas.

"Good night, Emma. Thank you for a great day."

I smiled and let my hand hover above my phone for a minute, a quiet caress I felt in my heart no matter how irrational it was, and I wished I could give it to the man who had sent the message.

Every evening for the next several days, we went out exploring. We played chess in Washington Square Park while eating pizza we'd picked up from a corner pizzeria. In Central Park, he showed me little-known nooks and secluded treasures. He took me on a tour of the General Grant National Memorial, which was a place I'd never even heard of. And he took me to the cloisters, where we viewed medieval and gothic architecture and tapestries. I'd given up the idea of taxis during the evening. He bought us both metro passes, insisting that freedom of travel was better claimed when you had a metro pass.

Saying good night at the end of our days together seemed strange. We awkwardly stood at our doors, our demeanors suddenly stiff and uncomfortable as we nodded and parted ways to our individual rooms. It was probable that the discomfort existed only on my side. So much of what we did felt like dating. I didn't mean to think of it that way, but what else could I call the fun activities we'd done, the time we'd spent getting to know each other? Every new thing I learned about him as we scouted the city made me like him more than I knew was appropriate when there were so many strikes against us. And every night, Lucas sent me a good night text.

To my relief, Blake also still texted me, reminding me of how my lingering thoughts of Lucas belonged to me only. Lucas would never tread in my direction when his brother still wanted me. I was also glad to think about the little girl in the slum apartment because it reminded me that Lucas was flawed and not someone I wanted to be with beyond our current professional capacity. I clung to those thoughts whenever I pondered what would happen if I broke that barrier and reached out to hug him good night. Thoughts of Blake and April kept my arms firmly at my side. But they could not stop me from smiling when Lucas sent his good night texts.

They did inspire me to text Blake a few times, not with anything too promising, but it helped take my mind off the brother in the next room. Through that little bit of communication and the stories Lucas shared with me, I found I wasn't mad at

Blake anymore. Via text, we even seemed to be getting along. Blake asked me questions about the sites we were considering and offered his own input and viewpoint, which helped me see things from a fresher perspective. He warned me to not let Lucas bully me into decisions I wasn't comfortable making. The warnings felt like he meant more than just the decisions with the company, but he couldn't possibly mean anything else. Just because I felt guilty for liking Lucas didn't mean Blake knew of my guilt.

With Lucas's expertise and Blake's added input, it took some effort for me to distill my own opinions so I could be certain my objectivity remained intact. However, Blake's perspective on the locations opened up my ability to question everything and come up with conclusions that might have eluded me otherwise.

After several days of going back and forth between locations and Skyping meetings with the team at home, where I gave full reports and analysis on everything Lucas and I did throughout our days, the team picked a site, taking Lucas's suggestions and recommendations more seriously than they'd ever taken anything of mine. I thought the team's decision felt rushed, but Jared and the rest of the executives all agreed — a thing which hardly ever happened — and they wanted us acting on their decision immediately. My jealousy of the praise spooned over Lucas could not be allowed. It was okay for him to receive the praise for the location — that was his primary job function, after all. With his job done, it was my turn to really shine.

Jared went to work on finalizing the contracts and details and aligning ourselves with the suppliers we wanted stocking the retail store and restaurant, and I went to work getting all the materials we needed to effectively market an experience health facility to the people of Manhattan.

Lucas and I celebrated the success by taking the "best free ride in all the United States" according to Lucas. The Staten Island Ferry. Because we were on the water, the temperature cooled to something bordering on tolerable. We both leaned our arms on the railing and stared out over the waters of New York Harbor. The smell of fish and salt mingled in the humid air with the industrial smell of the ferry.

Lucas was particularly chatty, delving back into the personal stuff we — or at least I — had been trying to avoid. "I used to ride this thing all the time when my mom first brought us here. Once I realized it was free,

I would bring my homework and stay on it all afternoon after school. I didn't care that they kicked me off at each stop. I just gathered my stuff, went back through the terminal, and got back on. Once we moved to the shelter, it was too far away to ride very often. I really missed the peace it offered during that time."

"What brought your mom to Manhattan?" I hated calling the woman who'd ditched him at a homeless shelter his "mom." It seemed like a slap in the face to the real moms who stuck with it day in and day out and made stuff work. Yet, I still called my mom *Mom*. Maybe that made me a hypocrite to judge his mother so harshly while still feeling the need to protect and justify my own.

"She had a boyfriend. He worked in a warehouse somewhere in the Bronx. He actually married her, which was kind of a surprise to me — to her, too, I think. When he ended up in prison for drugs, we ended up at a family shelter. It wasn't a terrible place. Not really. I was still able to go to school, and I wasn't hungry very often there. There were some pretty good teachers at the Bronx Middle School, and the walk was easy. I'd been to other places where I wasn't so lucky. Most places we ended up were because my mom was following some boyfriend or another. My mom had a thing for guys who usually ended up in jail."

"Have you ever thought about finding your biological father?"

He laughed and turned his head to me, his hair fluffing up in the wind as the boat sliced a path through the water. "No. No real reason. My mom gave me a name and a phone number once. I was dumb enough at the time to call the number and hope a father answered."

"What happened?"

"When I told him who I was, he called my mom some names that were not things a kid should ever hear and told me to tell her that she owed him and she knew what for. Then he hung up on me."

"Did you give her his message?"

He shook his head, his smile soft, sad. "Nope. Some things are better left alone. If he said she owed him, she probably did. I didn't want to know what she owed him for."

"I'm sorry, Lucas." I really felt sorry, too. Knowing people in the world had crummier backstories than my own and hearing those stories up close and personal were two totally different things. Feeling his compassion the few times I'd given in and shared my own story with him had forged a bond with him I knew I shouldn't foster.

He shrugged off my sympathy. "At my high school graduation, when I was standing in line to receive my diploma, the kid in front of me said, 'Can you believe we made it?' And I answered, 'Statistically, I have no business being here.' He had no idea what I meant. Everyone thought I was just another rich kid. A Hampton. No one knew about my past."

I expected him to tell me about the Hamptons again, to tell me how they had saved him, how Blake was the equivalent of a superhero, how Blake was the best brother in the world, how Blake really cared about me, and how I should give Blake another chance. I expected those responses because they were the usual ones Lucas gave, but even as I waited for them, I realized Lucas's praise of his brother had waned during our time together in New York.

I watched him as he watched the water and wondered why he'd stopped sounding the trumpet of his brother's perfection. I wondered if maybe he felt some of the same bonding I felt, if maybe he felt any of the same growing emotions I kept trying to talk myself out of feeling, if maybe he didn't want me to want his brother anymore. I leaned closer to him so our arms were touching. Did he understand the deliberate move for what it was, even if I didn't understand it myself?

My phone buzzed in my pocket. The sound startled both of us. I jerked away from him as if caught doing something wrong and pulled out my phone.

"Blake?" Lucas asked, his voice hoarse.

I checked the screen. "No. My friend Silvia." I sent the call to voice mail. "I'll call her back later."

Either way, the conversation and mood shifted. Both Blake and Silvia were like guardians of my emotions, and once again, they kept me from tangling myself into something that would be messy.

The scare of his brother calling returned our discussions to the light and trivial.

I hated the trivial a lot more than I wanted to admit. I hated the way we moved forward and back from real to fake. At least we'd accomplished our tasks in New York. Once we got the ball rolling with Boston, we could return to California, and I could pawn off the consultant to the lower tier of management. Lucas could consult with the supervisors over the different departments, and they could bring those consultations to me. The thought of having a buffer between us made me breathe easier. An earthquake with fissures cracking open was safer ground than being with Lucas Hampton.

Our trip back from the ferry was more subdued. A simple phone call had jostled us out of the bubble we managed to create every time we were alone together; it was exactly what we needed. I would have to call Silvia and thank her for her amazingly good timing.

The awkwardness between Lucas and me didn't stop him from sending his good night text, though. I smiled as I went to sleep, holding my phone to my chest.

The next day, Lucas joined me in the sitting area of my hotel room so we could make sense of our Boston schedule from all the spreadsheets I'd tried to organize. I spent the majority of our time mentally chanting the reasons why he was off-limits to me. *He has a child he doesn't take care of. He's Blake's brother. He has a child he doesn't take care of. He's Blake's brother.*

Being alone together in my hotel room turned my shaky ground to roiling hot lava.

He has a child he doesn't take care of. He's Blake's brother.

"I don't get it," Lucas said after we'd been working for a short while. His interruption yanked me out of my mental chant.

"Get what?"

He pointed to my copy of *Pride and Prejudice* on the end table by the couch. "Why someone of your education and position could like the Regency time period. It's nothing but barbarism dressed up as elegance and sophistication. Like vampires. One second they're wearing a coat and tails and the next they're draining you dry." He made a sucking sound and smirked at me.

"Jane Austen is nothing like vampires. The Regency period *is* beautiful and graceful and charming."

He snorted. "Yeah, charming. How charming for a scullery maid and a gentleman to fall in love but then never able to be together because she's beneath his station. And then the only way they *could* be together would be secretly where he uses her up, all while wining and dining and introducing the 'real' ladies to his mother."

We were both sitting on the floor, separated by paperwork. The *whop-whop* of police sirens and the horns from impatient drivers floated in through the open window. I'd technically given him the day off, which meant he'd entered my room by his own free will and choice, not out of professional obligation.

I stared at him for several moments before looking back down at the paperwork in my hands. "If we're being honest, things in society haven't changed that much, have they?" I felt his stare of incredulity burning a hole in my forehead. I didn't dare look up to face it directly, but I didn't back down from my statement, either. Tiny April standing in the hallway of that apartment building kept coming to mind. Hadn't she been the reason I worked so diligently to keep my emotions away from him? Wasn't it important that I say something? Wasn't it important that I pled her case to the one person who could make her life okay again? Lucas was a decent guy in every other aspect. I had to make him see the error of his ways with his daughter. Or at least, I had to understand why he was neglecting her the way we both had been neglected as children.

"I'd say they've changed a lot — and in ways that a modern, intelligent woman like yourself should appreciate." The low timbre of his voice told me he took his viewpoint seriously. "Women can own land, they can vote, they can have a hot bath without cutting down a small tree for firewood and drawing water from a well and carting it a half mile to the house. Men and women can marry who they want, regardless of race, wealth, and prospects. It's no longer about how you're born, it's about how you live."

I knew he was thinking about himself and the statistic he *hadn't* become. This was the moment, if ever a moment were to exist, that I could make him see his mistakes with his daughter. He could turn things around for her and keep her from becoming a statistic, too. He could realize what he was doing to her and erase one of the excuses I'd made to keep from falling for him.

How much I wanted that excuse erased surprised me. "If all that's true, then what happened between you and . . . Denise? Was that her name? And April." I asked my question quietly, as if it could be made less obtrusive if it was somehow smaller. Even as I said the words, alarm bells rang in my head, warning me that I had no right, that it wasn't my business.

For a moment, he seemed perplexed by the question. But then he sucked in a resigned breath and said, "I know what you're saying. But Denise made different choices than I made. There wasn't anything I could do for her. She was so much younger than I was. I didn't even know where she was for half her life since our mother took her with her when she left me at the shelter.

My mother poisoned her before I had the ability to do any good in her life. And short of turning my own sister in to child services — which I would do if I thought it would help, if I thought I would get custody without dragging April through a huge emotional and legal fight — there isn't anything I can do about April, either. And trying might cost me my right to see her at all."

My eyes flew up to meet his, the shock of his explanation dousing me like ice water. "Your sister?" For a beautiful, brief moment, hope swelled inside me. He had erased one major issue that kept me from loving him.

"Yeah, my sister. Who else would we be talking about?" His eyes narrowed even as mine went wide as that hope plummeted.

My face flamed to scorching hot.

"Wait a minute. You thought Denise and I were . . . what? *Together?*"

What had I done? His eyes showed that he fully understood my meaning and couldn't believe I'd said such a thing. How could he love me after such an accusation? Now that I knew I could love him, the heightened color in his neck and cheeks proved he could not love me. He understood my comment completely. There was no way to backpedal from this moment.

"It just seemed like . . ." I faltered. Every answer available to me made me sound like a prejudicial gossip.

"You thought April was my daughter?"

I nodded slowly.

"How could you think that? What would make you think that?"

My face grew even warmer. "When I saw you and Denise fighting that night in the hall, you just looked like . . ."

"Like what? What did we look like?"

I flinched. He wasn't shouting, but his harsh, clipped words shattered against me. "You looked like you had history."

He narrowed his eyes further as he rose up on his knees, his hands sweeping aside spreadsheets. "We do have history," he whispered. "Because she's my sister!"

He rocked back on his heels and shook his head, raking his fingers through his hair and then curling those fingers into a ball that likely would have been a fist if he was the sort of guy to throw punches. He scrambled to his feet, the paperwork he'd been poring over fluttering around him like startled birds. "And you thought I was the sort of guy who would just leave my own child in the worst situation possible even though it would be obvious that if I had *any* parental rights, the courts would give me custody? You thought I was the sort of guy who wouldn't want custody of my own child?"

I didn't nod but instead felt frozen to the spot, unable to tear my gaze from his, unable to flee the guilt laid at my feet.

"I cannot believe that this is what you think of me. That anyone could possibly think — Do you know what I've done for April? All that I've tried to do? I'm a certified foster parent so that if she's ever pulled from her home in an emergency, I will be the one they call and not a stranger. I've worked closely with April's social worker for years, ever since a teacher reported signs of neglect. I've done all that because I care. I am not a monster, Emma."

His face twisted into a pained expression that told me everything.

Now that I felt free to fall, he had retreated from my reach. I ached with what I had lost.

His trust.

His esteem.

His friendship.

And all the possibility that crackled between us when we allowed ourselves to be real with each other.

My comments didn't help April's life to be any better. Instead, they revealed me for the kind of judgmental person who had likely tried to hold him back his whole life.

"I was wrong about you," he whispered. "You're . . . Never mind. It doesn't make a difference to me who you are." He left my room without another word, the papers settling to the ground as the door slammed shut.

CHAPTER NINE

"It was badly done, indeed!"
— JANE AUSTEN, *Emma*

I sat on the floor of my room, surrounded by work, and felt the weight of my accusations towards Lucas press in on me from all sides. "What have I done?" I asked the room that felt so much emptier without him in it.

I'd hurt him in every way possible. That much was evident in the way his pleasant, open features fell and dimmed. In his words, low and angry.

"It doesn't make a difference to me who you are."

Those words sliced through me and left me bleeding out.

"What have I done!" I shouted, then pressed my lips together tightly. He probably heard my outburst. But what did that matter? How could he think any less of me than he already did?

My eyes fell on all the papers spread out over the floor. Would he tell Jared? What would Jared think? We had work to do, and I'd insulted Lucas so completely that he would likely never talk to me again. But what did Jared's opinion or the work really matter? The one thing that had held me back from *really* falling for Lucas was how he had handled the situation with April. With that out of the way, leaving me open to think of him as I wanted, he likely hated me. I heard his voice, saw his face. He definitely hated me. *His niece.* How had I missed that?

How had I allowed my prejudices to blind me so completely? I dragged my hands down my face, my eyes landing on my book. Prejudice.

Curse you, Jane Austen!

This was all her fault. If I hadn't spent half my life wanting to be Elizabeth Bennett, I wouldn't have held my own prejudices so dear. I wouldn't have taken pride in my own clever snap judgments to like and dislike at a whim. Besides, it was the topic of Jane Austen that had started the ill-fated conversation.

How had an author who'd been dead for so long get me into so much trouble?

How could I expect any less after what

happened to Catherine Morland in *Northanger Abbey* when she accused Mr. Tilney's father of killing his mother? I'd read the book a dozen times. How did I not learn anything from it? People can't run around flinging accusations at other people just because things look suspicious.

I stood and paced, not even caring that I stomped over all of the paperwork on the floor. I would eventually have to reorganize and smooth out the wrinkled mess, but what was paper to me when I had to reorganize and smooth out the *people* first. I picked up the offensive Austen paperback and tossed it into the trash can.

Lucas. I had to fix things with Lucas.

But how?

My phone rang, and I answered it without even looking. "Lucas, I am so sorry!"

"Sorry for what?" Debbie asked.

I pulled my phone from my ear, saw her number, and realized my error. My jumbled mind had derailed any common sense. Why would Lucas call me after I insulted the very fabric of his integrity?

I certainly wouldn't call me.

"Debbie! Hi!" I changed my tone to something light, breezy, professional. "Sorry. You called as I was running late to start the day. Lucas has been waiting on me so we could leave." The lie had to be told. Debbie enjoyed gossip way too much. If given a whisper of a rumor in the morning, it would be declared on every news station as fact by the evening.

"Oh. I thought maybe I was interrupting something . . ."

You are, I thought but said, "Just getting ready. I *am* in a bit in a hurry, so what's up?"

"Jared wants to know if you've made any headway regarding the foundation idea. He wants something that shows the unique aspects of Kinetics while maintaining our brand."

"Right. I've got some thoughts I've jotted down. What about you guys back home? Any ideas you want to add to the list?"

"We brainstormed a bunch at the last couches meeting."

"Great. Send them to me and make sure to credit the person who came up with the idea. Also, let the team know I plan to incentivize this, so if their idea is chosen, we'll throw in some kind of bonus."

"A good bonus?" she asked.

I heard Lucas's door open and shut and hurried to peer out of the peephole to see where he was going and if he was coming to my room. I didn't want to be on the phone if he was knocking. I didn't want to be on the phone at all.

He did not come to my door but passed by without even looking in the direction of my room. His mouth was clamped shut, his shoulders were squared, and all his body language screamed anger and irritation.

"Yes. A very good bonus. But it has to be a very good idea that gets it, so put them to work and email me the results." I slid my feet into dress flats and cut Debbie off before she could ask or say anything else. "I've gotta go. It's time for us to leave. Thanks for all you do, Debbie. It's nice to count on you."

Ending the conversation with a compliment would make it so she didn't feel the brush-off as deeply as I meant it. But I needed to go. I had to make things right with Lucas.

He had a right to hate me. I had accused him of something terrible. How did we move on from that?

I grabbed my messenger bag, flung it over my shoulder, and hauled after Lucas before he could disappear in Midtown congestion. The elevator doors closed just as I rounded the corner. The stairwell beckoned to me but in no real-world scenario would my legs take me down forty-two floors before he made it to the bottom. I hit the down button for the elevator multiple times, hoping the other side would come for me while Lucas was still in transit.

When the second set of shiny metal doors slid open, I silently thanked the planets that aligned to help me redeem myself. I promptly pressed the CLOSE DOOR button repeatedly until the doors actually did what they were told.

Then the planets that had aligned suddenly scattered to the four corners of the universe. When the elevator stopped on floor twenty-seven, I had to bite my tongue to keep from telling the elderly couple who got on that I despised them. When it stopped again on floor fourteen, the man in the suit received the full measure of my glare. He frowned as he turned his back on me to face the front.

Floor fourteen. Whatever. Everyone knew that was just a pretty way of keeping floor thirteen from always being empty. The suit was definitely a thirteenth-floor demon because he put his hand out to stop the doors from closing so a middle-aged woman in activewear could get on. Like it mattered if she caught the elevator or not. She was wearing activewear, for pity's sake! She should have walked the walk by taking the stairs. She was only thirteen floors up.

Finally, the doors opened on the main floor, and I bulldozed my way through my crowded elevator so I could be the first off.

The apocalyptic emptiness of the front lobby sunk my heart into my toes. How would I find Lucas in the city? I pushed through the front doors and checked both directions on the street only to discover what I already knew to be true: Lucas would not be easily found. I tugged my phone out of my pocket and called him.

My eyes scanned the street. First ring. What should I say to him? Second ring. Start with an apology. Yes. Do that before anything else. Third ring. Or maybe start with an explanation so he'd know where I was coming from? Fourth ring. No. Definitely apologize first.

Voice mail.

I hung up.

And I might have growled. I didn't remember actually growling, but the way the woman in the activewear jumped and then sidestepped me on the street made me believe that I must have done something to freak her out.

Standing on the street without Lucas at my side when I'd been expecting him by my side made me feel incredibly exposed.

Did I look like a child lost in a mall? Not sure what else to do, I forced my feet to the curb. I couldn't spend the day looking for him in the city. Manhattan itself had more than a million people in it; finding one person in a crowd would be impossible.

I hailed a cab. Lucas or no, I had a job to do and couldn't count myself as off the clock until after five. I called Silvia once my cab pulled back into traffic.

"He hates me!" I wailed as soon as she answered.

"What? Who?"

"Lucas. He hates me because I was so wrong. And I was, Sil. So, so wrong."

She calmed me down enough for me to unload the whole story while the cab driver wove through the dense morning traffic. Once she'd heard it all, she said matter-of-factly, "I thought I told you that you weren't allowed to fall for your ex-boyfriend's brother."

"I'm not calling because I fell for him. I'm calling because I accused him of being a deadbeat dad! I offended and hurt him, and I don't know what to do about it."

"You guys are there on business. Stop acting like it's high school and get to work. Where are you now? What are you doing?"

"In a cab. On the way to the real estate

agent's office to get a few more details on timeline."

"So you *are* working."

I nodded.

Though she couldn't see me or know that I nodded, she said, "Good girl. Look, I'm sorry he's upset, and, yes, you were wrong to make accusations when you didn't know the whole truth, but he won't stay mad forever because he'd never given you any reason to believe anything except that he was a deadbeat dad. After you told me the whole story of the crazy lady with the daughter, I thought she was his kid too. Don't beat yourself up over it. What else were you supposed to think?"

The cab driver cleared his throat and gave a meaningful look to the curb. We'd arrived at the agent's office. "But after getting to know him and finding out how great he is, shouldn't that have been a clue to me?" I unbuckled myself from the backseat, handed the money over to the driver, and got out of the cab.

Silvia said the hardest thing I ever had to hear. "Clue or no clue, hon, none of this changes the fact that he is Blake's brother, and that means he can be Superman, but he's still off-limits to you. Okay?"

"I know, but he's out there and hating me

right now."

"And he's off-limits while he's hating you, okay?"

"Okay." I stood on the curb and felt like a fool. I kicked at some litter, then rolled my eyes at myself and picked it up and dropped it into the can that was less than two feet away. What was wrong with people? Was it really that hard to throw away your own junk? "But I still have to work with him. And he still hates me."

Silvia made a psh noise. "I hate half the people I work with, and we still get our jobs done."

"But do any of them hate you back?"

"Definitely. I can hand you a list right now of a dozen people who would pay money to party on my casket."

"But have you ever legitimately cared about any of the ones who hate you?"

"*Legitimately cared about . . .* What does that even mean, Emma? Are you trying to say you think you might love the guy?"

It was a wretched way to confess, but I had felt stirrings for days now. Did I love Lucas?

No, not love, maybe not yet, but I felt like I *could* love him, that I could be happy loving him, that he would never leave me stranded or let me down the way I had let him down. "I really care about him, Sil. I don't know what that means, yet. It might not mean anything. It might mean everything. I just don't know."

Silvia's silence carried for far longer than I anticipated. Instead of giving me the expected flippant answer of *"You were dating his brother just a few weeks ago, so slap yourself out of this,"* she said softly, "Love is a bruise. The best way to let it heal is to stop touching it."

Her voice dripped pain, causing me to worry. "Is something going on, Sil? Are you okay?"

She snapped her response. "Why are you getting weird on me? Of course I'm okay." It sounded like the biggest lie ever. But she insisted she had to go and hung up before I could dig further.

In spite of Silvia's warnings to leave Lucas alone and let things be, I sent him a text. *Lucas, I am so sorry. You're right. I do know you well enough to know you're a good person. I hope you can forgive me.*

With no other real options, I went into the real estate agent's office to get answers to Jared's questions.

Lucas did not return my text.

By lunchtime, I figured he would remain absent for the day, which was fine, professionally speaking. It wasn't like I didn't know what needed doing or like my capabilities were in any way lacking, but the calm, humorous companionship we had developed was truly missed. By evening, I picked up some dinner from a food truck and took it to my room to eat.

I stopped at Lucas's door, my hand hesitating just short of a knock before I decided that backing off and letting him have time to be angry was the best option. He had my apology. He could do what he wanted with it.

Feeling offended by his being offended was clearly a childish response, but his offense was over me not believing he was a good guy. Wouldn't he want to prove his good-guyness by picking up my olive branch and making peace?

I rested my palm on his door. More likely he would slap me with that olive branch if he picked it up. And who could blame him? I could hold a grudge with the best of them. Anyone who didn't believe me could ask the mother I refused to forgive.

Not one child therapist in all of Southern California could make me say the words *I forgive my mother.* I didn't. Why lie about it? I accused Lucas of the worst neglect conceivable to parenthood; to expect him to forgive me in under the course of a single day was simply too much to ask.

Even forcing him out by saying we had to work wasn't really an option since we were scheduled to leave for Boston the next day and I'd already told him he could do what he wanted until then.

I slid my hand down the door and hung my head to do the walk of shame to my own room.

I deserved his silence and anger. Once inside my room, my eyes fell on the paperback in the garbage can. I pulled it out and smoothed my hands over the cover and whispered a soft apology to the book. I felt certain it would forgive me when humans failed to. Jane and I were still on the rocks, but I really needed Darcy.

Lucas and I left for Boston the next day. We took the train, which I suspected was something Lucas had arranged with Katie so he didn't have to fly any more than necessary. He was polite when we met in the lobby, luggage in tow. All business and no play, banter, or deep conversations.

I understood his reasons and didn't press for more than I deserved. The very fact that he'd decided to be polite was better than the situation called for. I wish Katie hadn't been so efficient by booking all of our tickets together. The three-and-a-half-hour train ride would have been far more comfortable sitting next to a stranger.

Lucas remained entrenched in his book, leaving me to pretend I was reading mine as well, though not a single string of words made any sense to my jumbled thoughts. I went ahead and used the app on my phone rather than pull out the Austen paperback I kept in my bag. No reason to pour lemon juice on a fresh wound.

I gave up reading after the first hour and gazed out the window. The green of New England flew past as the Amtrak cut through the undergrowth on smooth rails. At some point, I must have dozed off because the next thing I knew, Lucas's hand was on my shoulder, gently shaking me awake.

"I'm sorry, Lucas. So sorry," I whispered, my brain still caught in the dream catcher of sleep.

"Emma. Emma? Ms. Pierce!" He said the last louder, and my eyes popped open. It took several moments of being awake before my brain registered that he'd been talking to me and what exactly he'd said.

Had I apologized out loud or just imagined it? His hand was still on my shoulder as if stilling a child who'd awoken from a bad dream. When my gaze flicked down to his hand, he removed it immediately, cleared his throat, and said in a colder tone than he'd used when saying my name, "We're here."

"Oh. Right."

He refused to meet my eye as we gathered our things and exited the train into the world of the Back Bay.

We headed straight to the pick-up area, where a shuttle waited to take us to the car rental place where Katie had reserved a car for us. Though I hadn't wanted to drive in Manhattan, I had no such inhibitions about driving in Boston. I didn't ask if Lucas knew the Back Bay area, not wanting to seem like I depended on him for directions. I was a big girl who knew how to work the GPS on my phone.

As if prompted by my not asking for advice on directions, Lucas resolutely refused to offer any. But he huffed at a few of the turns I made and outright grunted at one of them.

Aw, heck, no. Blatant passive-aggressive behavior had no place in my car — even if it was a rental. Outright aggression, fine. Even the quasi-passive-aggressive silent treatment passed muster, but the little mutters and grunts were not happening.

"Do you have something to add to the

GPS directions?" I asked.

"Just that if you stayed on Storrow, you'd have cut five minutes off the trip."

"Good to know. But since we're already off Storrow, would you like me to back-track?"

"No. Not now."

Then shut up, I thought. But my brain filter had apparently engaged because the words didn't leave my mouth. Then came the self-admonition. *You can't be mad at someone for being mad at you. It doesn't make sense.*

But I *was* mad at him. Sense be hanged.

Jane would have disapproved my less-than-ladylike behavior. But Jane be hanged, too.

"Do you want to eat first or check into the hotel first?" I asked.

He stared out his window. I resolutely stared out the windshield and followed the GPS with the loyalty of a dog at its master's heels. Even so, I heard his teeth grinding next to me. "If there's a restaurant at the hotel, I can just take dinner in my room."

"Oh. I see. Well, then we can go check you in, and I can drop you off."

He stayed silent. Well, silent aside from the teeth grinding and minor mutters.

At the hotel, I parked the car in the guest

check-in area and went to the front desk. Once we were handed our room keys, which led to the discovery that Lucas was, once again, the boy next door, I asked about restaurants. When the front desk clerk went on for several minutes about the awesome food amenities of their establishment, I turned to Lucas and said, "Just charge what you need to your room. I hope you have a nice, peaceful evening." I tried to smile but failed since my conscience had kicked in again, returning me to my earlier state of wretched guilt.

I turned and closed my eyes briefly before starting back toward where I'd left the rental.

"You aren't even going to take your bag up?" Lucas asked from behind me.

Why? Why talk to me now? He had nearly four hours today on a train to talk to me. He had almost all day yesterday to talk to me. And now? About luggage?

"Nah," I said, hoping I sounded casual. "I'll bring it up later." I started walking again.

His footsteps followed behind me. "Let me get your bag for you. I can take it and drop it off in your room."

Yeah, right. I was *not* going to hand over my room key. After what I'd said to him yesterday, he had every reason to booby-trap my bathroom, not that I thought he would. I was done misjudging him. He wasn't a villain. But to have him in my room without me present felt intimate. After realizing that I could really come to care for him and then making the worst-ever-out-loud mistake possible, the idea of any kind of familiarity made me sad. "It isn't a problem for me to take them up later. There's no reason for you to bother."

He either didn't hear me or ignored me outright. "Leaving bags in the car is a bad idea because it inspires smash-and-grabs."

"From in the trunk? Where no one can see it?"

"Where are you going?" he asked.

"The Liquid Art House. Thinking about trying something new." We were now at the car. He stood by the trunk as if waiting for me to open it so he could take my bag. The stubborn part of me had decided that no way was he getting my bag, even if it was entirely my fault I'd upset him. He didn't get to be the nice guy and make me feel worse about being the bad guy.

He narrowed his eyes at me. "The Liquid Art House?"

"Mm-hm." I lifted my chin.

"You probably need reservations for that

restaurant."

"Good thing I made them, then." I hit the unlock button with my thumb so I could just get in the car and drive away. I felt stupid and angry and sad and *stupid.* He confused me in every emotional way possible, and I confused myself when I was with him. His decision to be nice and take my bags like he was some kind of servant just made everything worse. Why couldn't he go sulk in his room and let me go sulk in the city, and we could each be miserable on our own?

But he apparently had no intention of any such thing.

He opened the passenger door, got in the car, and belted himself in.

I opened the driver's door and poked my head in. "What are you doing?"

He didn't look at me. "When did you make your reservation?"

"A few days ago. They had a cancellation, and I was able to slide in. What does the timing of reservations have to do with the price of tea in the Boston Harbor?"

His lips, which had been tensed and pursed since I accused him of single-handedly destroying the dreams and hopes of a little girl, softened at my cultural pun. "It matters because you likely made a reservation for two. And if I know anything about you, Ms. Pierce," he said, finally facing me, "it's that you're a woman who keeps her commitments."

He held my gaze for a long time, long enough that I was pulled into the car behind the driver's wheel. "I *am* sorry," I whispered.

"I know."

He looked away. I started the car, and we went to dinner.

Chapter Ten

"A large income is the best recipe for happiness I ever heard of."
— JANE AUSTEN, *Mansfield Park*

That was as far as we got to giving and accepting apologies. *I know* was kind of a punk answer, but I let it pass, recognizing it was as good as Lucas could do. Obviously, no one ever gave him the lesson I got from my father that when someone apologized, you had to forgive them. That was the grounds I used to not forgive my mother. She had never said she was sorry.

Dinner was fine, but any stories from childhood or hopes for the future were silenced, replaced with actual eating, admiring the art gallery in the restaurant around us, and talking about the new location, which was beachside and beautiful. We discussed its merits until it seemed we were in a competition of who could admire it most.

The way things were going, it would be just my luck to show up at the site tomorrow to find a big SOLD sign on it.

By the time we ended up back at the hotel and were saying good night at our rooms, I wanted to apologize again. I wanted the relationship we had before the insult and offense.

I wanted to tell him that I knew it hadn't been true. I knew his character and heart would never allow him to leave April the way our mothers left us. That, of course, I'd known all along.

But if I had known, why would such accusations ever enter the conversation?

He offered me a tight smile as if reading my thoughts and coming to the same conclusion I had.

I hadn't known, hadn't trusted him, and that was why we could never be anything but a string of farewells and good nights at doors.

My heart sank to my toes when he gave voice to my thoughts. "Good night, Emma."

"Good night, Lucas."

He sent no text that night.

The next day, we visited the site. The perfect weather made me wish we were out walking the rocky coastline and not in the building. The longing looks Lucas tossed from the windows to the surf showed he felt the same way.

The real estate agent led us upstairs, then left us for a moment while she answered a quick call. I entered a room that had floor-to-ceiling windows all along the back wall. The windows all faced the ocean, and I imagined how lovely sunrise would look from such a room.

"The yoga classes," I said. "This would be perfect for sunrise yoga classes."

"Yes," he agreed. "Perfect.

"It almost has a feeling of being in the sky," I continued. "If we built out and did an entirely glass room, it really would feel like being in the sky. That would shake things up and add the edge we needed to win over people who already have a morning yoga routine."

"A glass room sounds . . . precarious." Lucas edged away from the wall of windows as if they might shatter at a glance.

So, not just planes for him — heights of any kind freaked Lucas out. I would have laughed except the friction stayed warm between us. Those friendly terms we'd been on before were gone.

We took pictures and video footage and

discussed all the build-outs necessary to make the current structure work, took copious notes, and then allowed the agent to take us to several less-worthy locations where we tried to pretend to do the same for them, but our hearts weren't in it. The first was the only one worth talking about.

There were no bantering texts exchanged behind the agent's back.

That evening, Lucas stayed with me while I traveled up the coast, taking in the tourist attractions. Every once in a while, he shifted and inhaled like he was about to share something with me, but then he quieted and looked away, and I knew I had missed out on something.

Jared hired Lucas because he knew the East Coast intimately. That was how we landed the best real estate agents in the business. That was how we were allowed access to great properties that fit our business model. This meant he knew things about the locations we stayed. He proved as much when he took over my travel plans in New York. But in Boston, he left me to whatever I could find online and be guided to with my GPS.

"Is there anything you want to see?" I asked several times.

"Nah. I'm just along for the ride," he'd

say, and that would be the end of it. I wished he would have stayed back at the hotel so I could enjoy the city on my own, but that would hardly be fair to him because I had the car. Since he asked to go with me, leaving him behind would be inexcusable.

Kinetics agreed with our assessment on the location and went to work finalizing the deal. That left me to get the ball rolling for preliminary advertising and marketing.

Lucas came with me this time, in spite of my protests.

"Jared asked if I'd give my input."

Of course Jared asked for that. Of course Lucas, grand consultant to East Coast marketing, would have to be available to consult on all the details, not just the location. I was surprised Jared hadn't scolded me via text for not including Lucas in my meetings in New York with the various media outlets. Perhaps Lucas hadn't mentioned I'd left him out. It was the only explanation

"You must be magic," I said to Lucas as we retrieved the car from the valet at the hotel.

"Why? You looking to make something disappear?"

Yes, I thought. *I want the tension between us to disappear.* Or maybe I wanted him to disappear. Or maybe I wanted *me* to disappear. "The executive team at Kinetics is a slow, slow machine. They argue in tactical meetings as if the fate of the world depends on their decisions. And that's just when it's about what to order for lunch. It took four months for them to pin down the La Jolla location. You point at a property and say, 'Make camp there,' and they fall all over themselves to agree and sign the papers. It's magic."

"It's just knowing the area."

"It's more than that. It's knowing the market and how the communities will perceive our company when we move into the neighborhood. It's impressive."

Lucas made a little head jiggle that may or may not have been an acknowledgment of my compliment. It was as if he didn't trust anything nice coming from me. I wondered if I felt overly complimentary because I was trying to compensate for my earlier gaffe. Not that the compliments weren't meant, but they might not have been voiced out loud without my determination to mend past mistakes.

The double-edged sword of complimenting him on a job well done added aggravation to my existence. For every great idea of his, my own less-great ideas felt overshadowed. The other executives appreciated the value of his opinion, and they couldn't even be blamed. He had some genuinely good thoughts.

His coming on as consultant had bugged me at the first, and, yes, even threatened my confidence and security over my position in the company. But once we'd become such good friends, I'd forgotten all that. Or maybe hadn't really forgotten, but I didn't let it get under my skin the way it did now that we were painfully professional towards one another.

Some part of me wanted to throw my hands up in the air, admit defeat, and book the next flight home. I could have my office packed and an updated résumé live on LinkedIn by the end of the day. Other parts of me wanted to stay and prove myself better and more capable than Lucas. And other parts still, the ones that seemed to hold the greatest sway over me, wanted to stay anywhere close to where Lucas was, just so I could be around him. Even if he only spent time with me out of some sense of moral obligation to the company or some chivalrous need to make sure the girl didn't go out exploring the city on her own.

I lined up some television interviews with a few of our ambassadors. I also signed us up for several local health-related events and went to a number of high schools and colleges to see about partnering with their sports teams to help their athletes train. The training-athletes idea belonged entirely to Lucas. With his continual apathy toward me, my irritation and need to compete with him grew.

On our last night in Boston, when going over highs and lows with Jared, my boss poured so much praise over Lucas there was a very real possibility Lucas would drown in it all. Or maybe I would be the one drowning.

"And Lucas's sky yoga room! Simply brilliant." Jared crowed. "Best money we ever spent was hiring him on. I might have to find a way to keep him when his contract runs out."

"He is a great find, and he does have great ideas," I agreed, "but the sky yoga model was mine, sir."

As if I hadn't spoken at all, Jared plowed over the top of me with all the great feedback coming in from the rest of the board — who never praised anything.

Had he heard me? Did he know that the sky yoga concept came from me and not Lucas? I wasn't so competitive as to claim any ideas that weren't mine, but I'd be hanged if I allowed someone else to get credit for what rightfully belonged to me. If he *had* heard me and I mentioned it again, I would end up sounding petulant and greedy for acknowledgment.

Before Jared hung up, he reminded me that he expected to see the foundation concepts in his email box soon.

I growled at the phone after hitting END, and then panicked as I rushed to make sure I really had ended the call. Explaining a growl to my boss would certainly make for an uncomfortable conversation.

Between Jared and his praise of Lucas, and between Lucas and the awkward tension between us, I decided I needed a Lucas-free day once we got back to New York. We had finished up early enough in Boston that we would gain an extra day in New York City before we flew out. Katie had us flying out of the same city we flew into because the flights from Boston were all red-eye, and Jared didn't like his employees flying red-eye. He believed it messed up our chakras. The extra day in New York meant we would be able to relax a bit. Certainly that would be good for our chakras.

Not that I had any intention of relaxing. I spent the quiet train ride back to Manhattan plotting out my time for the last day in the city.

Once we were back at the New York hotel and standing in the hall, I plastered on my brightest smile. "You have the day off tomorrow," I told him.

"Off?"

"I have meetings with some magazines and MTA so we can get some teaser posters going. Go sightseeing; have lots of fun." I wanted to make it sound like I was doing him a favor, like this was somehow a perk for him, not a time-out for me. But the thought of being away from Lucas made me feel incredibly depressed and made it hard for me to pretend any other emotion.

He considered his day off for a moment, his face clouded with an unreadable expression. "Jared asked me to be available for those sorts of meetings so I could give my input."

"That was for new concepts and plans. This is old hat, something we do day in and day out. I am the chief marketing executive. It's not like I don't know how to broker advertising space with magazines." I felt him tighten more than actually saw the movement. He must have sensed the challenge in my voice, so I tried to soften it. "Trust me. The last thing you want is to be stuck indoors while we haggle pricing and spacing. Seriously. Take a day. You've earned it. We'll be heading home soon enough, and then it's back to work."

His hooded expression made me feel guilty and enhanced my own disappointment at not having him with me, especially since he had as much right to be in my meetings as I did. He was the consultant, and Kinetics was paying him a lot to offer advice. They likely wouldn't be happy to hear I'd cut him out of the process for a day, but I needed a day to get my head back together, to figure out why I was jealous of him, resentful of him, and on the verge of seriously caring for him while knowing he harbored no such feelings for me, not after my wild accusations.

"Oh," he said. "Okay."

We were given the same rooms in the Manhattan Hilton that we had vacated the week previously. We parted ways at the doors, and, as had become my habit, I slumped against mine with all the weight of my personal angst and frustration. "Shake it off, Emma," I chided myself before stepping away from the door, out of my clothes, and into the big, freestanding bathtub.

I'd taken care to turn out all the lights in my room first because the tub faced the floor-to-ceiling windows, and I wanted them open so I could enjoy the world outside, but I wanted it dark so I could also enjoy my privacy. Being on floor forty-two gave me a unique perspective on the city below. Soaking in the tub with the lights of the city offering their illumination, I felt better prepared to handle the next day — the one that did not include Lucas. The one that did not include me reaching out to him — to either slap him or hold him.

I would be strong. I would resist.

Halfway into the next day, Lucas's absence was a thing to mourn. The meetings were long and filled with miserly little grabs at marketing dollars for overpriced ad spots. Did these people really think I'd show up without knowing what things cost on their side of the country?

It would have been nice to have Lucas's input. And then the evil part of me thought about how nice it would have been to have Lucas see me negotiate like a boss. He would have been impressed if he could have seen it.

By the end of the workday, my mind felt hollowed out by figures and dates and ad space sizing. I really wanted to see Lucas, wanted to tell him all about the day and the people and the way they thought they could steamroll over the little California surfer girl.

So, being the mature, intelligent woman I was, I ignored common sense and texted Lucas. "Want to meet up for dinner?"

After I hit SEND, my brain finally figured out what I was doing and began howling misery and mistake at me. Too late. The message was out there.

I paced in tight little circles out on the street while waiting for his answer. I looked down into the stairwell leading to the subway and shook my head. No way was I going to try to tame that monster on my own. If he agreed to meet somewhere, I was taking a cab.

Many minutes ticked by with no response.

What could he possibly be doing that was more important than answering my text?

My phone buzzed.

Debbie's name flashed on my screen. I growled at it in frustration but figured reading her text was better than pacing and willing an answer from Lucas to appear. She wanted to know what we should do about the Kick It! line in our retail stores; a lawsuit had been filed against them based on materials in their products. Debbie worried the lawsuit could affect our branding.

I sucked in a deep breath, not really caring either way but knowing that not caring was the wrong answer. I was a professional. Caring about the brand was my job. But the only thing that held my focus was my screen and the lack of Lucas's name.

I texted Debbie back and told her to call Kick It! about their stance on the lawsuit. Abandoning them based on a frivolous lawsuit by some money-hungry firm looking for deep pockets would be worse press than anything the actual suit could do. Our other suppliers might lose faith in us for not standing up for one of them. I told her to make sure we had all the facts before making knee-jerk reactions.

My phone buzzed again.

I expected to see Debbie responding, but joy of joys, Lucas's name flashed in all its digital glory on my screen.

He texted, "I have plans already for dinner with some people."

Joy burned down into ash. Plans? With some people? Did he really have plans with someone else, or was this code for *Emma, I think you're a monster even if you did apologize, and I'd rather gargle broken glass than eat with you?*

But this city had once been his home. It only stood to reason that he would have friends here, maybe girlfriends. I squared my shoulders, determined not to get jealous over a guy who didn't, couldn't, wouldn't belong to me.

"Oh," I texted back. "No problem. I'll see you in the morning, then. We should be in the taxi by seven in order to make the plane on time." Maybe it was a cheap shot to mention the plane and invoke his flight anxiety, but I ignored my own culpability and raised my arm to hail a cab to take me back to my hotel. I had half talked myself into taking in a Broadway play when his response buzzed in my hand.

"Would you care to join me?"

Relief surged through me and settled in my belly as I contemplated what his wanting me to meet his friends might mean. And then I rolled my eyes at myself. "You are going insane, Emma, you know that?" I said aloud.

"Sure," I texted back as if it was no big deal. It felt like a huge deal. The invitation into his personal circle couldn't be anything but a big deal.

He sent me the address, which I gave to my cab driver. He eyed my business suit and my tidy bun and leather briefcase and said, "Are you sure that's where you want to go?"

I confirmed, and he shrugged.

When he pulled up to the curb in a neighborhood that echoed the neighborhood Lucas had taken me to that first night when I met April, I shuddered. What did I really know about him anyway?

He could be involved in drugs or other nefarious activities. Any kind of illicit activity could be going on inside the building that seemed to be guarded by the few homeless people milling about in the yard.

I got out and paid the fare.

"Want me to wait?" the driver asked.

"No," I said, hearing my own uncertainty. I could have seen a play on Broadway. I could have gone to a movie. I could have done a million other things besides step out of a cab and onto a street that looked like it had seen better days. "I'll be fine."

I walked up the front steps and entered the building.

Laughter hit me square in the chest when the door opened. Bubbling, happy laughter. The sound felt so incongruous with the environment that I frowned, but I followed it to a large open room set up with tables and chairs.

People sat at the tables eating pizza and chugging root beer, if the smell was to be believed. And they all looked happy. The room was a gigantic roar with the noise of mixed conversation, children laughing, and people just being people.

My eyes scanned the crowd, trying to pick out the one person in the apparent pizza party who I actually knew. He was at the front of the room, standing behind a table loaded with boxes of pizza. Many empty boxes were underneath the table — a testament to how many people had already eaten.

Lucas wore plastic gloves, which looked silly as he waved them around, using his hands to tell a story to the woman next to him. Her gray hair and wrinkled face showed the age that didn't show anywhere else. So he *was* with a woman, but not the sort I could feel jealous of.

Seeing him there was too perfect. Before anything else, I took out my phone and snapped a picture of him.

The rumpled, smudged clothing of the people around me testified of the poverty that consumed them. But none looked forlorn or disheartened by their lives. The general mood was the satisfaction of a good meal and the pleasure in good company. The laughter in the room told me everything. These people knew what it was to feel genuine happiness in spite of their trials or the things that might come tomorrow.

Wealth existed among the impoverished.

Lucas must have felt my gaze on him because he turned and smiled at me, beckoning me forward with one plastic-covered hand. It wasn't a dining hall with cloth napkins and candlelight, but I found I didn't want to be anywhere else than in this homeless shelter with Lucas.

Chapter Eleven

"Were I to fall in love, indeed, it would be a different thing; but I have never been in love; it is not my way, or my nature; and I do not think I ever shall."
— JANE AUSTEN, *Emma*

Lucas had apparently taken my invitation to do what he wanted on his day off to mean spending the day at the family shelter helping them with anything they needed and then buying anyone and everyone pizza and root beer for dinner.

I slid my hands into a pair of plastic gloves and helped to serve the people still entering the dining hall. "This really wasn't what I expected when you asked me to join you for dinner." To keep myself from staring at him in awe, I focused on the pizza boxes.

"Totally better, right?" he said, his eyes filled with a happiness that had been missing during our time in Boston.

"Totally better."

The line got busy again as another wave of people picked up paper plates and smiled at us expectantly. So many of them wanted to talk, to have someone listen. We served more than food while in that line; we served our attention by the plateful. And unlike the pizza boxes, it seemed that the more we gave, the more we had. With each person and the stories they shared, I found myself so caught up in the moment I actually forgot about the man at my side who made my stomach flutter in a way I didn't want to admit to anyone.

At least I forgot about him until someone plugged a phone into some worn speakers of questionable sound quality. The static-hum of a phone jacked in hissed in the room before music blared through. The playlist was fun — punchy, upbeat folk music, the kind you'd hear at a coffeehouse near a college campus. A few kids began to dance. Our line for pizza dwindled to stragglers who were in animated conversation with the older woman next to Lucas. She must have worked regularly with them because it seemed they all knew her.

Lucas grabbed my hand, and the little flutter that occasionally beat its wings in my stomach became a desperate, full-on flight.

I turned to him, my mouth open in surprise, when he said, "Let's dance!"

And then we were doing exactly that. He spun me around the table and to the middle of the floor so fast the movement didn't even register in my head until we were already there, already dancing. His one hand in mine. His other on my waist. His smile like sunshine breaking through a cloud-bruised sky. With his face so close and him not seeming to mind, I felt he'd truly forgiven me for my cruel accusations.

The folk song turned to a rap dance song. Lucas had no trouble shifting styles and tugged me along. "C'mon, Ms. Pierce! You got this."

I snickered at his calling me "Ms. Pierce" and followed his lead as best I could. My herky-jerky movements made me look more like a drunk scarecrow than a rap-song dancer, and Lucas laughed, the belly kind of laugh. The kind that said he enjoyed being with me at that moment as much I enjoyed being with him, the kind that said we'd moved into a kind of comfortable companionship that allowed us to get silly without being embarrassed. Why not? How could I embarrass myself more in front of him than I had by exposing my prejudices?

By the time the third song came on, a lot

of the kids had joined us in an impromptu dance off.

Though Lucas could hold his own with them, he'd been out of the dance scene for far longer, which gave the kids the clear edge.

The song ended and another started. When Lucas and I left the floor, a couple of tweens tried to stop us, teasing Lucas about being too old to handle the moves, but Lucas waved them off and pointed at me. "I don't want her to feel bad. So I better go with her."

"Oh, right, blame your weakness on me?" I balled my hand to throw a playful jab at him, but he caught it and tucked it against his chest to keep me from squiggling away. Heat from the exertion of dancing and his rapidly beating heart pulsed through his shirt to my palm, the sensation knocking me so off-balance I wasn't ready when he rolled me up tight against him.

We were so close.

So. Close.

He was still laughing at the kids who'd kept dancing with the new song when he turned to face me as if pulled by my stare. His laughter faded when our eyes met.

"I'm sorry you're mad at me," I whispered.

"I'm not mad." His words were soft, a gentle breeze washing over my lips, promising something more.

"Yes, you are."

"I was. At first. But the fact that you cared enough about my niece to call me out shows a lot of strength on your part. How could I ever stay mad at that?"

He'd come impossibly closer, yet the only contact between us was my hands on his chest and his hands on my hands. How had he done that? How had he crossed so much distance and still made no contact anywhere else?

This was a bridge moment. I could feel myself tensing for the jump. I couldn't stop myself from leaning in, from wanting his lips to settle on mine, from wanting to forget what I had said to him or how much all the executives liked him and focus only on what I *felt* about him. Under my hand, his heart rate increased. Did he feel this, too? Did he care for me, too?

"Emma, I . . ." His warm breath against my lips made me rise on my toes a little, hoping his lips would touch mine. "Emma . . ."

His eyes, the ones that were a pale blue color, soft yet strong, locked with mine in a way that made me feel he might never let me go. *Jump now.* I pushed up higher on my toes and closed my eyes in preparation for the moment of impact.

As if we'd crossed through some forbidden door and tripped an alarm, my phone trilled from inside my pocket. We broke apart immediately. I tugged my phone free and glanced at the screen. "It's Blake," I announced, more from confusion than any real desire to confess that Lucas's brother was on the phone at the same instant I had been about to kiss him.

He wiped his hand over his mouth as if I actually *had* kissed him and he wanted to clean away any evidence.

"I . . ." I began, not sure how that sentence should be finished.

"Emma," he said, his voice strained and thick and . . . sad, maybe? "Emma, do me a favor."

The phone trilled again.

"What favor?"

"Talk to my brother." He stepped back, farther away from me. "Just talk to him. He really does care about you."

I looked at the phone in my hand, a poisonous snake that had struck and left its victim numb and confused. By the time I looked back to Lucas, he had moved behind the tables and was stacking empty pizza boxes for the trash.

A third ring.

I swiped the screen and put the phone to my ear. "Hello?"

I glanced back to where Lucas had been, but he was gone.

"You answered." Blake's surprise could only be equaled by my own.

I covered my other ear with my hand to muffle the music. "Yeah. I guess I did."

"Are you okay? Where are you? What's all that noise?"

I glanced to the people, the young and the old, the smudged and street worn. "Pizza party at the family shelter."

Blake laughed. "Luc dragged you to his old stomping grounds, then, huh?"

When I didn't answer, he kept talking. "Did he take you upstairs? There's a plaque with my mom's name on it."

There it was. The difference between Lucas and Blake. Blake used his mother like a gardener might use a shovel. She was a name to drop, something to use to impress people.

Blake was still talking, as if making sure to remind me where Lucas came from. Was he worried that Lucas and I were here together on the opposite side of the country without him? Did he worry our rooms were separated by only a wall and a door? Blake let out a small laugh. "Ever since she found Luc there and brought him home, that place has been a pet project for her and her foundation."

Her foundation . . .

I shook myself out of the strange need to hang up and go find Lucas to see if he was okay, to apologize for being too forward and for making him uncomfortable, but Blake's words made me stop. The foundation.

Jared wanted a foundation for Kinetics.

Blake's overt competitive feelings toward Lucas awakened my own need to compete.

I'd thrown the foundation puzzle to the team so they could brainstorm ideas that fit the Kinetics model and ended up with suggestions from Nathan on fighting against diseases such as cancer and diabetes, from Alison on fighting mental and emotional troubles like depression and suicide, and from Jeremy, who wanted to have a foundation that lobbied against children and politicians. Jeremy's suggestion came with a list of reasons why politicians and children were similar enough to be considered identical enemies. He used words like whiny, fibbing, tantrum-throwing, stinky, and sticky. He apparently had his brother's kids staying at his house again.

I glanced around the dining hall to the faces of people who were in transient lifestyles, the kids with nowhere to go, and remembered how Lucas said he used to do his homework on the ferry after school.

"Emma? Are you still there?"

"Blake." I'd almost forgotten the phone in my hand and the person connected to that call. "Yes. Still here."

"Are you all right?" He sounded worried, a tone I'd not often heard from him in any of our past dating.

"Fine. Just thinking."

"Oh? About me, maybe?"

"Actually about your mother." *And trying not to think about your brother.*

"Oh."

I hated it when he acted disappointed. And then wondered at how often I *had* heard that tone. How good of a girlfriend could I really have been if my boyfriend constantly found himself disappointed by my words and behavior? How much of the breakup was actually me?

His disappointment prompted me to explain myself. "You've talked a lot about your mom since we've met, about her work with charities and so forth. You mentioning her reminded me that I'm supposed to help Kinetics start a foundation — one that builds our brand and is marketable. That's all."

Blake never missed opportunities. That made him a perfect son to inherit the Hampton fortunes. He saw my need as the opportunity it actually was. "My mother could probably help you. She's a master at that sort of thing. In fact, I was planning on heading to my parents' for the weekend in a couple weeks. You should, or is it too much to ask — I mean, you could come with me."

How did I go from nearly kissing Lucas to getting another invitation to the Hampton family home from Blake in less than five minutes?

"Emma?"

Even hearing my name from him couldn't push words past my lips.

"I understand if you'd rather not. It's totally fine. I just would love a chance to do our relationship over, to make things up to you, to prove myself. But this doesn't have to be a do-over. It could be no-strings-attached if you want. My mom really could help you. She knows everyone worth knowing when it comes to charities. You can meet with her and not feel like you're obligated to be with me."

Why couldn't he have been like this before things became so complicated? Why couldn't he have felt this way before I met his brother? The same brother who evacuated the room as if someone had called a fire drill. The same brother I'd already decided against due to my accusations, the golden-boy love the other execs gave him, and the fact that he was my ex-boyfriend's brother. But it was also Lucas's past that drew me to him. Only an abandoned child could understand how another abandoned child truly felt about anything. We had an unmistakable connection that made me care about him in spite of everything else. And even with the other execs heaping praise over Lucas, I'd stopped feeling like he was my competition and feeling more like he was my friend. My close friend. My friend with possibilities . . .

But Lucas asked me to answer this phone call. He had wanted me to talk to Blake, which meant his feelings for me were not as deep as my feelings for him. Would he want me to accept Blake's offer? Would he be hurt if I did? Would he care either way?

"If I go with you to your parents' house, are you saying they will actually be there this time?"

Blake laughed, the kind of laugh that spoke of relief, gratitude, and a smidge of triumph.

"I promise I'll give you a proper introduction, Emma. And the whole family will be there. It's Mom's birthday."

I considered that information. A family event meant Lucas would be there, too. Would he feel like I was intruding on something private if I showed up as a tagalong? But how could he feel like that when he'd asked me to answer Blake's call as a favor to him?

"Meeting your mom would be great. Thank you for offering. I have some ideas and would love to have input from someone who understands what's needed."

Blake seemed to be waiting for something more from me, for some sort of signal that this was about him, too, not just work.

"And it's probably a good idea for us to talk," I added. "To figure out . . . things."

Things like Lucas and me. And Blake and me. And why dating felt like making caramel: a sticky mess where the chances of getting burned were likely. Maybe Jane knew what she was doing by staying single, after all. Maybe I shouldn't have been so quick to break up with her. But clearly I wasn't committed to staying broken up with anyone since I was so willing to be amicable with Blake. I glanced around the room, noting how many people had siphoned back to the rooms they slept in or to the outdoors. Very few people remained. And still no sign of Lucas.

"I agree," Blake said. "And, Emma?"

"Hm?"

"I still love you. Nothing's changed there. Tell Lucas to take care of my girl."

He hung up before I could squeak out any kind of response, likely because he wasn't sure of what kind of response I might give.

How could he be sure of my reaction when I wasn't sure of it?

Whoever had jacked the phone into the speakers unplugged the device and drowned the room in the silence of my uncertainty. There was nothing left to do except find Lucas and go back to the hotel.

The thought of facing him after I'd leaned in like some desperate flirt filled me with dread of the worst kind. Was it any wonder he wanted me to get the phone and talk to Blake? Lucas was not the sort of guy who backstabbed his brother. What must he think of me? Puckering up like he was the first customer at my personal kissing booth?

"You are such an amateur, Emma!" I whispered to myself.

But standing around and waiting for Lucas to return wasn't exactly a great plan either. The few remaining lingerers to the

Lucas Hampton Pizza Party whispered among themselves and cast meaningful "get the heck out of our space" looks at me.

I complied and found Lucas dribbling a basketball with a bunch of the same kids who'd been dancing with us. He rolled the sun-faded ball off his fingertips in a perfect throw that swished through the metal hoop and through the chain basket that half dangled from its few remaining rusted links.

He high-fived a few of the guys and fist-bumped another before he saw me. His demeanor went from casual to hooded in the blink of an eye. "See you around, guys," he said to the kids, who continued the game without him. He stuffed his hands into his jean pockets and sauntered my direction.

"So . . . how's my brother?"

"He sounded fine," I said, wishing I had worn jeans instead of my black business pantsuit. Very few of my dress pants gave the benefit of pockets, and I suddenly wanted a place to stuff my hands as well, a place to keep them from feeling floppy and fidgety.

I folded my arms, and we began walking.

He lifted his arm to hail a cab, but I protested. "What happened to the subway being the only real ride in Manhattan?"

"Maybe we should get in early tonight."

Was he mad at me? My face felt hot with embarrassment. This was a business trip. Nothing more than business. We were here to get work done, not date, not like each other, not anything that wasn't business related. Besides, he'd already told me he wasn't mad at me. So why go back to mere civility instead of friendship? Why not put his arm over my shoulder and meander to the subway where we could sit close on the train? Why not make the good-bye scene at the door something worth dreaming about?

I knew why.

He loved his brother.

And his brother, according to the phone conversation I'd just had, loved me. How did I feel about any of that?

I didn't know. My time with Lucas had reminded me of all the good things I liked and admired about Blake. Hearing the stories of all Blake had done for Lucas helped me to remember that Blake hadn't been a monster while we'd been dating. But my time with Lucas also showed me all the things to like and admire about *Lucas.*

Was I really that girl? The fickle one whose heart was so easily turned? I had never thought so before, but now . . . now, I was pathetic.

Lucas being my competition in work and

my ex-boyfriend's brother didn't feel like enough to keep me away from him. But it clearly was enough to keep him away from me.

He held the back door for me while I folded myself into the cab and then he got in the other side. I sat silently next to Lucas while the car eased out into the street. Silence settled between us in a way that forbade breaching. Not until we were off the elevator and walking to our rooms did I see the truth for what it was. We would go back in the morning, and we would become distant coworkers.

I didn't want to go home that way.

I wouldn't go home that way.

I stopped. Lucas did too once he realized my feet were no longer in rhythm with his. "I'm going back out tonight," I announced.

"You're what?"

"Times Square is just a short walk away, and it seems wrong to not visit on the last night here. People back at the office will expect to see pictures."

He shot a longing look down the hallway to where his room waited for him. "We have lots of pictures."

"But none of me or you or *us*. And certainly none of us actually doing something fun. All our pictures are various angles of buildings and neighborhoods. We came all this way and never got one fun picture of the two of us? That's insane."

"Going out when we have to catch an early flight is insane," he said, crossing his arms over his chest.

"We can sleep on the plane. Heck, for you, sleeping on the plane is the best idea. It'll take your mind off the fact that you're miles above ground with no parachute. We should actually probably see about getting you a prescription for antianxiety medicine if you ever have to fly again."

"Emma, we can't go out tonight."

He had to be considering our almost-kiss. He had to be mulling over the fact that I'd leaned into him; my intentions in that moment weren't exactly hidden. When his eyes dropped to my mouth, I realized I was biting my lip just thinking about the way the heat from his chest felt against my palm, the way the rhythm of his heart vibrated through my fingers.

Lucas was a good man, the kind of man I wanted for myself. He was educated and intelligent, fiercely loyal and painfully polite. I stepped away from him, back in the direction of the elevators.

I would not kiss him, would not think about that ever again. But I would go to

Times Square and spend my last night in Manhattan doing something fun and exciting, even if I had to do it alone, even if being alone wasn't fun or exciting.

"We really can't," he said as I took another step back.

"I can," I responded. And with that, I turned on my heel and marched right back to the elevators. "And I will!" I called over my shoulder as I hit the down arrow.

"Emma!" Lucas shouted.

I ignored him.

"Emma!"

"Sorry, Emma Pierce is out right now actually living her life. If you want to talk to her, leave a message at the beep." The response was obnoxious in every way, but there was some serious satisfaction that, right at that moment, the elevator doors slid open with a chiming beep. I stepped into the elevator and turned to face him. "If you don't want to leave a message," I said with a shrug, "then you'll just have to come with her."

He was still down the hall, far enough away that it seemed unlikely he would join me. The idea made me sad. Not one person on this planet made such a great travel companion as Lucas did, at least when he wasn't fuming at me for being stupid. He may not care for me like I cared for him, but he could still be my travel companion. We could still have this connection of understanding and empathy and friendship for a little longer if he'd only come with me. We had this one night. One night to be genuine friends. And he was missing it.

The doors began to close.

I released the breath I'd been holding. He really wasn't coming.

But then his hand slid between the two doors, stopping them and bouncing them back to an open position. "I hate leaving messages," he said as he took his place next to me.

The doors slid closed after a brief hesitation, and the mirrored silver revealed the two of us, facing forward and smiling.

"You don't have to be so smug," he said.

"I might not get another chance," I responded, feeling the truth of it. *I might not get another chance.*

We walked, a thing I only planned on doing if he came with. Had I done this alone, a taxi would definitely have been part of the plan. No one could actually call it a long walk — maybe a mile — but in that mile, Lucas loosened up.

Granted, he had to be goaded into loosening up. When he kept his hands in his pockets, I knocked into him a little and said, "You know, if I shove you down, it's unlikely you'd get your hands out of your pockets fast enough to catch your fall. Smashing into the cement would really mess up that pretty face of yours."

He jerked his head to look at me in shock. "Are you saying I'm pretty?"

I rolled my eyes. "Yeah, pretty. Pretty annoying."

"You're the one who dragged me out of a perfectly good night's sleep."

You're the one who asked me to take a call from your brother instead of letting me kiss you. But I didn't say it out loud. My word filter must have been exhausted from biting back so many, many things.

We made it to Times Square just before midnight. "Look at the screens," I said, counting down the time until the screens all changed.

"Why?"

"What? You mean I know something you don't know about this city?"

He lifted his eyebrows and finally took his hands out of his pockets, but only so he could raise them in a gesture of confusion.

"Midnight Moment?" I asked.

He shook his head, and his hands went back into his pockets again.

"Really? C'mon, Lucas. Do you never go on TripAdvisor before you leave town?"

"Apparently not."

"Well then." I grinned. "Let me show you something new." There were forty-eight seconds until the screens changed. I walked us to a place where we would have the best view of all the screens at once. "Here's where we're getting our picture. It only lasts for three minutes, so we'll have to do it fast."

"What only lasts three minutes?"

I held up my hands and counted down the last ten seconds on my fingers, then pointed to the screens.

They all changed at the same time.

All the advertisements and news feeds vanished, replaced by the theme of the day: waterfalls.

The digital art gallery showcased some of the most exquisite pictures of waterfalls I'd ever seen.

I exhaled with a quiet, "Oh."

It was lovelier than I had imagined. With all the screens filled with images of various waterfalls, it actually appeared that water was spilling out into the center of Times Square.

"Oh," Lucas repeated just as quietly, just as surprised.

I lifted my phone above us and scooted

closer to Lucas so he was in the selfie. My short arms could not stretch high enough to get his head in the frame. "Do you have to be so tall?" I demanded, feeling anxious to catch the moment while it lasted. Seconds were ticking away. The waterfalls would be gone soon.

With a grunt, he tried to scrunch down, but it didn't matter. My arms were no match for his height. I stood on my tiptoes and nearly fell off the curb into the street.

Lucas's hand shot out of his pocket and caught me just in time to safely settle me back on my feet. "Here," he said, taking the phone from my hand.

His other arm wrapped around me to keep me from falling again, and he lifted the phone high enough to get us both in the shot as well as the wall of waterfalls surrounding us. It was probably just my wishful imagination, but his arms felt like they tightened around me as if he were holding me — not just holding me up, but holding *me.*

I leaned into him, and I couldn't help it; my eyes fluttered closed at the feel of his arms around me. When I heard the *snick* of my phone taking a picture, my eyes popped open. He hit the button three more times, and I brought myself back to the moment enough to smile for those pictures. And then the screens flashed back to their original states.

He handed me my phone. I grinned at him, showing all my teeth. "Well?" I said.

He rolled his eyes. "Okay. Fine. That was worth it."

He didn't put his hands back in his pockets.

"Yes, it was," I said.

CHAPTER TWELVE

"Friendship is certainly the finest balm for
the pangs of disappointed love."
— JANE AUSTEN, *Northanger Abbey*

"I'm a prophetess," I said miserably to Silvia over a plate of pad Thai noodles. She came over for dinner a week and a half after I returned home. To celebrate getting to hang out with her again, I made her favorite meal and dessert, and we planned to settle in with a good movie to take the edge off what Silvia called a terrible week at work.

She snorted at my declaration. "It only took you three weeks away from me for you to get a big head?"

"I'm serious."

She smirked. "So am I. So tell me, oh huge-headed prophetess, is the weather going to be good tomorrow? Because I need to go surfing in the morning."

"It's perfect surfing weather tomorrow.

See? I'm really good at this prophetess thing."

She downed the rest of the Diet Coke in her glass and shook her head. "Watching the Weather Channel is not even close to the same thing as being open to revelation."

"Oh, yeah? Well, how about the fact that even though Lucas and I became real friends on our trip, I knew when we got back, we'd regress to being indifferent coworkers. And here I am, nearly two weeks later and getting nothing out of him aside from a murmur of assent and a nod when I propose new ideas. Or sometimes a shake of the head when he disagrees with me. And worse than that, Jared is under the impression that all my good ideas belong to Lucas. It shouldn't make me furious, but it totally does."

"Lucas hasn't corrected Jared?"

I swirled the noodles on my fork, released them, and swirled them up again. "I think he's trying, but you know Jared has a nasty habit of interrupting people. Jared's always in the middle of something else when Lucas brings it up. And we haven't been able to get him in the office, so Jared's only communicated with anyone via phone, and Lucas can't seem to get a word in at the time."

"Crap excuse. Lucas could send Jared a

text and explain it to him, or he could send an email. Or did his fingers break on the trip and he's lost his ability to type?"

"He's had a lot of responsibility dumped on him since we got back."

"Was that an excuse I just heard you making for him? 'Cause it sounded like an excuse. Another crap one." She dropped her head to the side and gave me a long sideways look. "You ignored me. You ignored me and totally fell for him, didn't you?"

"Of course not." Noodles had never seemed so interesting. My eyes stayed focused on the contents of my plate rather than meeting her eye.

"You are the worst liar. You've always been the worst liar. I should've bagged the two weeks' notice and insisted on coming with you for the trip so you had some protection from yourself."

I laughed and hated interpreting it for the nervous noise that it was. "I just feel like there's all this tension between us."

"What tension?"

The kind where he avoids me whenever possible. The kind where, on the flight home, he kept his hands clasped together in his lap instead of letting me hold one to comfort him during takeoff. The kind where he hasn't actu-

ally met my eye since we parted ways at the airport.

But what I said was, "He won't really talk to me. And it's hard to get our work done when I feel like he's aloof and avoiding real conversations."

"Call him on it," she said and took a huge bite of her noodles.

Silvia's strength inspired me. She was always ready to call people on their crap, always ready to jump into the snarls and untangle them one strand at a time. She despised emotional games and messy lives due to no communication. When her parents experienced a blip in their marriage, Silvia, at the age of twelve, ran her own brand of intervention. She packed her bags and set them by the front door, then made her parents sit next to each other on the couch while she explained that the first of the Four Horsemen in relationships was contempt and she was tired of seeing them toss contempt at one another when they both had things to work on. She told them if they couldn't get it together and act like adults, she'd stay with me and my father.

Maybe her technique wouldn't have worked for everyone, but it worked for her mom and dad. They opened up. They ended up seeing a counselor and talking through the things they'd let build up over the years.

They credit Silvia with the lives they'd managed to happily live since then.

But I didn't think calling Lucas on his status as an office-mute would change anything. "How do you suggest I do that?" I asked her.

"Corner him in his office and tell him you've developed feelings for him and ask him to dinner. Or you could cut to the chase and just kiss him and see what he does with that."

"Silvia!"

She smirked. "The thing about calling people out is that you have to be open and honest, too. Crap-calling is a two-way street."

"I can't."

"Can't or won't?" She tossed her napkin on her plate.

I frowned and stared at her napkin because it was easier than facing her directly. "I've been seeing Blake this last week."

Silvia didn't speak for several seconds, likely as surprised by my admission as I felt. "Seeing? The ex-boyfriend?"

I nodded.

She drummed her fingers on the table. "Dating one while you're moping around about the other?"

"We're not dating. We're . . . *seeing*. Seeing if we fit, if we have any reason to keep pursuing each other. We have an official date tomorrow night."

She blinked several times and put her hands up to ward off my words. "I'm not going to lie when I say that I fully expect you to feel some sort of moral conflict over this whole thing, because really . . . this story gets sadder every time you update me."

"I know."

"Why are you accepting dates with Blake anyway, after what he did?"

"He apologized for that. He says he really didn't think it was a big deal, just dinner, and that it would never happen again. He wants to make it up to me. He wants to prove himself to me."

"And so you said yes? Even though you're feeling all kinds of mushy gushy feelings for his brother?"

"I never said I felt mushy gushy feelings about anyone." I stood to clear my plate and, in the process, clear my guilt. As much as I admired Silvia's cut-to-the-chase way of speaking, I didn't love when she used it on me — especially when I deserved it.

She stood as well, carrying her plate to

my sink. "So what do you see in all this seeing?"

I scrubbed my dishes harder. "I don't know. I like Blake. I care about him. And he seems genuinely committed to the idea of us in a way he never did before . . . but there is the moral conflict that his brother is always a centerpiece in my head."

"So all this seeing has rendered you completely blind."

I didn't turn away from the dishes. "It's not like Lucas and I even had a chance to explore anything. Like you said, I was dating his brother just a month ago, and not just dating but about to say yes to his proposal."

"The marriage proposal that didn't happen?"

"The point is," I said, trying to speak over her, "is that if I felt that sure about him then, isn't it fair to give him a chance to prove himself better, now? Are the feelings I have for Lucas just a rebound attraction that need to be ignored because they aren't legitimate in the long-term?"

"All feelings are legitimate in the long-term, sweetie. All feelings stir together the seconds and minutes and hours that make us *us.* It's not fair to take away the legitimacy of each moment's feeling by saying it doesn't count."

"Even if the feelings are misplaced?"

"Especially when they're misplaced. The misplaced feelings help us find the real ones."

Silvia was right, as always. But she was also not telling me something. She had no problem meeting my eyes when we discussed my misfortunes in love but blatantly refused to look my direction when we discussed her.

"So what misplaced feelings are making up your current moments, Sil?" I asked. I knew I was on the right trail when she took over the task of doing my dishes. Silvia avoided dishes as much as possible. They grossed her out almost as much as feet.

She blamed all her weirdness on her job and the transition and her fears that they'd figure out she was a fraud as soon as she started her the new position with Portal Pictures.

All of which was reasonable enough that I didn't notice how she changed the subject back from her to me and my betrayal in accepting Blake's invitation to be *seeing* anything. Since she felt so strongly about my time with Blake, I left out the fact that on Friday, I would be doing a repeat performance of the weekend getaway with Blake and his family. I only hoped more of the cast showed up this time.

The *seeing* we'd been doing was really to just test the waters, to see if I could handle a whole weekend with Blake or to see if the whole thing needed to be called off. If that was the case, I'd just have to make an appointment to meet with Caroline Hampton in some other way. Spending small bites of time together played a pivotal part in the weekend's fate. But telling Silvia any of that would require me to admit to the weekend at all. If she knew about it, there was a very real possibility she would chuck her fake eye at me.

Silvia and I settled in to watch several films done by her new employer. "It still weirds me out that you take notes while we watch movies," I said as her eye brightened in admiration of a particularly clever scene change.

"It still weirds me out that you promote a healthy lifestyle for a living." She said this around the donut stuffed into her mouth.

"Not gonna lie, that weirds me out too."

"And yet, you're not partaking in the donut love. You've been drinking the company Kool-Aid."

"It's way too late to put that kind of sugar in my system."

She laughed, the kind that spoke of comfortable pleasure, and turned her attention back to the romance movie.

Silvia and I were suckers for romance. Romance and the lasting love it promised were all I had ever really wanted out of life. My father never had that for himself. My mother apparently didn't have it either, or she would have stayed.

Maybe that was why I felt the need to take Blake up on his dating offer. With Lucas neglecting me, I wanted to feel datable in some sphere.

Was I rebounding from Lucas with Blake?

Had I been rebounding from Blake with Lucas?

Was rebounding even a real thing, or was it just some psychological garbage that someone who'd been crossed in love made up to keep other people from exploring the happiness they could never have?

I pinched off a chunk of donut and stuffed it in my mouth. Silvia noticed, her one working eye glancing over me while the other stayed trained on the movie. I didn't apologize for the sugary snack or make an excuse. Sometimes a girl needed something sweet in her life from somewhere. If it came from our buddy Dunkin' the Donut King, so be it. Silvia had called it donut love, after all. And love was the one thing I was missing, the one thing I'd always wanted.

Love's elusive properties forced me to action; they compelled me to accept the mini-dates with Blake. If I ignored real chances at happiness, I would end up like Jane Austen: alone.

My thoughts pecked at me until Silvia left my apartment at one in the morning. They stayed with me at work the next morning, distracting me enough that Jared scowled in my direction from the other side of the long table in the boardroom. I was grateful he didn't say anything to draw attention to my distraction.

After the meeting was over, Lucas called out to me as he gathered up some paperwork from the table. "Hey! Emma! Wait up!"

My heart rate increased. Lucas actually acknowledging me? How was such a thing even possible? I halted and hated how quickly I obeyed. He had ignored me for nearly two whole weeks, and I forgive and forget and stop and wait?

Apparently. Because I kept waiting until he caught up.

He smiled, all sunshine and oblivion to the slight he'd given me for days on end. "Jared wants to meet for lunch. He wants to talk over your idea about the sky meditation room."

I bristled. Lucas wasn't talking to me because he wanted to. He was talking to me because Jared wanted him to. *And* because they wanted to discuss something Jared continually gave Lucas conceptual credit for. "I can't make it today. Besides, I really don't think you guys need me at that meeting."

He blinked, clearly surprised by my flat refusal. "Of course we need you. This is your idea, your baby."

"My baby? Are we talking about the one Jared kidnapped and gave to you to raise?" There. The words were out. I'd bitten them back for days. They tasted just as sour exiting my mouth as they had when I swallowed them down.

His eyes widened, and he crossed his arms over his chest in a classic business defensive move. "He did not *give* the idea to me. Though I admit, he did try to hijack it for a while and not give you the credit, but I set him straight. All that's done, now."

All the excuses I'd made for Lucas when talking to Silvia the night before came to mind. I had wanted this side of him to be true, wanted to defend him to her. But I felt irritated that he was only talking to me because Jared asked, and I no longer felt like defending him or having him prove himself to be who I had made him out to be in my mind.

"I'm already working through my lunch hour to finish other things so I can leave early tonight."

"Right. Big date tonight."

I glanced around the hall to see who else could have heard. Debbie was talking with Jeremy, which surprised me since Jeremy usually avoided Debbie's sunny, overbearing disposition.

They both glanced my way and then hurried to look away, which meant they were definitely talking about me. The last thing — like end-of-the-universe last thing — I needed was anyone at work finding out about my date with Blake. For anyone to discover I was going back to the guy who jilted me after a nonproposal would make me the most pathetic boss ever.

No one could respect a woman who acted like a schoolgirl when it came to love. I couldn't respect myself knowing that I was such a hopeless closet romantic.

How did Lucas even know? Were he and Blake discussing me?

"Emma?" Lucas said, pulling my attention back to him and the fact that I had a date with his brother.

"Hmm?"

He shrugged. "Nothing. Not really. I'll make an excuse for you to Jared, something good so there won't be any issues. It's important you get out of here early enough."

"Why?" I asked, unsure of what I meant. If my life could be wrapped up in one little word, it would have been that one.

Lucas waited for me to explain, but I shrugged in direct imitation of him.

"Why does my *date* matter to you?" I finally said, figuring it was as good a why as any of the other dozens running through my head.

He held my gaze and waited a long moment to answer.

In that moment, I felt something coming from him, something I didn't understand, not really. It felt like regret and love and admiration and a lot of other things rolling my direction in waves that cemented me to the spot.

I remembered the way his chest rose and fell under my palm when we'd been dancing. How he'd held my hand there, sharing a heartbeat with me.

He swallowed hard and broke eye contact. "Blake told me about you the night you walked out on him, about how you have such big dreams and goals, how you rise to challenges, how you make him feel happy in a way no one ever has. He's not ever felt serious about anyone before. Not ever. To hear him talk about you like that . . . he just . . . I just . . . My brother's a great guy. I love him."

So that was all.

"Oh." Why did his declaration of love for his brother disappoint me? Brotherly affection was admirable. It gave credit to both brothers. Why did it make me want to cry and run away from them both?

"So . . . I'll cover for you at the meeting?"

"No," I said, changing my mind, knowing I could delegate to Debbie and Jeremy and rearrange my schedule so I could at least make it to half of that tactical meeting and still meet with Jared. I don't know if it was because I wanted to see for myself that Jared knew where credit needed to go or if I just wanted to spend time in the same room with the guy who ignored me except for when he wanted to play his brother's advocate.

"Beet and avocado salad for your lunch order?"

I gave a tight smile of acceptance, hating that he could order the lunch I would've ordered for myself and then wondering if Blake could've done the same. Did Blake know me well enough to order my favorites? Had he ever paid attention to that sort of thing? He knew about my disdain for fish, but that was only because he thought it an oddity and liked to make fun of me for being so picky.

Lucas smiled, almost like he had read my thoughts. We each went our separate ways: me to hurry along the meeting with Debbie and Jeremy, him to presumably order my lunch.

I poked my head in Debbie's office. "Meet me in my office in three minutes. Bring all the content prepped for this month's magazines, including the trades as well as the billboards and posters we're doing for both the East Coast and Southern California."

She nodded her understanding at the same time she immediately tapped up commands on her keyboard to ready the materials I needed. "Why the hurry?"

"I apparently have a lunch meeting with Jared and Lucas I have to go to."

"I *hate* being forced into meetings with people who can broaden my horizons," she said with a smirk.

I narrowed my eyes at her. "What was that?" Was she thinking I was using Lucas to help me get back with Blake? She heard us talking about the date Blake and I were going on. How pathetic did it make me look if I had to use Blake's brother to finagle a date?

Her smirk vanished, and red bloomed in her cheeks. "Nothing."

Debbie and I were friends, but I was also her boss, and I understood her inference well enough to make sure she understood she meandered on crumbling ground. The look that passed between her and Jeremy in the hall was enough for me to know that the rumor mill was in full operation. And it needed to be closed down.

"Let's make sure it stays nothing," I said.

She nodded again and tightened her lips together.

I left her office and went to Jeremy's. "Meeting has been moved up. See you at my office in two minutes. I need the stats across all platforms, and I'm curious how our last email campaign went, so those stats, too. Thanks, Jer."

"I hate meetings, you know," he called to my retreating back. "Making me interact with the team is bamboo shoots under the fingernails. I don't get paid enough to have to talk to you people."

"Yes, you do," I called back over my shoulder.

Jeremy avoided anyone with a pulse. For

being a social media manager, he didn't love most social environments. At least not the ones in real life. But for as often as he acted as though he didn't enjoy most of the people in the office, he was also the first to donate money to people who had kids doing fundraisers. Even after working with the company only a few months, I saw the quiet things he did for his coworkers' benefit.

Once they both sat in my office, Debbie handed over the tear sheets from the previous months' ads as well as the design concepts for the upcoming months. I looked them over while Jeremy explained that the last campaign brought in more than eight thousand new likes on the Facebook page and also bumped our engagement, allowing our online operatives to write up new memberships. The whole thing had been a great success. That, coupled with the clever slogans and calls to action with the design pages, meant we were definitely on the right track.

"I'm meeting with Jared in a few minutes, and all of this is excellent. Thanks, guys, for taking such good care of your teams and keeping them all on track as we add new locations and flirt with new markets. Everything here takes us from flirting to relationships." I saw a look pass from Jeremy to

Debbie, but she widened her eyes and shook her head. Apparently, making dating references around these two was taboo since they acted so concerned with my dating life.

"One last thing before we break," I said. "I've got some great leads for the foundation Jared wants and wanted your feedback before I move forward. We already have a youth program in place for teens who want to prepare for athletic achievements within their schools, but it's a paid-for subscription like it is for everyone else. This eliminates kids who might want to enhance their own performance with extra workouts and proper equipment but who can't afford it. What if we do an earned subscription where kids can earn their right to the equipment, the pool, the meditation rooms, even the climbing wall?"

"How do they earn it?" Jeremy asked. "Mop floors?"

"Yes, and clean windows," I said, rolling my eyes. "No. With grades. We can create a study room in each facility, somewhere kids can come and have a quiet, peaceful place to get their brains in the game. And then they can reach privileges based on grades. The privileges can level up — better benefits as they get better grades."

Jeremy nodded while Debbie scribbled

notes. "This is great," Jeremy said. "The tier idea is really great. And maybe if they can show consistency, like two semesters in a row with a 3.8 and above, they can redeem one skydiving tunnel coupon, since seriously, that's one of our biggest attractions for youth."

Debbie tapped her pen on her tablet. "And the campaign can revolve around what you just said: 'Get your brain in the game.' "

Jeremy bobbed his head in agreement. "Right. We can run ads online in places kids go and on the social media platforms they use the most. The events manager could run events in schools to promote and recruit students who are candidates. We could run a competition, like an Olympics between schools in the surrounding neighborhoods. We can do a few humorous YouTube videos, see if we can get one to go viral. It could be good."

"Very good," Debbie confirmed. "Nicely done, boss."

Her calling me boss felt like a dig at my earlier admonishment, but better a dig than the continued comments earmarked for insinuation. It pleased me that she liked the foundation idea. "So we're good to present this to Jared?"

They both agreed that we were.

Jeremy tossed over a dubious scowl. "I feel like Jared is asking more from the team than he should. Do you know how to start a foundation? I know I don't know anything about it. Your idea sounds great — don't get me wrong — but how hard or easy is this going to be to execute?"

I sucked in a deep breath. "Well, you're right. I don't know a lot about starting a foundation."

"This isn't meant to be a critique on you, Emma," Jeremy said, "but Jared sometimes doesn't understand our roles and jobs."

Jeremy was right. "No offense taken. But it turns out that this will work okay. I managed to procure a mentor for this endeavor. I'll spend the weekend with her and have been promised she'll walk me through the process and be available afterward for any follow-up questions."

"That's great! Who's the mentor?" Jeremy asked.

I sketched a glance from him to Debbie. "Caroline Hampton."

Debbie's mouth fell open. "As in Blake Hampton's mom?"

My ear tips went fire hot. "Yes."

Her eyes widened, and I saw her connecting the other dots in her mind. Caroline mothered not only Blake Hampton but Lucas Hampton as well. Debbie must think I was using the whole family. With a self-restraint seldom exercised, Debbie let the subject drop.

She even changed the subject. "Hey, I need pictures of the new locations," she said. "Didn't you say you had those for me?"

"Right — sorry. They're on my phone." I handed her my phone so I could take the last few precious moments doing what I was supposed to be doing by reviewing the tear sheets. "Email them to yourself before I forget again."

She took my phone from me while I finished going through the stack.

"How often are we running in *Oxygen* magazine?" I asked.

"Six a month."

"Cut it to four, and add two to *Weight for It.*"

"Got it." She had a knowing smile on her face as she handed back my phone.

I pocketed it and narrowed my eyes at her. "What?"

She shrugged. "Nothing. I just think it's great you'll get to know Caroline Hampton better."

I sighed. Debbie and her romantic plans for me. "It's business." And yes, it was also an exploration of what might still remain between Blake and me, but mostly it was business.

"I know." She scooted out of my office in an obvious attempt to avoid having to hear more of my denials that I was not trying to get back with Blake through his mom.

With a growl and a scowl, I gathered up my notes to meet up with Jared. And Lucas. Lucas with his fair hair and serious pale blue eyes. Lucas, who threw an impromptu pizza party for the homeless. Lucas, who knew what it was like to be left behind by a mother who didn't want you. Lucas, whose heart had pounded so furiously under my palm.

I swallowed hard and stood outside the meeting room set aside specifically for lunches. Only after my insides felt less shaky did my feet carry me inside where Jared expected too much of me and Lucas saw too little in me.

My lunch was set out already, the salad the way I liked it, the water with a lemon and a lime squeezed into it.

I wondered again if Blake knew those details about me. Had Blake paid that kind of attention? The time we'd spent together the past two weeks felt stilted and overprocessed. It was hard to determine what he knew about me. Or what I knew about him.

Lucas had awakened my good memories of Blake, and he'd talked my ears to bleeding about how Blake really hadn't thought the fish incident was infidelity so much as it was just making fish. I had to explore the possibility that maybe I hadn't listened to Blake before I stormed out of his house, that maybe some of the situation had been my fault, that maybe those good feelings needed to be reevaluated to see if anything existed in them.

Some part of me also hoped that perhaps the attraction I felt to Lucas would disappear if I reacquainted myself with Blake. Everything about my love life was spinning out of control, and I was the one who had yanked the wheel to the side to start the spin. But I couldn't force it to straighten out now or I'd be guaranteed a crash.

When I'd been six, my dad taught me to ride a bike. I crashed on every corner I took until he said gently, "You've got to lean into the turn. Let the curve happen. You'll be able to right yourself when you're on straight road again."

I'm leaning, Dad, I thought as I offered a tight smile to Lucas, whose return smile felt strangled.

The meeting began benignly enough.

Jared wanted explanations of everything, details about the details. He received all the information with his eyes closed and his hands cupped open and placed face up on the table in front of him. He believed this made it easier to receive new information and process whether the information was any good or not.

In reality, his posture made me feel like he'd gone to sleep while I was talking. Jeremy once suggested throwing our peas at Jared during meetings just to see if he was really awake or not.

No one ever threw peas at Jared, but I was tempted and suspected I wasn't the only exec who daydreamed about such behavior. The thing about climbing a corporate ladder, even if it was a small ladder within a small company, meant that you wanted the guy in charge of stuff to notice the awesome things you did for that company.

Jared never really seemed to notice. Because he had his eyes closed.

Not for the first time, I wondered what a red beet would look like sliding its way down his forehead and over his blousy linen shirt while he meditated away the information we fed him.

He opened his mouth after I gave him the briefing, the one I'd been prepared to give him for days but that he hadn't shown up to work to receive, and finally spoke. "Well done. Well done, both of you — especially you, Lucas. I told them hiring you was a stroke of genius."

"Emma did all the groundwork, sir," Lucas said, scurrying to deflect the compliments in my direction. So much for his straightening everything out with Jared.

Jared didn't open his eyes, but he kicked his chair back on its wheels so he could pull up his legs and sit cross-legged on the chair. "Right. Emma. How are you coming along with the foundation, Emma?"

I explained my ideas. He nodded a lot and murmured assent until finally he popped his eyes open and pinned me to the spot with his stare. "This all sounds great, but it also sounds excessive. I can't envision how to begin. I can see it going along smoothly once it has a start, but I cannot see the start."

This was Jared-speak for "I don't get it."

"Honestly, Jared," I said, "I don't see the start either because I've never done a foundation before." The guy had my résumé. He knew this information already. "But," I continued, "I do have some sources who can help me. I just need a green light from you for basic groundwork to begin."

"Who are your sources? How soon can you bring them in to work for us? When will all of this get started?"

My shoulders straightened, and I lifted my chin. "I'm meeting with Caroline Hampton at her estate this weekend to go over the details. I've been promised help and support."

The all-seeing eye of Jared's gaze slid to Lucas. "Isn't that your mother?"

"Yes, sir."

Jared nodded. "Good job, Lucas. I appreciate how you've taken our little starling and given her flying lessons."

He was really giving the credit to Lucas? Lucas had nothing to do with my meeting with Caroline.

I looked to Lucas to correct Jared but was met with his openmouthed stare from across the table. Lucas was apparently too startled to speak at all.

Had he not known about my visit to the family estate? He knew about my date tonight, which led me to believe he knew about everything else, too.

"It's my mother's birthday this weekend," Lucas said to me through pale lips.

"Yes. I know. Blake said he'd already talked to her, though, and she was fine with me crashing the party to talk business. Do you . . . not want me to come?"

His eyes stayed unreadable and as mute as the rest of him.

"Well?" Jared prompted. "Is there a problem with Emma spending the weekend with your mother?"

That startled Lucas out of whatever funk he'd thrown himself into. "Yes. I mean no. No, there isn't a problem. Yes, of course, she can come. No one had told me the plan before now, is all. I just needed to take a mental walk-through of all the schedules to make sure everything fit."

"And does it fit?" Jared asked.

"Like a glove." His bark of laughter was so sharp he could've cut himself on it.

As soon as the meeting was over, Lucas bent his head, avoiding eye contact with me, and shot off in the direction of his office, which unfortunately sat right next to mine, which meant I had to go in the same direction.

Not liking the together-but-separate sojourn to our own personal corners, I caught up to him and fell into step beside him. "So . . ." I began. "Why the radio silence?" Why not just ask outright? Wondering without at least asking was only driving me crazy.

Did he actually hasten his steps?

I lengthened my stride to keep up. "Well?" I prompted.

"I don't know what you're talking about." He was almost to his door and all but leaped forward to try to reach it faster.

"You talked a lot to me while we were on the trip. We were friends, I thought. Now . . . nothing. That's what I'm talking about. And you're a smart guy. I know you know that."

He stopped at the threshold of his door and turned slowly. "Okay. I do know. So here's the deal . . ." When his eyes fell on mine and pinned me to the spot, my breath hitched in my throat at his intensity. "I am careful about who I form attachments with. You, better than anyone, should understand that about me. Where I come from, what I've been through . . . I've never met anyone who understands all that."

I nodded, understanding perfectly. How could we not have some kind of bond or attachment when we shared so much similar history? That was why his silence hurt so much.

But if I was being honest with myself, it hurt because I felt more for him than I should, more than was work appropriate or personally appropriate, considering the circumstances.

"The truth, Emma, is I've never met

anyone who gets me like you do, and it's unraveled my careful-about-attachments policy."

A part of me lit up inside, hoping to hear him say he had come to care for me in the last month we'd worked together, that he felt we had a future together, that he wanted to spend time together to see what that future might be.

What he said was, "I'm sorry if this comes out wrong, but I just need to be where you are not."

With that, he stepped into his office and closed the door.

CHAPTER THIRTEEN

"His apparent partiality had subsided, his attentions were over, he was the admirer of someone else."
— JANE AUSTEN, *Pride and Prejudice*

I stood, lungs not breathing, heart not beating, for a long time in that hallway. Processing his actual words proved impossible. Lucas keeping his distance because he cared about me had made it to the top of my list of possibilities, of my hopes. Him resenting me because I'd accused him of being a deadbeat dad? Yes. I had expected that, too, even if he did say he wasn't mad anymore.

But for him to say he needed to not be where I was?

What did that even mean?

Whatever it meant, the words changed everything for me.

Or maybe they changed nothing.

It's not like he actually spent any time

talking to me anyway. Him not wanting to be where I was could have no effect on the silence we currently found ourselves in.

But why? The why was still out there. Did he hate me? Did he not want to be where I was because he found me irresistible? I laughed at myself and shot down that idea immediately. He sounded so angry before he shut his office door that it could only stem from the fact that I was invading his space, his beloved mother's birthday party, his family sanctuary.

But now that he'd confessed the difficulty of being around me, visiting his family during his mother's birthday party weekend seemed entirely foolhardy. Family get-togethers were awkward enough without flippant women crashing the party. At least that's what Silvia always told me and what I witnessed from the two reunions she'd dragged me to.

Sometimes being alone in the world when it came to relations wasn't such a bad thing.

I felt a strong need to visit the Hampton estate again, cautiously hopeful that the weekend would help me know how to feel about both brothers. The time spent with Blake so far reminded me of all I liked about him. But it also reminded me of all I didn't like about him. It had me comparing the brothers and my compatibility with each. Lucas was easier, more relaxed and comfortable — at least when he wasn't slamming doors on me. I hoped that being with Blake for a long period of time like I'd been with Lucas during our trip would help me see him as clearly, would help me understand how I felt about him, help me know if I needed to cut and run or swoon and stay.

Would Lucas being there muddy the water or clear it up?

But Lucas did not want to be where I was.

I closed my eyes and tried not to think of another door shutting me out. Lucas's door shut, the front door of my childhood shut. Both of them shutting over and over in my mind in a dizzying confusion.

I remembered Blake's voice on the night of the fish incident: *"There's no need to get hysterical about it. This isn't some manifestation of your mother's abandonment."*

But it was.

"Emma?"

I jumped at Jeremy's voice. He smirked when he realized he startled me.

"Jeremy!" I was about to tell him he scared me, but he already knew it, so there was no reason to hand him the satisfaction.

"Are you okay?"

281

"Of course. I'm fine. Why?"

"Because you're standing in the hallway as if you've had an alien visitation — or expecting an alien visitation."

"Just thinking."

He lifted an eyebrow. "Okay. Well, while you're thinking, can you sign these?"

He had a stack of invoices that needed approval for accounts payable. I signed them all while barely seeing them and sent him on his way. After he'd gone, it still took me several moments before I could force my feet to do their job and walk me into my own office, where I paced and cursed and wondered what to do next.

I did not call off my date with Blake, though my fingers hovered above his name on my phone on several occasions during the hours between the moment Lucas shut his office door and the moment Blake rang my doorbell that night. What would I have said anyway? *Hey, I'm uncertain about how I feel about your brother, and he apparently hates me right now and doesn't want me anywhere near him, so how about those Lakers?*

Not calling the date off meant I had to answer the door when Blake rang the bell. I almost laughed when I saw him. He wore his impress-the-ladies, slim-fit, button-up blue shirt. Did he realize what he'd done?

He lowered the flowers in his hands, the ones I hadn't even noticed at first because of my attention to his shirt, and said, "What's funny?"

"Nothing. I was just remembering something."

"Oh. Well, a good memory is a good start to the night, right?" He handed me a small bouquet of pink roses. I had to give him props for not going straight to the red rose, which would have been overreaching for this first test date, and also for not undermining himself by going with a yellow friendship-type rose either. Pink was a nice settling point. Romantic without getting carried away. And a bouquet of three roses was attentive without being overbearing the way a dozen would have been. This moderation was a new feature of Blake's personality. He was usually an all-in or all-out kind of guy. I opened the door wider to let him into my apartment and went to put the flowers in water before we left.

When I returned from the kitchen, I suppressed another laugh at his blue shirt and wondered at the fact that the shirt, and the memory of that night when I'd been so humiliated, didn't bring anger bubbling up to the surface of my emotional state. His dark brown eyes met mine and, with a smile, he reached for my hand.

I let him take my hand because months of habit made pulling away an unnatural response, but the driving need to have him hold my hand wasn't there the way it had been when we'd dated before.

I surveyed him while we walked down my front steps. Blake was a photo negative of his brother, a dark contrast to Lucas's fair features, definitely more striking visually, more handsome in the basic ways one could expect.

But that blue shirt would have brought out the blue in Lucas's eyes.

"You look beautiful," Blake said, yanking my mind from the path it had wandered down.

I had dressed carefully in a black pencil skirt and a loose gray pullover that was dressy enough for anything he might have in mind but casual enough to be comfortable. I'd worked for moderation like he had done with the flowers. We were in an awkward place of in between: afraid of doing too much and afraid of doing too little.

"Thanks. So . . . what's the plan tonight?"

"I figured we'd do dinner and see where things were at after that."

I wasn't hungry. The knots in my stomach

failed to leave room for digestive purposes. I just wanted to talk to him, to gauge what conversation could be like after everything. But he was right. Talking with a food distraction might make talking easier — less intimidating. Though we'd been together several times in the last two weeks, this felt different because of the label we'd put on it. This was a date.

We went to Cicero's — another moderate, safe choice. It was the one restaurant we both always agreed on. The Kalamata olives were salty, and the Alfredo was creamy. The conversation stayed to safe topics: weather, jobs, how the upcoming season looked for the Lakers.

Talk of basketball made me remember everything Lucas had told me about Blake helping him with the game and by so doing securing him a place in the family.

"I've missed you." Blake's voice broke into my thoughts.

I stared at Blake, hearing Lucas's words, *He practiced with me every day after school to help me figure out how to work a backboard to my advantage,* in my mind and saw Blake through the loving lens Lucas used to view him.

"I've . . . missed you, too," I said and felt some truth in my words. I had missed a lot of things about Blake, missed as in hadn't understood or hadn't seen certain aspects of him.

Before, I'd always seen him as one of the heroes in one of my worn paperback Austen books — the romantic love interest who was wealthy, handsome, and basically good. How did I see him now?

I saw him as a man who had once been an unspoiled, unselfish little boy. The sort of boy who saw a kid his own age and, instead of feeling territorial of his family, opened his family circle wider because there was enough room in their lives.

"Lucas talks a lot about you," I said.

Blake lifted a shoulder in kind of a bashful shrug. After months of dating, I'd never seen that movement from him before. Blake wasn't bashful. "Luc is an excellent photographer of my character. He always manages to capture my good side."

"You've talked about him before when we were together, but you never told me he wasn't your natural brother." To be honest, back then, he'd never even told me his brother's name.

"That's because he *is* my natural brother." Blake grinned at me.

"You know what I mean."

Blake speared an olive and popped it into

his mouth before spitting out the seed. "I know what you mean. But really. As far as I'm concerned, he's all Hampton. About a year after we got him, they found his mom. My dad hired better investigators than the state did. Luc and I were afraid they'd make him go back with her, and so we sneaked out of our rooms one night and went to the basketball court. I pulled out a knife and dragged it across the palm of my hand, then handed him the knife so he could do the same. Then we locked hands. We figured if we became blood brothers, they had to keep us together. We were old enough to know better, but it didn't matter. We were also young and afraid. Becoming blood brothers was as much control we dared to take for ourselves."

"That's sweet," I said.

He chuckled. "Yeah, sweet . . . until we both realized how long wounds of that nature took to heal and how hard it was to do anything — especially basketball — with a jacked-up hand due to self-inflicted cuts across the palm. We should've at least done our left hands instead of our right ones."

I laughed at that, picturing two lanky, gawky kids instead of the men I knew.

Blake laughed, too. "Mine got infected, probably because I was the one who opened the back door of the house afterwards. Open wounds and doorknobs don't really mix, and it got us into trouble because Mom saw the blood and insisted on knowing what we did. After she dumped alcohol on our hands, which she did to teach us a lesson because I know we had triple-antibiotic gel — the stuff that doesn't hurt to use — she made me clean the doorknob."

And there she was: the mother Blake mentioned finally matched a little of the mother Lucas had mentioned. "So what happened with Lucas's birth mother?"

Blake shrugged. "My mom was pretty upset they'd actually found her. She had no intention of giving Luc back. Mom would've torn that woman's hair out before ever turning Luc over to her. They asked her to sign away her parental rights. And, for once, she did something good for Luc. She signed the papers and walked away. The decision couldn't have been too hard. She *had* left him in a homeless shelter, after all."

The waiter came over at that moment, and I realized that I had leaned so far over the table to hear the story that my hair hung down in my soup. I hurried to pull it out and wipe up the soup drippings with my napkin while the waiter distracted Blake.

When he turned back to me, I dropped

the napkin back to my lap. "I'm surprised she didn't ask for compensation," I said, thinking she sounded like the kind of person willing to sell a child for profit.

"I'm pretty sure Dad gave her some money to help her get back on her feet when it was all done. But the money was an afterthought for him, not part of the agreement. Never let it be said that the Hamptons bought a kid off the street like a stolen television."

"No. Of course. Never let that be said." I agreed, even though it sounded like that was pretty much what happened. I wanted to ask if Blake ever met the woman who had left her son at a homeless shelter, if he knew what she looked like, if he ever talked to her, but I left all those questions unasked. This dinner wasn't about Lucas.

Except that it was.

Because Lucas did not want to be where I was. And through the course of the evening, I knew I couldn't bring discomfort to their family home. "Blake," I began, "I don't think this weekend will work for me to meet your mom."

"What? Why?" His dark eyebrows knit together in a knot over his nose.

"I just feel like Lucas and you and your parents would rather celebrate your mom's birthday without a stranger present."

He laughed, the kind of laugh that said I was being silly. "You're not a stranger. Luc's told Mom all about you."

"He has?"

"Sure. She asked how his trip went, and he told her. You were part of the trip, so naturally you were a part of the discussion."

Lucas had told her about me.

Not Blake.

Why hadn't Blake been the one to tell his mom about me? Blake had said the words casually enough, but enough bite existed behind his words to make me wonder if he was annoyed that their mom found out about me from Lucas and not him.

"But to mix business with a party environment isn't fair to your family."

He laughed again and waved my protests away. "You've met half my family. We're all about business. We can't help it. It's in the blood. Trust me. We prefer things that way."

I tried again. "I make the party number uneven. I don't want Lucas to feel uncomfortable, and —"

"Nope." He cut me off. "The party will be uneven if you *don't* come. Luc's bringing a date."

I blinked and almost leaned too far and ended up with hair in my soup again.

"What?"

"Yeah, the punk texted me this evening with some lame excuse about not coming. It'd break Mom's heart, so I told him he had to come. He said he had a date. I told him to bring her since I was bringing you. It's all settled. And Mom wants you to come. She never could have kids after I was born and never got daughters. She loves that she's actually meeting the women in our lives."

His words implied that her boys never brought women home to meet the family. It also meant that this date of Lucas's was serious enough to count as a woman in his life. If I felt sick before, I felt plague-ridden now.

Blake asked about the trip but didn't notice how I glossed over the details, didn't notice how I never mentioned Lucas even though he was such a huge part of everything that happened during that trip, didn't notice that I'd come down with the plague.

If I had been an outsider looking in on our date, I would have called it a raging success. I would have seen the couple as compatible and happy and well on their way to something more settled and serious.

But I had insider information. And the plague. I had that, too.

The image of shutting doors still spiraled in my psyche. Each slam sent a shudder through my spine.

Lucas had a date.

And not just any date. He had one he was willing to bring home to meet his mother, which, according to Blake was a first for both of them.

If not for that news, the entire weekend, at least my part of it, would have been cancelled. But Lucas was bringing someone. And I had to meet her, see her for myself. Blake grinned with delight at my willingness to change my mind. And the rest of dinner went on as before: polite, unchallenging, no debates or interesting discussions. Just dinner.

The time with Blake had been nice, even relaxing, but at the doorstep when he moved in to kiss me good night, I moved aside, forcing his kiss to catch air. He stiffened. "I probably should have expected that," he said with a laugh that said he was cringing on the inside.

"Probably," I agreed. "Let's take things a day at a time."

He bit the inner side of his cheek. "Do you not love me?"

I sighed and leaned against my doorframe. "Of course I do. I love a lot of things about you. I love that you're a good brother, a good son. I love that you know business and rock it like a boss."

"Loving things about me isn't quite the same as loving me, though, is it?"

Another sigh. At this rate, I'd have to go to the doctor and see if a person could spontaneously come down with asthma without ever having had signs of it before. "I do love you. But I'm still not sure about being in love with you. I don't exactly trust you, yet. And," I hurried on before he could go into another lengthy apology and excuse, "I don't know that loving you is quite the same thing as being in love with you. I want to take this all very, very slowly."

He frowned. "That's Silvia talking."

I shrugged but didn't argue. "Silvia's a smart woman."

"You're a smart woman," he countered as if somehow that would change things and get him a kiss good night.

"Yes," I agreed. "A smart woman who takes good advice from other smart women."

"You know I'm going to treat you so well this weekend, you'll be begging me to kiss you by Saturday."

Blake loved a challenge. Me not kissing him good night represented a problem that needed solving, an obstacle to overcome. His drive to win enabled him to be an excellent businessman. But the trait made him a less-than-ideal boyfriend — especially when I was as competitive as he was and liked to win as much as he did. Putting a kiss up as the winner's mark made him unlikely to be kissed ever, let alone by the middle of the weekend. "Let's just see how things go, okay?"

He gave one nod of agreement, but his eyes had the steel of a champion entering the ring with his sights on winning.

I sighed a third time but only because I felt certain if someone placed a mirror in front of me, my eyes would have the same hard-focused glint. Normally I liked Blake's drive to never quit until he got the prize, but it didn't sit well with me when I was the apparent prize.

He bit the inside of his cheek again. "In the spirit of full disclosure and wanting you to trust me, I need to tell you that Mom's party is more than family. The weekend is family, but the party is everyone. Trish will be there, as will everyone from Dad's businesses."

"Trish the Fish?"

A laugh of equal parts incredulity and horror bubbled out of him. "Tell me you don't call her that."

I shrugged and didn't even feel ashamed that my filter broke. It had worked overtime and deserved a break.

"She's just my friend and a coworker. Don't read too much into it."

I did read too much, but only because I said all the same things about Lucas. And because Blake's voice softened when he said her name. And because his eyes lit up at the same time his voice softened. I let it all pass, though, determining that my heightened emotional state left me vulnerable to faulty interpretation. The big surprise was that I felt more anxiety over Lucas bringing a girl with him than I did about Trish the Fish showing up again.

"I'll pick you up tomorrow." He took my hand and bent to kiss it.

"You're a cheater," I said and then blushed, hoping he knew I wasn't referring to the fish situation.

The fish apparently never crossed his mind because he said, "Not yet. *This* would be cheating." He turned my hand over, his breath hot on my skin as he pressed a kiss to the middle of my palm, and then traced several more featherlight kisses up my wrist. I equally hated and loved that he knew how to do that to me. I shivered in spite of myself, and he left my porch steps with a skip to his step and a wolfish grin on his face. Physical touch was definitely one of my love languages, and he knew it.

Fine. Round one to Blake.

Chapter Fourteen

"A mother would have been always present.
A mother would have been a constant
   friend;
her influence would have been beyond all
   other."
   — JANE AUSTEN, *Northanger Abbey*

I went inside my apartment and shut and bolted my door, thinking of how Lucas would have waited for me to be safely behind my door before leaving my porch. It might have been old-fashioned of him to think I needed that protection, but I didn't mind the gesture. Instead Lucas's simple act of respect and concern had warmed me from the inside out. Blake never waited for me to go inside first.

The moral dilemma of thinking about one brother while seeing the other bothered me as much as Silvia said it should.

Shaking my head over my own weakness,

I pulled down my hair — too many pins were jabbing my head at various angles — and kicked off my shoes. I sat at my computer and palmed it on. I didn't go to Blake's Instagram feed to see what he might have to say about our first official date since I'd stormed out on him, and I didn't go to look at Lucas's Twitter feed either. I'd meet his date soon enough.

Instead, I went to my dad's Facebook page.

The last entry had been me wishing him a happy birthday even though he'd been gone for four years and would celebrate no new birthdays. At least, he wouldn't be celebrating with me and would never be able to click the heart button to say he loved my birthday wishes for him.

"Out of all the men in my life, Dad," I told the screen, "you're still the only one I can trust."

His profile picture was of the two of us on the beach at dawn. We were smiling, dripping wet, and shivering in our wet suits. We'd gone surfing because he loved it. It still baffled me that a man as physically fit as he was could die from something so contrary to his lifestyle. He ran marathons, surfed, mowed his own lawn, and was willing to do yoga with me when I came to visit.

His only vice was Dr Pepper, and that certainly wasn't enough to stop a heart as big as his. After digging through his stuff after I'd sold my childhood home, I found that his mom had also died of a heart attack and his father had died from a stroke. Apparently, the grandparents I'd never known left him with a bad-ticker legacy. I wondered what my mom's parents had died from. Did faulty hearts come from both sides or just the one? Maybe Mom was already dead, too.

I touched the cover photo close-up I'd posted on the day I'd announced he was gone. He was laughing in the picture, his salt-and-pepper hair windblown, his eyes and smile bright. I wondered if my mom ever stalked him or me on the internet. Sometimes, back before Dad died, I posted comments about how great my life had been because my father walked it every step with me. I sent him digital Mother's Day cards for his wall, hoping in a way to sting her.

I stopped that nonsense once he'd gone and I accepted my newfound orphanhood. It seemed impossible she could exist in the world if he didn't.

"So, Dad," I said to his smiling face. "There is this one guy . . ."

I must have fallen asleep because the next

thing I knew, my phone alarm was buzzing on the desk next to my head. I jolted up and gasped out of a nightmare that, even seconds out of it, fled until I couldn't remember anything of except the feeling.

I dragged my hand down my face and felt the imprint of computer keys in my skin. "Really, Emma?" I said out loud. The computer page showed I had posted a long series of garbled letters to Dad's Facebook page. Classy.

Once that was deleted and the computer checked for anything else that might have happened while my head used the keyboard as a pillow, I took a shower, hoping the heat from the water would plump up my skin enough to erase the dents.

I was only working until noon, and then Blake would be ringing my doorbell and dragging me off to a weekend I no longer wanted to participate in but which I couldn't seem to muster the strength to decline. Lucas had a date. I wanted to meet her. Blake had issued a challenge. I wanted to win. Caroline Hampton had knowledge. I needed to learn.

So I scrubbed out my dented face, dressed carefully, and went to work expecting to see Lucas but found he'd decided to play no-show for the day, which just irritated me. I finished the tasks that required my presence, sent everyone home early to enjoy their weekend, and left the office two hours earlier than the earlier I'd already planned.

At home, I packed and paced.

Realized that packing to impress a man was ridiculous.

Unpacked, repacked, and paced some more.

Then I gave in, turned on my computer, and went to Lucas's social media pages. I stalked him like a starving tiger hunting a gazelle, searching for any evidence of his date for the weekend, of some relationship meaningful enough to merit a meet-the-parents scenario.

Her name was Stephanie Kent. Brunette. Brown doe eyes. Working for social services helping children.

I hated her immediately.

Which was totally unfair. I had no reason to hate a woman of obvious intelligence and with enough goodwill in her heart to help those less fortunate than herself. But she was pretty, and selfless, and in one picture had her hand hooked over Lucas's arm in a way that made me feel downright violent.

Not that I would ever get violent, because he obviously liked her or he wouldn't have invited her home. Didn't I want him to be happy and have what was best for him? And wasn't I going to be there as his brother's guest?

Right.

Perspective.

I figured Stephanie was the one Lucas would be taking since she was the only girl who had been on his Facebook in the last six months. The proof of her being "the one" wasn't because he'd posted anything, but because she had. And she did it while I was online looking at his page. The post materialized out of thin air like a mean-spirited curse.

"Going to San Diego for the weekend for a much-needed vacay with surfer-boy hottie. Yes, Lucas, that's you." She tagged Lucas and marked the whole post with a heart.

I tried not to feel superior to a woman who used terms like "vacay" and "hottie" when the words sounded so juvenile. With my suspicions confirmed, I meandered over to her page and perused the last year or so of her life. Her page led me to believe she was likely April's social worker. Lucas had said he'd worked closely with April's social worker, who had helped him become foster-parent certified.

I had admired him for taking such pains to guarantee he could swoop in when April's mother failed her. But now, I felt irritated. What kind of guy got chummy with his niece's social worker? What kind of woman left her entire profile set to public so anyone could find her?

What kind of woman cyber-stalked other women who were innocent of any wrong-doing?

That last question made me shut down the computer.

By the time Blake came to pick me up, I was a frenzied mess who had repacked for the third time. This time, both sensible and not-so-sensible clothing made the cut, meaning I had to shove all my weight against the suitcase to make the zippers come together.

"Everything okay?" Blake asked as I tugged my bag behind me to the car. He clicked his key fob so the trunk opened, the linked rings from the shiny Audi symbol momentarily reflecting the sun back in my eyes. I remembered Lucas's car had been posh, with buttery leather seats and all that. But was Lucas a luxury-car guy or just a nice-car guy? My time with him in his car had been a blurry sort of panic. The brothers shared similar tastes in many things. Lucas had a few of the impress-the-ladies-slim-fit-buttoned-up shirts that Blake loved. It would make sense for them to have similar tastes in cars. As I slid into the passenger side of Blake's silver Audi, I realized it didn't matter what car Lucas drove because he hadn't invited me to be sitting in it with him. Well, he had, but that had been nearly two months ago, and he'd only offered out of obligation to get an angry woman safely off his property.

I tried to stay engaged in the conversation with Blake as we navigated midday traffic to San Diego. But my brain flitted back and forth between the brothers and how I felt about each and why I was doing all of this to myself.

Forget the brothers, Emma. You're here for the mother. And with that thought, my brain settled down enough to hear the tail end of Blake's monologue regarding the entertainment industry — something Hampton enterprises dabbled in from time to time.

"Don't you agree?" He glanced from the freeway to me.

I nodded. "Yes." I willed him to look back to the road. Blake had a habit of looking at you when he was talking to you, not a great trait when you were both in a car and he was the one driving.

"Just yes?" he asked, still looking at me and not the road.

"Why? Is yes the wrong answer?" I asked, willing his gaze to go back where it belonged. And wondering what he'd actually been talking about.

"It's not the wrong answer, just a short one. I would've thought you'd have more to say. After all, you're the one who is constantly crying foul over the lack of women in the management hierarchies of the film industry. You're the one saying Silvia isn't getting a fair shake because of her gender. I just thought you'd have more to say on the subject."

I lifted my hand to point to the glowing red taillights in front of us, but he wasn't slowing because he didn't see them since he was looking at me. "Blake . . ." I shook my hand to call attention to the front of the car.

Blake finally put the brakes to use hard enough that my seat belt was also put to use keeping me in my place.

"Silvia *was* overlooked due to her gender." The words came out breathlessly since my life had been on the line for a moment. "But good news! Silvia is actually the new film editor for Portal Pictures. She starts Monday."

His eyes went to me again, his smile bright. "Hey! That's great!"

"Mm-hmm." I tightened in preparation for impact, my eyes wide and staring at the traffic in front of us. One of us had to watch the road, and since he didn't feel an obligation, it had to be me. "Blake, that guy needs to get over."

Blake's eyes snapped back to the front. "Oh. Right. Sorry, man." He apologized to the car though the driver couldn't hear him.

By the time we arrived at the wrought-iron gate leading to the Hampton Empire, my nerves were frayed little wires sparking out their last displays of life.

Blake punched the button on his visor, and the gates slid open.

An electronic voice chimed into his car. "Welcome home, Mr. Hampton."

Blake grinned at the greeting. "I created an app to do that for me when I enter the gate. Coming home is a huge stress release, and I like to have something to herald the occasion."

His car eased forward onto the cobbled driveway and up to the garage.

Coming home was a huge stress release for him? This was something I knew in the basest of ways. It was something he'd said to me over two months ago when he tried to get me to spend the Fourth of July at his childhood home. But until that moment, when an app sighed out a cheery welcome because he'd programmed it to, the realization of how much he loved and needed this place hadn't occurred to me.

I cast my thoughts back to when he'd invited me to his home the first time. He'd been stressed. One of the companies at the Hampton Corporation had been going under, and Blake couldn't seem to save it. People were going to lose jobs. Not a lot of people since the company had been small. How many was it? Twenty? Thirty?

But people.

And it had made Blake very unhappy.

I pressed my lips together and watched Blake from the corner of my eye. "I'm sorry," I said after a moment.

"About what, babe?"

"For not listening to you when you needed me to." He got a pass for calling me *babe* even when things remained so unsettled between us.

He made a *pshaw* sound and scrubbed his hand through his hair. "When don't you listen? You're always listening, even when I talk about stuff I know you don't care about. It's part of the reason I felt so devastated when I thought you'd walked away forever."

Devastated? Lucas had said Blake felt

devastated, but I hadn't believed him. Not really, not until this moment when, for the first time in maybe ever, I wasn't just listening but actually hearing. Maybe Blake had really needed to go home that weekend and my denying that one thing had been a rejection of him.

Silvia's voice in my head warned me that I was making excuses and shifting the responsibility to my own shoulders, but didn't every relationship bear the burden of dual responsibility? Maybe inviting the fish-female over for dinner was a bad choice, but couldn't I see the path that led him there?

"Well, I'm sorry."

He glanced at my hand and gave me a look as if asking for permission to take it. I gave a single nod. He took my hand, pressed a kiss to my knuckles, and said, "We're okay. You don't have to apologize to me. I know what I did was pretty stupid, so the apologies get to be all on my side. The forgiveness and forget-ness" — he gave my hand a squeeze — "is all on you."

I felt like I had the forgiveness part down. But the forget-ness, as Blake put it? That was harder for me to find.

He slid his car into an empty space in the garage that appeared to have been waiting just for him. As big as the garage was, the space probably did belong to him. Being my father's sole heir meant I got the life insurance and house and everything when he died. I sold the house, unable to fathom living there without him, and put the money in a bank account labeled "When I Need This Someday." Landing the job at Kinetics paid nicely, so I enjoyed a lot of benefits of living comfortably, but the Hamptons were on a whole different level of living.

My last visit to the Tuscan palace had been an emotionally heightened experience and not much of it was memorable except the emotion, which consisted of confusion, hurt, and incredible amounts of anger.

But now, stepping out of Blake's Audi, the classic and modern architecture and elements blended together into a creamy Old World feel all while exuding a fresh newness.

The custom-crafted natural limestone and marble mingling with the terra-cotta floor and roof tiles eased some of the tightness behind my eyes. If eyes could make happy noises, mine would be sighing.

"So?" Blake asked after popping the trunk. "What do you think?"

"Wow, Blake. Really. Just . . . wow. This place . . ."

"I know. I never get tired of it. Lived here my whole life and still feel instantly better just by being here. Everyone needs a happy place, Emma, and this is mine. But it's so much more than what you're seeing now. Just wait. I'll show you."

Blake popped the trunk, but moved to the backseat to retrieve his own bag rather than moving to the trunk to help me with mine. Not that I needed help, but if spending time with Lucas taught me anything it was that a man helping a woman by holding a door or getting a bag was a way to show her respect. After all, Lucas held open doors for men, too. I shook the thought from my head. Comparing the brothers against each other was not part of the weekend plan.

I pulled my bag out of the trunk, hating how it was heavier for this single weekend than it had been when I'd traveled across the country for nearly two weeks. An overweight suitcase was a sign of a seriously insecure woman.

I was suddenly glad Blake hadn't helped. He'd definitely wonder if I'd packed cinder blocks.

Blake led the way into the house, entering with a loud, "I'm ho-ome!" as we stepped into a mudroom-styled hallway.

A beige ball of fur blurred through the

310

room and bounded straight into Blake's chest, making him drop his suitcase with a *thunk* on the tiles so he could pull the dog off him. Not a Doberman but a Wheaten Terrier. Silvia had had one while we were growing up. And from the way the dog Blake referred to as "Chester" wagged his tail, licked the air all over, and barked and jumped, spastic behavior was apparently a breed defect; I'd thought it had only been Silvia's dog.

"Who's a good boy? Chester's a good boy!" Blake said over and over again while rubbing the dog's ears and trying to keep Chester's tongue from making contact with his face.

"You don't visit nearly often enough," a woman's voice said from the entrance to the hallway. "Chester has never gotten over being a puppy, and I have to walk the little monster every day or he chews up my couches."

If *Vogue* did editions dedicated to the graceful middle-aged woman, Caroline Hampton would have been their cover model. Her long, seafoam-green chiffon tunic hug over slender hips and the top half of her white pencil skirt. Her strappy sandals showed off a pedicure of pink polish with little white flowers and jeweled stones decorating the big toes. She was tanned, lean, and had longer hair than I imagined a woman of her age and rank to have. Most wealthy, business-savvy women I knew wore their hair shorter, but Caroline's dark hair hung down her back in a casual style that other women likely spent hours trying to replicate.

"Hi, Mom," Blake said, sounding legitimately happy and as playful and hyper as Chester acted. He moved Chester off of him and said "Down!" and "Stay!" as if the dog cared anything about those words, and went to hug and kiss his mother.

Chester immediately jumped up on me and managed to get a full lick of my cheek before I could block him.

"Get down, Chester!" Caroline Hampton scolded while she pulled the dog down and held his collar so he couldn't make a second jump. "You must be the Emma Pierce my boys have told me so much about."

Her *boys* had told her about me. Not one, but both. The knowledge of both of them talking to her about me when I had such churned feelings made me swallow hard. I knew I needed to meet her eye.

A smile wobbled out onto my face and I said, "Yes. That's me." I put my hand out, but she moved passed it.

"I know you're here on official business, but you're also here as a guest of my boys. That makes us family. We hug in our family. All of us." She wrapped her arms around me.

At first, I froze. How long had it been since I'd received a parental embrace, let alone one coming from a mom? Silvia's mom often filled in for me during the years, but I hadn't seen her since Silvia and I graduated high school and they moved to San Francisco to be close to Silvia's aging grandmother. And my own father . . .

After last night when I'd found myself talking to his memorialized Facebook page, I really needed to be held by a parent. To feel comfort. Tears leaked from my eyes as I softened into her hug, one that went on long enough to make it seem like she knew how much I ached and wanted to press all that ache out of me.

"Welcome to our home," she said, giving me another little squeeze before releasing me. "And you!" She turned to Blake, distracting him and herself long enough to allow me to mop my face with my sleeve. "You never come home."

"Yes, I do. You're just always gone." Blake defended himself.

She gave him a narrowed look. "You know

313

when I'm here and not here. You choose to come when I'm not here. I'm starting to think you're avoiding me for some reason." They linked arms and left the hallway. Caroline looked back and motioned with her head for me to follow. Chester's ears pricked up and, with a curious expression, he trotted after his family, leaving me to do as Caroline directed and follow.

The hallway led to the kitchen. The kitchen I had been in once before when Blake had tried to placate me and hide me away. I saw the other hallway that led out to where I knew the front door to be.

Caroline said something quietly to Blake, who nodded, and then turned her attention back to me. "Let me show you your room, and then we can settle in and talk shop."

"Oh, there's no rush, Mrs. Hampton," I started to say.

But she interrupted me with, "Of course there's no rush. But tomorrow's my birthday, and I want to watch the boys shove each other in the pool and eat too much food and compete with each other about who does everything better in business and who has the better car and explain to me why, if they're both so wonderful, they aren't married and giving me grandchildren yet."

I smiled. "Understood completely."

"Right. We work today and play tomorrow." She linked her arm with me. "You know, I do think you're the first young woman Blake has brought home since high school."

I sketched a glance to Blake, who looked away immediately. We both knew that wasn't strictly true. There had been a certain woman who had been *no big deal.*

"Funny I had to hear all about you from Lucas first and not Blake. Small world that you two ended up working together."

"Yes. Small world."

She led me up a back set of stairs tucked on the other side of a large pantry. The stairs had two landings before we reached the top. At each landing was a large stained-glass window with various blue-and-white panes set into rangoli patterns that looked like flower petals. They didn't quite fit with the décor, but they also totally belonged.

When I stopped to admire the windows, Caroline smiled. "Aren't they lovely? I ordered the first one when I was pregnant and found out he was going to be a boy. I figured that the stairs from the bedrooms to the kitchens would be often used by my children, and I wanted something beautiful and peaceful to shine light on them when they came through here. The stairs were really quite dark before. I had the second window installed when we brought Luc home. Two windows for my two boys."

She didn't mention Lucas being adopted or coming home in a different method than Blake. They were simply her two boys and that was that.

She took me to a room decorated with an Italian flair that matched the rest of the Tuscan style and told me to settle in and then meet her out back.

I unpacked my suitcase and hung up my clothing in the closet, hoping that gravity would pull the wrinkles out of them. Returning to the stairs we'd come up, I allowed myself another moment to take in the two windows Caroline had commissioned to commemorate her sons. Each window represented a celebration of the two boys in her life. The beautiful gesture swelled my heart. A mom who loved being a mom. What a novelty.

Back in the kitchen, now empty of people, I realized I had no idea how to get to the backyard. I assumed, wrongly, that there would be a door from the kitchen, but the light coming from the back wall was all windows. I finally found the way out by heading to the front door and then going around to the back. A set of French doors stood open, allowing the warm, fresh air to fill the house.

I followed the breeze and found myself in an oasis of pools, fountains, and greenery. Caroline Hampton sat under a patio umbrella at a table. She had a laptop open in front of her as well as several sheets of paper held down by a glass ball that was probably just a table decoration when it wasn't pulling double duty as a paperweight.

I sat at the table when she inclined her head for me to do so, settled my own laptop close to her, and we went to work.

And did Caroline Hampton know how to work. I had never met anyone who kept the focus on the task at hand the way she did. I didn't know where Blake might have sneaked off to since Caroline hardly gave me a moment to breathe let alone to allow my mind to wander.

When she finally said, "I think that's a good start, don't you?" I looked up from my laptop, which was stuffed with notes about the foundation's vision, purpose, and goals, to find that the sky had darkened and the lights surrounding the pools and gardens had flickered on. I stretched my back and shoulders, my spine popping and cracking into alignment.

The file on my computer was filled with how to be a successful 501(c)(3), a tentative mission statement, an entire page of name ideas to take back to my team, articles of incorporation, and several pages of bylaws and ideas for bylaws, and all the government agencies and permissions I needed to move forward. Just as Lucas had taken weeks' worth of work tracking down properties and squeezed it into a few hours, Caroline had done the same with the foundation. No matter how good Mr. Hampton might be at business, the magic I witnessed at the patio table was proof that Mrs. Hampton had trained her boys in organizational skills.

Now that we'd swept off the business masks we'd been wearing, Caroline leaned back in her chair and surveyed me under a different sort of lens. "Lucas told me about your background, about how Blake deserves a time-out for his treatment of you, and about how you remind him of me."

My ear tips turned to fire. He said I reminded him of his mom? This powerhouse who had just coached me through an entire semester's worth of information in less than an afternoon? "Oh, well, that's quite a compliment to —"

"To me," she interrupted. I'd discovered

quickly that Caroline interrupted a lot when she thought it would save time by getting to the point quicker. I never felt insulted or cast aside when she did it. Often, I felt relief to have her find such economy in conversation.

"The compliment is all mine, I can guarantee you. If you ever find yourself unhappily situated at Kinetics, come find me. I will always find a way to utilize talent and organizational skills like yours."

I gave a depreciative laugh. "I actually really like my current career choice, but I appreciate the offer."

She tsked and lifted a shoulder in a half-shrug. "Well, you never know what business will rain down on you. It's best to keep an umbrella tucked in your bag just in case."

I saved my documents for the last time and made sure they loaded to the company cloud before closing down my laptop. In no way could this storm of information be repeated, and losing the information would be devastating.

She fixed me with a shrewd, investigative gaze once my laptop was closed and settled in my bag. "Perhaps you can solve a puzzle for me."

"Puzzle?"

"Mm-hm. A mother knows things about

her children, reads things between the words they say and even more between the words they don't say. She knows what to do to ensure her children are happy and successful in life."

Clearly, Caroline had never met my mother.

She leaned forward, a fierce determination to uncover a hidden truth radiating from her. "So how did you come to be here with Blake tonight and not Lucas?"

CHAPTER FIFTEEN

"I do suspect that he is not really
necessary to my happiness."
— JANE AUSTEN, *Emma*

Sweet mercy, she knows.

She knew how I felt about Lucas. And now she was calling me out on it. How she knew was unfathomable since I was only figuring it out myself. But now she'd probably have some security guard I hadn't met yet haul me off the property and banish me from the presence of all Hamptons, now and in the future.

I straightened from where I'd zipped up my laptop bag and stared at her. "Excuse me?"

She tilted her head as if she didn't understand why I questioned her question. I opened my mouth, not sure what to say, when Blake's voice called from the French doors. "Luc's here! And Dad's home. Also, dinner's ready."

She rolled her shoulders, finally showing a sign of wear and tear from hunching over laptops all afternoon and into the evening, and smiled a fresh, cheery smile at me. "I really miss my boys when they aren't home. I don't know how I got lucky enough to get one who loves to cook and one who loves to clean. It's every mother's dream come true." She patted my knee. "Hungry? Blake is a sorcerer in the kitchen."

It was like the question she'd asked before Blake's interruption had never happened.

Strangling on an answer I still couldn't come up with, I nodded and followed her inside.

"Luc!" Caroline spread her arms out wide. "My sweet little boy! What took you so long?" She wrapped him up in a hug, leaving me a view of the woman just behind him.

Stephanie Kent.

She wore a linen summer dress, the kind Lady Kate might wear to a tea party in the Queen's garden. She didn't see me since her focus was all on Caroline and Lucas. Her not seeing allowed me to watch her watch him. The way her eyes stayed trained on him proved her interest in what she saw, hard-core.

"And who's this?" Caroline asked as she pulled away from Lucas's bear hug.

He put his hand on the small of Stephanie's back and moved her forward to meet Caroline. "This is my friend, Stephanie. She's been helping me with April."

Stephanie stuck out her hand just as I had, but when Caroline moved to hug her, Stephanie pulled back with a tiny laugh. "I'm not really a hugger."

Caroline gave her own laugh, one that said, *"Don't mess with me, girl,"* and hugged Stephanie anyway. "But I am!" she said despite Stephanie's protest.

Unlike with me, Caroline kept her hold on Stephanie brief. A catch-and-release to put Stephanie out of her misery as painlessly as possible.

Stephanie laughed again, each titter a neon sign pointing the way to awkward. And at that moment, Lucas looked up and saw me standing in the doorway. "Hello, Emma."

"Hello, Lucas."

"It's good to see you."

My belly burned with the lie he just told. Hadn't he, not much more than twenty-four hours ago, told me he didn't want to be where I was? The burn in my belly shivered down into my legs, forcing me to use the doorframe to keep myself steady. I smiled at him and hoped the smile didn't get wobbly on me. "It's good to see you, too." The difference between us at that moment was that I meant it. Seeing him filled a hole in me that I hadn't known existed until his presence patched it all up.

"Did no one hear the call to dinner?" Blake asked from an arched doorway I assumed led to the dining room. "And where's Dad?"

A man with light-brown hair that silvered at the temples walked down the stairs. "I'm coming!"

Lucas looked at Blake. "Game?"

"Cubs."

Lucas twisted his face in disbelief. "He hates the Cubs."

Blake shrugged. "He's been a little more forgiving since they won the World Series."

Lucas scowled at his father as he descended from the last step. "Aw, Dad, don't tell me you're one of those."

"One of what?"

"A bandwagon fan. They're the worst."

Allen Hampton blew a raspberry. "No, the worst is being forced to endure baseball while waiting for basketball season to kick in. Hey, buddy." He wrapped an arm around Lucas's neck and kissed his forehead. "It's good to see you."

Lucas hugged him back, this father who was nothing like the other father figures he'd told me about in his life. I smiled at the affection in the greeting, the genuine love in the family.

When his father pulled away, he said, "Are you going to introduce me to your friend?"

Lucas's eyes went to mine, and he opened his mouth as if he was about to introduce me, but then he turned and said, "Dad, meet Stephanie."

Allen Hampton let her get away with a handshake, which I thought was a good thing because she'd have probably passed out if he tried a hug. He turned from her to me and said, "And this is — ?"

Before Blake could join me at my side, I stepped forward. "I'm Emma — Emma Pierce." I was about to reach out to shake his hand, but he gave me a one-armed hug like he'd done with Lucas. "Emma Pierce, the girl with grit. We've heard all about you, kiddo."

I returned his quick hug, grateful it hadn't given me a meltdown the way Caroline's had. I felt the dad hug as deeply as I'd felt the mom hug, but I was in better command of myself for this one.

"I don't know what you've heard, but it's

325

all lies," I said.

"Hampton boys don't lie," he informed me.

But they do leave out the truth every now and again, I thought, considering how events had turned out the last time I'd stood in this house.

"Blake might exaggerate a little," I said.

"He might, but he wasn't the one doing all the talking. Luc here was the one who told us all about you. Seems you've got an admirer on your hands. And all while you've been kept such a secret from us."

I stiffened. Caroline had said it was Lucas doing the talking about me before, had even gone as far as to ask me the awkward and unanswerable question of how all her knowledge of me came from the wrong kid. I'd just forgotten her question in the wash of new hellos.

Now here it was again.

But if I stiffened, Stephanie, who had been smiling at the interaction between Allen and me, turned to stone.

"She's not a secret, Dad," Blake said. "She's a fantastic surprise. Luc just likes to spoil my surprises."

"When have I ever spoiled a surprise?" Lucas asked.

"The time I caught a frog for Mom and

326

you ratted me out."

Caroline interrupted. "A frightened frog jumping out of a pencil box at me is not a surprise. It's a nasty shock, for both me and the frog."

"Well, I'm making up for it, now." He hurried next to me, put his arm around me, and moved me forward to the full center of attention, as if displaying a trophy won at school. "She *is* a good surprise, isn't she, Mom?"

Blake's appraisal didn't thaw Stephanie's stance. She only melted back into pliable human form when Lucas touched the small of her back to guide her into the dining room. She smiled for him but cast an unreadable glance my direction.

As we sat at our places around the table, she opened up the conversation. "So you're Blake's girlfriend?"

Everyone seemed to stop what they were doing as if awaiting my answer. I met Blake's eyes over the dinner table where he settled a plate of something covered. He lifted his shoulders and the corners of his mouth at the same time as if to say, *"You're on your own to answer this one."*

"Blake and I have dated in the past." There. They got the truth without me having to define anything happening in the present.

My phone buzzed in my pocket as Blake settled in next to me. I ignored the alert since pulling out a phone at a family dinner seemed like the fastest way to be invited to never come back. It buzzed again at the same time someone's foot kicked me under the table. I looked up, startled that Lucas would kick me. He looked down at something in his lap. His phone?

Really? Lucas was texting me now, here, at dinner with his whole family?

I slid my phone out and skimmed my finger over the screen.

The text was definitely from Lucas. "You get my vote for president. I've never seen such diplomacy before."

How had he texted all of that without anyone noticing?

"You've got to try this," Blake said in my ear as he nudged a plate of food in my direction.

"What?" I'd been looking at my phone, but he didn't seem to notice.

"I did a balsamic reduction glaze over the Brussels sprouts. It's really good."

I ladled some onto my plate and passed the dish to Caroline. Balsamic? Had he been paying enough attention to know that was my favorite way to flavor anything? Blake

328

had made dinner for me on several occasions, but he seldom used foods I liked or asked my opinion on what I wanted. He liked to experiment with foods, and usually those experiments didn't incorporate foods I'd even heard of, let alone enjoyed.

"So," Allen began after passing the plate of fresh rolls. "Stephanie, is it?" When she nodded, he continued. "How do you know our Luc?"

I bent my head to hurry to respond to Lucas's text while people were distracted with Stephanie. I'd written only a few words when I stopped and listened with interest to Stephanie's response.

"We met several months ago, after there were some charges against his sister and the state was considering removing his niece from his sister's care."

I deleted the snarky joke on diplomacy I'd been texting and instead wrote, "Is April okay?"

He glanced at his lap a second later and then met my gaze across the table. He gave a single, short nod.

"I know it's been a while since you've been home, but surely you would have told us. Do you have custody?" Caroline asked.

"No," Lucas answered. "Not yet. I'm still working on it."

"I'm sorry, Luc," Caroline said sincerely.

Allen shook his head. "How does that girl avoid prison? How does no one turn her in?"

Blake shot a meaningful look at Allen, who pointed his fork at Blake. "That was different, son. She's Luc's sister, and she was living with us at the time, so that made her family. You try to work things out with your family before you call the police on them."

"Even after she stole several paintings and pawned them for drug money?" Blake asked.

"It's just stuff, Blake," Caroline gently reminded him.

"Yes, just incredibly valuable, irreplaceable stuff," he shot back, which made me shift uncomfortably in my seat. I hazarded a look at Lucas, who didn't seem offended by Blake's accusations towards his sister. The brothers were in complete agreement regarding Denise.

"Well," Stephanie announced, "she's in jail now. She was arrested a couple nights ago."

A bomb couldn't have created the commotion that Stephanie's news did.

"Where is April, then?" Caroline demanded to know.

"Finally!" Blake declared.

"On what charges?" Allen asked.

The answer to the question on charges was, of course, drugs. Not just possession but distribution. Stephanie did all the talking. Lucas stayed silent. His jaw flexed just in front of his ear, a sure sign that his teeth were being ground into powder.

Stephanie offered what answers she could to the family's questions as they debated and discussed the fate of Lucas's sister and his niece. Since Stephanie did social work for a living, she probably had to often ask uncomfortable questions and give uncomfortable answers. Clearly she had no inhibitions about butting into the conversation tonight, especially since, apparently, one of her cases was involved.

Blake eyed the table and hissed low under his breath.

"What?" I asked.

"I left the carrots in the warmer in the kitchen and just remembered."

He had been talking about Denise and all her issues with Stephanie and didn't look excited to exit the table where so much gossip and information could be found.

"I'll get it." I pushed back my chair and stood, almost dropping my phone on the ground in the process. That's right, Lucas had been texting me. I'd forgotten.

Catching my phone and sliding it back into my pocket, I slipped into the kitchen. For reasons I didn't understand, the conversation at the table disturbed me. The sadness that always seemed hidden in my bones swelled up and flooded me.

That poor little girl.

In the kitchen, I found the warmer Blake mentioned and peeked inside. The glazed carrots weren't in a dish, and I doubted Caroline Hampton was the sort of woman who allowed cooking dishes to do double duty as serving dishes. I began opening cupboards to find an adequate serving bowl.

"Need help?"

I whirled to find Lucas standing in the kitchen doorway. He held himself rigid, tensed.

"Yes. Thank you. I need a serving bowl."

As he crossed the kitchen to a different set of cupboards, I said, "I didn't know Denise had ever lived with your family."

"Yeah." He opened a cupboard and began sifting through its contents. "Denise found me here at the Hamptons when she was sixteen. I was between semesters at the time and working in Dad's offices for my summer job when she just showed up," Lucas said. "She played all of us, giving us a song and dance about not wanting a life like our mom's and wanting to finish high school or maybe even go to college like I was. We all wanted good things for her, but not too long after she moved in, I found drugs in her room and hundreds of dollars went missing from my dad's dresser."

He slid a large terra-cotta bowl from the cupboard. "She went through the typical excuse that the drugs were her friend's, not hers, and all that, but I grew up in a life like hers and knew all the excuses and signs of an addict. I told my parents she was lying. When we confronted her, she was pretty mad. She took off — along with several works of art, which Blake is obviously still bitter about."

He handed me the bowl. "Do you need something like this?"

I nodded and went back to the warmer to transfer the carrots into the bowl. I thought Lucas would leave once his job of helping me was accomplished, but he leaned against the counter and kept talking.

"Denise was apparently pregnant with April at the time she took off. I wonder if maybe I'd given her the benefit of the doubt instead of assuming she was like my mom or like Mom's boyfriends I could've helped her. Helped April."

"Where is April now?" I asked.

"They took her to an emergency foster home since Denise was arrested in the middle of the night. I've met with child services, and they've agreed to let me take her until things are figured out with Denise since I'm her uncle and foster certified. I can pick up April in the morning."

I nodded, processing the information. Once I'd finished with the carrots, there was nothing left to do but head back to the dining room.

"At least you've got help to navigate through all of this," I said, hating that his help came from a woman who was actually pretty likable, all things considered.

He touched my arm, pausing me before my feet crossed the kitchen threshold. "Am I doing the right thing by taking her? I'm a single guy. I don't know anything about kids or what they really need. My parents' concerns make me concerned."

My eyes locked on where his fingers touched me. Heat shivered through my skin and into my heart. "The safest place for her is with you. I would absolutely do the same thing if a chance like this was given to me. I'm not saying it won't be hard — of course it will — but it'll be totally worth it."

His breath of relief to have someone else agree with him made me wish I could put down the bowl and just hold him until he felt okay. "Thanks, Emma, for listening." He smiled at me. "You'd make a good consultant. I didn't mean to come in here and dump all this on you. I just wanted a disinterested third-party opinion. Thank you." His hand left my arm, and I shivered again but now because his absence left me cold.

I wasn't as disinterested as he thought.

But I smiled because even though he'd said he didn't want to be where I was, he had sought me out. My opinion still mattered in some small way. We still had friendship. Sure, the friendship felt shaky, but it existed.

We returned to the table where the conversation was in full swing. Blake peppered Stephanie with all kinds of legal questions, implications of custody, rights of the new custodial guardian should Denise get out of jail, expectations of the temporary custodian should she end up in prison long-term. This was a family of analysts. Every subject was tasted and tested from all sides before they made any kind of judgment call on anything.

When Lucas took his seat, Stephanie smiled up at him.

I placed the carrots on the table and forced myself to look away.

"And you're picking the kid up tomorrow?" Blake asked Lucas.

"At nine in the morning. Is it okay if she's at your birthday dinner, Mom?"

"Of course. Birthdays are always better with children around. That poor, sweet little girl," Caroline murmured.

With that mournful declaration, everyone fell silent.

Finally, the conversation wandered away from the topic of Denise and April, though I very much doubted it wandered away from any of our minds. The family asked me about my trip back East with Lucas and about my work, about how Blake and I had met and about our relationship, which I evaded discussing as much as possible. Blake, being a smart man, followed my lead.

We were on such precarious ground that to commit to anything in front of witnesses would be the worst idea ever.

When those same questions were put to Stephanie, her answers were pretty direct. She'd been attracted to Lucas from the first moment she saw him and was thrilled when he finally asked her out. She loved her job working with children and loved being a part of helping Lucas navigate the system with April.

Lucas said nothing to refute her responses

but silently pushed his food around his plate with his fork. Stephanie had, in a way, staked a claim, and he didn't argue that claim. I thought that would help me know how to act, but instead, I felt displaced and incapable of any kind of action at all.

After we'd eaten, conversation drifted back to April, which was natural since Lucas would be picking her up in the morning.

They discussed what room they would set up for her and asked if Lucas had a place prepared for her in his town house, which he did.

Finally, Caroline sucked in a breath as if to ask the question of her life, but it was Allen who gave it voice. "Are you sure you're prepared to take on a child with no previous experience at child rearing? You're kind of on your own."

"Oh, he won't be alone," Stephanie interjected. "I'll be there every step of the way."

She might have meant "there every step of the way as a guidance counselor." That would have made sense and seemed to be the way the family took her meaning. But I knew better because as she said the words, she turned to me and smiled.

Her smile wasn't the smug smile of a competitor who'd won; it was the hopeful smile of someone who desperately wanted to be telling the truth and wanted me to confirm that she was right. Instead of offering her anything, I stood and began clearing the table.

Blake took the plate from my hand and set it back on the table with a shake of his head. "This is Luc's job. He gets mad when any of us try to take it from him."

At my protest of picking up the plate again, Lucas stood and took it from me, though he had to wrestle it away from me harder than Blake had. "Blake cooks; I clean. We've been doing it that way since we were, what? Fourteen? Fifteen?"

Caroline offered a laugh, playful and adoring. "Fifteen. You were chumps who made me do it all before that."

Neither of them argued the point. Stephanie was on her feet and helping to clear away the dishes alongside Lucas. It irritated me that no one tried to stop her from helping.

Everyone except Lucas and Stephanie moved to the family room to continue talking where it was more comfortable. Blake discussed the birthday party for the next afternoon and asked how many guests they were expecting.

His father's answer confirmed that the

party was a social event, which made Blake's explanation of inviting Trish seem entirely reasonable. I felt a wave of relief that I had packed and repacked and packed some more. It meant I had brought a party-appropriate dress with me to San Diego. Just because I felt out of place, at least now I didn't have to look out of place, too.

Not that anyone had done anything to make me feel out of place. Up until the moment Stephanie had shown up, I felt completely comfortable with the Hampton family. I looked at Blake, who was still talking, and forced myself to pay attention.

He was talking about some old friends of his. "You've gotta remember Gary. He's the reason Lucas and I got into so much trouble in high school."

"You two were troublemakers?" I asked.

"No!" Lucas insisted from where he'd just entered the conversation. Stephanie was only a step behind him. They both settled on the couch across from where Blake and I sat.

"Only when Gary's around," Blake insisted.

"Good thing he ended up at another school, huh?" Lucas said. His arm hung over the back of the couch, which Stephanie must have taken as an invitation since she snuggled herself down into the crook as if she belonged there.

Why am I noticing those sorts of things? I shifted my body so I was facing Blake, which made it harder to see anything Lucas or Stephanie were doing.

"He's posted some old pictures of us on your Facebook page," Blake said.

Lucas rolled his eyes. "What are you doing stalking my Facebook page, you creeper. Even I never go to Facebook."

"Oh! I want to see!" Caroline cooed, clearly delighted with the idea of pictures she hadn't known existed before.

And then they were turning on the TV and switching it to Internet so they could find the pictures from the past.

They went to Lucas's page, but the most recent picture on his wall wasn't of him with Blake and some childhood friend pranking kids in high school.

The picture was of him with me.

CHAPTER SIXTEEN

"The more I know of the world, the more I
am convinced that I shall never see a
man whom I can really love.
I require so much!"
— JANE AUSTEN, *Sense and Sensibility*

It was us in Times Square with the waterfall
art on the digital screens in the background.
It was the one where I had closed my eyes
and leaned in to his embrace.

Everyone in the room went from laughter
at the anticipation of silly teenage antics to
silence.

To be fair, the picture was actually really
nice. If Lucas and I had been a couple, it
was the sort of selfie that was good enough
to be a photo on an engagement announcement.

Since we were not a couple, it was kind of
horrible.

"Oh," Caroline said.

"Huh," Allen said.

What came out of Stephanie was a gassy sort of hiss between her teeth.

"Nice picture," Blake said.

Neither Lucas nor I said anything at all.

"Did you put this up?" Blake asked Lucas.

"No!" He insisted. "I don't go to Facebook. I haven't even seen the picture since we took it. That was several weeks ago."

All eyes went to me.

"I didn't post it," I immediately spat out, quick to defend myself against the guilt of creating such a public display of . . . what? Behavior that was certain to be deemed inappropriate for the workplace?

Blake clicked on the picture to make it bigger, which seemed to shrink me in reality as I sank into the sofa cushion.

The caption read, "Look what I found on my boss's phone! Looks like the company consultant consults on snuggles as well. How cute are they?"

Debbie.

Debbie had done this to me.

And she'd actually tagged both of us.

She was so fired when I got back into the office on Monday.

"Looks like you both are having a great time." The stilted words indicated Blake didn't like the close proximity of our faces in this picture. He didn't like it at all.

"Yeah," Lucas said, trying to ease the discomfort. "It was a lot of fun. They actually do this thing in Times Square. What was it called, Emma?"

"Midnight Moment," I answered, my voice too high, too strained for it not to be a loudspeaker revealing my emotional state.

But Lucas blazed ahead, either not noting the general discomfort or noting it entirely and doing his version of damage control. "Right. Midnight Moment. It's where they change all the screens in Times Square into a sort of temporary art gallery right at midnight. It only lasts a few minutes, so we really had to hurry to take the picture. So it's too bad we didn't have time to get one with Emma's eyes actually open, but we did the best we could."

He laughed. Stephanie did, too, though it sounded like a deflating balloon.

No matter what we said, the picture was a thousand words ahead of us. I wasn't caught in a blink. The camera caught me in a moment. A moment where I'd felt safe and calm and peaceful.

Lucas kept talking, trying to make it look like a blink instead of that moment. "We were already back at our hotel when Emma decides she's not done seeing the city. In the middle of the night, she drags me back out onto the streets to go see Times Square because she doesn't want to miss the Midnight Moment."

"Dragged you, nothing," I said, needing the whole thing to seem as innocent as it actually was. After all, nothing inappropriate actually happened. *Except I fell hard for my ex-boyfriend's brother,* I thought miserably. But, like Lucas, I pretended like it was no big deal. "I was perfectly willing to go alone. You were the one who insisted I needed a chaperone so the New York City thugs didn't get me."

Lucas laughed and pointed at me. "A woman with your spontaneity needs a chaperone. Who knows what trouble you'd have gotten into on your own?"

"Spontaneity? My Emma?" Blake put his hand on my arm, claiming ownership, and inserting himself into a conversation he desperately wanted to control. "You probably talked her into it. Emma never does things like that."

Lucas's laugh died. He seemed annoyed by Blake's assessment of me and of what had happened. He also seemed angry, not with me, exactly, not even with Blake, but just angry in general. Probably, if he felt

344

anything like I did, he was angry with Debbie. She'd be double-fired on Monday. He cleared his throat. "Well, brother, looks like you need to get to know her better because she *is* spontaneous when she wants to be."

His parents had moved their heads back and forth between their two sons as if they'd been watching a hypercompetitive ping-pong game. I knew this side of Blake, his need to win, to crush his competition, but I always imagined family to be off-limits when he set his targets. And I hadn't ever seen it flare up in Lucas.

But as quick as it was there in Lucas, it was gone again. He took a breath and tightened his arm around Stephanie's shoulder.

"That's really sweet of you to look out for your brother's girlfriend like that," Stephanie said.

"Right," Blake said, his eyes narrowed. "That's what he was doing."

I elbowed him.

His dad snorted and then immediately fell quiet, which made me wonder if Caroline had elbowed him.

Blake scrolled down Lucas's page. "Here we are. The pictures Gary posted." And everyone turned their attention back to the screen and pretended to have forgotten about the other post. But I knew the act was useless. No one could un-see what they had seen. I certainly couldn't.

And though it was horrible, it gave me something I needed.

Clarity.

Yes, I came to his parents' home to try to see where Blake and I stood together, but the fact was that I'd never felt that kind of peace or safety with Blake. I liked him, even loved him, but not enough and not in the way I needed.

With Stephanie tucked into Lucas's arm and the knowledge that me pursuing one brother would never be fair to the other, I understood how Jane had ended up alone at the end of everything all those years ago.

You can believe in love, believe that it works.

You can want love, want it with your whole soul.

But you can't force it. You can't force it on yourself. And you can't force it on anyone else.

I wanted love, the Jane Austen happy-ending love. But it wasn't here for me. Certainly not now. Now it was time for me to be a big girl and come totally clean with Blake. We weren't going to be together.

It was time to jump off a bridge.

Even not knowing if water or rocks waited for me at the bottom, the jump had to be made.

Some part of me wished I could slip away tonight before the festivities of the next day began and were ruined by my decision. But if I left tonight, who would open the gate? Who would drive me to the train station?

I peeked at Lucas, and, as if he felt my eyes on him, he turned to me. We both looked away at the same time.

No one.

No one would open the gate. No one would drive me to the station.

Caroline and Allen laughed at the images on the screen. They'd moved on from the Facebook page and gone to personal albums filled with dozens upon dozens of home movies the boys made when they'd imagined they could be the next Spielberg.

The movies were corny. In one, they were dressed in bathrobes for wizard robes and yarn for beards. There were several other people in the films they made, boys and girls from school, all laughing with the silliness that comes from being fifteen and not responsible for the world yet. I noticed that Lucas had a different kind of laughter. And, unlike the others, he didn't break out into hilarity at just anything. He reserved his humor like a kid who had seen a darker side of the world around him might do.

Blake's arm went around me, and he gave a squeeze. I eased out from under it, clueing him in that we were not to the place of cuddling.

Caroline glanced our direction, her face flashing with a hint of worry. She knew. Had known since probably before I walked in to meet her. I would definitely have to tell Blake as soon as possible, tonight for certain. After everything she did for me in helping with the foundation, the very least I could do in return was respect her son enough to be honest with him.

Stephanie knew, too. It was why she kept some part of her touching Lucas at every second. Though she could hardly be blamed for wanting to be where she was, I couldn't make myself not dislike her for it. She commented on the movies, made jokes about how gangly Lucas had been.

He didn't shy away from her touches or her comments but seemed to meet them head-on with the stoic resolution of a man determined to stay exactly where he was.

I could call for a driver in the morning, when the family would be readying the house for the afternoon party, when no one would really be paying attention. I could sneak away then.

But tonight, I would do as the kids in their silly movie roles did. Pretend. I would pretend a little longer that my heart wasn't breaking.

We went from home movies to a card game called Snake Oil. When I confessed to having never heard of it, everyone seemed appalled, even Stephanie, though I was pretty sure she'd never heard of it either.

"My dad and I never played games like this when I was growing up," I said in my defense.

When my phone buzzed in my pocket, I glared at Lucas. How dare he? He snuggled all night with his humanitarian girlfriend and then wanted a clandestine conversation via text? I lifted my chin and ignored my phone. I was heartbroken, not stupid.

It buzzed again.

And again.

And again.

Every time I looked at him, he was hands-free. Maybe he wasn't texting me? But then he looked my way and gave a smirk of a smile that said, yes, he was indeed texting, but he was sneakier about it than anyone I'd ever seen. I bet he never got caught with his phone when he'd been in school. I finally fished my own phone out of my pocket under the ruse of checking the time and read the three messages.

"No games?"

"Now that's just sad."

"You win Worst Childhood Award. I thought I had you beat with the stepdad taking me on drug deals, but no games???? You totally win."

I tried not to smile, tried not to let my heart pound with happiness at his attentions, but I failed. "We had games," I texted back.

"You just said you didn't."

"I said we didn't play board games or card games. We shot up zombies together in video games. Way cooler."

When he made a guffaw-snort noise on the other side of the table, we all looked up at him. Ha! Caught phone-handed!

"Put that away," Caroline said. "This is family time."

While they all looked at him, I slipped my own phone back into my pocket.

A few minutes later, my phone buzzed again. I ignored it. Then it buzzed again.

And again.

And again.

On the last one, I excused myself to find a restroom.

The five texts were all in regard to zombie games.

"Which ones?"

"*Left for Dead*?"

"*Resident Evil*?"

"*Dead Rising*?"

He ended with "*The Last of Us*? I hated that one, BTW. Stupidest ending ever. I was sorry I finished it."

I read through the list of zombie games and finally texted back, "Why are you texting me?"

A few moments later, he responded, "You looked sad. I wanted to cheer you up."

"Really?" I whispered to the bathroom. "How can he want to cheer me up when he doesn't even want to be where I am?"

I texted, "Don't worry about me. I'm fine." My phone buzzed almost before I'd hit the SEND button.

"I'm sorry Debbie posted that picture. I don't want to cause you and Blake trouble."

"She's fired," I sent back.

"Make sure Blake knows it wasn't anything. I think the picture upset him."

My phone went silent after that. I didn't respond, and he apparently had nothing left to say.

Make sure Blake knows it wasn't anything.

Yeah, right. Not anything. Just my heart

ripped out and fed to a pond full of piranhas. Not anything at all.

I planned on letting Blake know something to that effect, but it wasn't going to go the way Lucas planned. He could consult me on business, but he needed to butt out of my love life. I returned to the game of Snake Oil.

Allen Hampton explained the game. "Think slimy salesman from the Old West who goes through town selling people products they don't need. Each player takes six purple word cards. The customer for that round draws a customer card and shows it to the rest of us, who are salesmen for the round. We have to take any two of our six word cards and invent a product that the customer might want. The customer then chooses the product he or she is sold on."

A marketing game? Easy.

Stephanie paid close attention to the directions they gave me. Yep. That girl had never played before. I shot a look at Lucas and wondered if he knew she'd made the classic girl-blunder: lying to impress a guy.

I respected women who owned the lives they lived. No excuses, no lies, no games. But Lucas could pick whatever kind of woman he wanted. I wouldn't judge. Okay, fine; that was *me* lying. I was judging hard-core.

Snake Oil turned out to be fun enough to allow me to forget a little, to laugh a little, to get competitive a lot, and to win — much to the chagrin of the Hampton boys, who were working extra-hard to beat each other. More than once, Caroline had to remind them that they actually liked each other.

"I'm a marketing executive," I told them while they howled over my win. "It's my job."

"Your job is to sell dubious products to unsuspecting customers?" Stephanie laughed.

Funny how a simple card game could bring people together in intimate ways. Perfect strangers had become almost family in less than an hour. I laughed, too. It wasn't Stephanie's fault I dated the wrong brother first.

"For the game, yes. Dubious products. In real life, I sell stuff I can morally get behind."

Lucas shook his head. "I can't believe anyone voted for your animal broom."

"It helped that I was a schoolteacher at the time," Allen said.

"So why did you vote for her muscle whistle?" Lucas turned to Blake. "What does a prison guard need a muscle whistle for?"

"She had a good sales pitch. Besides, you were trying to sell a bathroom buddy. No self-respecting prison guard is going to buy something like that." Everyone laughed.

The laughter of comfort and belonging.

Once the cards were back in their box and Caroline and Allen kissed and hugged their boys good night, they also hugged me. Somehow Stephanie had escaped to the restroom during good nights, so she avoided the hug-fest. I savored the parental embraces while forcing myself to not cling too hard or for too long.

"It was nice to meet you, Emma," Caroline said. "I'm excited that we'll get to work together more on your foundation."

"It was nice to meet you, too. Thank you again for all your help today."

She patted my cheek. "It was my pleasure. I'm only sorry we didn't get some personal time to talk."

Recognizing the loaded question she'd shot at me, I only smiled and felt glad we hadn't had time to talk.

In the time it took Caroline to say good night to me, Lucas disappeared. Stephanie never returned from the restroom. I tried not to think about where they might have gone or how intimate or not intimate their relationship might be.

"Tired?" Blake asked me.

I was glad he appeared to be gauging only my own fortitude with the night, glad he didn't look tired at all. We needed to talk, and putting it off longer only made everything worse. I shook my head. "Can we go for a walk? The grounds are beautiful."

Not many "yards" were promoted to "grounds," and once we were out and walking in his, I felt maybe his "grounds" were due for another promotion — like to "state park."

An expanse of lawn surrounded a large terra-cotta-tiled patio covered by a network of pergolas. Flowered vines crawled up the sides and snaked over the trellises and hung down like fairy curtains over the back sides. Under the pergolas, tables and chairs had been set up — probably for the party happening the next day. All those chairs definitely elevated the party to an event.

They had an actual vineyard, a hedgerow maze leading to a fountain, and a lily pond not too far from where a sturdy playhouse had been built up between two sycamore trees. Blake talked nonstop about everything, about how even though he'd been thirteen when his mom brought Lucas home, they still did all the kid stuff. They acted like teenagers at school and around the other guys, but at home, they lived in childhood a little longer.

"We let ourselves give in to childish things probably because Lucas had never had a real childhood and I'd never had anyone to share childhood with. It was nice getting him right at that time, where we could still pretend and 'play.' " His fingers hooked air quotes. And then he gave me a look that said playing when you're a teen is not cool.

We settled on a wrought-iron bench near the lily pond. Actual frogs started croaking after we'd stopped moving and they felt safe enough to begin their nocturnal routines.

Blake kicked back on the bench, stretching his legs out in front of him and putting his arms behind his head. "I'm glad you came tonight," he started. "My family is pretty well perfect the way it is. It never occurred to me how bringing outsiders in could enhance that. But here you are, proving me that family can definitely be improved on."

That wasn't the perfect opening for me to drop my decision on him, but he made it worse by tacking on, "My brother is a great guy."

"Yes, a great guy . . ." I echoed. I opened

my mouth to just say it, say out loud that my feelings had shifted, that I didn't love him like I thought I did. That I was sure he didn't love me either, not really.

But the words strangled in my throat when Blake added, "He'll definitely be the best man at the wedding."

No.

He did *not* just say that.

Why would he say that? "Wedding? Wait, Blake —"

"I mean, after all, if it weren't for my brother, there likely wouldn't be any us. I was so mad at you when you left my parents' house that night. Mad that you showed up unannounced, mad that you overreacted about everything, mad that you expected me to be the bad guy in it all. But then Lucas came home and told me what a great girl I'd just kicked to the curb and chewed me out for a good hour until I realized he might be right. You were really great, definitely one of the longest relationships I've ever had, and it made me wonder if I'd let something important, something that could give me happiness, walk out of my life. When Lucas made me call you to apologize, he really set things in motion. I owe him big-time for making me see where I was wrong."

His words felt like static — the kind that came before the poltergeists. He was trying to, in a backhanded way, compliment me. But the undertone of his speech felt like a sucker punch. "Lucas made you call?"

"Yeah. He's like that. Always the first to apologize and send flowers and smooth things over. Such a lovable chump. That's why he's Mom's favorite even though she says she doesn't have favorites."

"What if Lucas had just come home that night and not said anything?" I asked. "What would have happened?"

He shrugged. "Nothing, I guess. But he told me if I didn't get smart and call you to make things right, then he was going to ask you out."

Lucas made him call me and had done so by turning it into a competition. It explained so much. And that meant it was time for me to explain as well. *Here goes the truth.* I stepped off the bridge. "Don't you think it's a shaky beginning to have to be talked into a relationship?"

He barked a short laugh that cut off when he saw I was serious.

"The fact is . . . the *truth* is, you don't really love me, Blake." I put up my hand to keep him from interjecting. "And it's okay. It's okay that we're not *that*. It's okay that we're just friends. So before you start planning on a wedding, which isn't going to happen, by the way, you've gotta ask the hard questions — the grown-up questions. Are you willing to stop flirting with other girls, even when I'm not around? Are you willing to put me first in everything you do and think and feel? Are you willing to set aside things you love because you know there is something I love and my happiness matters?" I covered his mouth since he looked alarmed. I knew that look meant he was about to start speaking over me. "It's okay, Blake. I know you aren't, and it's okay. I'm not that girl for you. But someday there will be a girl for you who is, and it would be a shame if you were with me when you finally found her."

His look of alarm turned to confusion. "Emma, I don't understand," he mumbled against my hand. I pulled it away.

"You shouldn't be with me because your brother goaded you into it. And I shouldn't be with you because I'm afraid to be alone — you were right about me in that way. My fear does come from my mother leaving me."

"I should never have said that," he started.

"Maybe you shouldn't have said it, but that doesn't make it not true."

Blake nodded. He liked to be right about things.

"The truth is that neither one of us wants this."

He opened his mouth, about to deny it, when I asked him a question. "Why did you invite Trish to have dinner with you all those months ago?"

"What kind of question —" He tried to sidestep the conversation, but I was ready for that.

"Blake. Seriously. I want to know. Not as a jealous girlfriend but as an interested friend."

"We're friends. That's all."

I waited for him to continue. When he realized I was waiting for him to continue, he blew out a long breath. "We're together a lot at work. This means we talk, and we discovered we have a lot in common and she seemed like she really needed a friend. Inviting her over seemed like a good idea at the time. That's all."

He had no apparent intention of saying anything more until I said, "I think you invited her because she really listened to you in a way I never really did. You love coming home to this place. You would only have brought someone into your refuge if that person made you feel safe outside of it, too."

He didn't deny it.

"Do you know your eyes light up when you say her name?" I continued.

"They do?" He immediately blushed at his own curiosity and tried to cover it up. "No, they don't."

I smiled.

His face burned bright red. Had I ever seen an honest-to-goodness blush on Blake before? "Am I that transparent?" he asked. He must have felt the heat in his cheeks and knew they were ratting him out, or he never would have given in so quickly.

"Like freshly cleaned glass."

We both slumped against the back of the bench as if the conversation had taken everything out of us.

"You aren't that transparent," he said. "I thought you were really into me, that you expected a full-on proposal from me this weekend."

"A proposal would have been crazy awkward. So glad you didn't do that."

We both laughed, the nervous laughter of people who had narrowly escaped something hideous.

"I do care about you," I said. "Just not in the way we both thought." I straightened on the bench and tapped my toes together, my nerves vibrating from the tête-à-tête and all that it meant. "We can still be friends, though, right?"

He put an arm around my shoulder and gave a squeeze. "Yeah. I think friendship would look good on us."

"And I think you should date your fish girl. She seems really nice."

He laughed and bumped my shoulder with his. "You do not."

"Really, I do. You already said you guys have a lot in common."

"Yeah. Well, if we're going to be friends, can you do me a favor?"

"Sure."

"Don't call her 'the fish girl' anymore. She really is a nice person and that dinner really wasn't meant to be anything more than dinner."

I nodded and apologized for being insensitive.

After several moments of silence that should have been awkward but really wasn't, he said, "Since we're being honest, her face was the first thing that came into my mind when you said I didn't really love you. I guess that means something, huh?"

I laughed. "Really? You're admitting that out loud?"

He shrugged. "You're the one who wanted to be honest."

We both laughed again, and I realized this might be the best time I'd ever had with Blake.

"What about you?"

"Me?" I stiffened. I thought about Lucas somewhere in that big house and thought about who he was probably with. "There isn't anyone."

He followed my gaze and smiled. "You may not be transparent, but you do have discernible shadows moving behind that frosted glass."

I pretended not to understand.

I pretended not to hurt.

CHAPTER SEVENTEEN

"Seldom, very seldom, does complete
truth belong to any human disclosure;
seldom can it happen that something is
not a little disguised, or a little mistaken."
— JANE AUSTEN, *Emma*

By the time I dressed the next morning, Lucas and Stephanie had already gone to pick up April. Instead of putting on the cute summer party dress that showed off my legs, I put on jeans and my dad's Dr Pepper T-shirt. The shirt offered the only emotional support available to me. I carried my suitcase downstairs so it didn't thunk on the tiled floor. Once in the kitchen, I pulled out my phone to call for a driver.

"They're out back."

I nearly dropped my phone and whirled to find Caroline with a mug of something steaming in her hand, leaning against the counter.

"Who?"

"Blake and his father. They're out back. Basketball."

"Oh. Thank you." I tucked the phone away, guessing that calling for a ride in front of my hostess would be rude.

"Do you play basketball?" she asked.

"Yes. I used to with my dad."

She took a sip from her mug, then set it down on the counter and smiled at me. "Well, then, boys against girls?"

I smiled, too. It was either that or go home and cry all by myself since Silvia had gone out of town for the weekend. "Sure."

If Blake was surprised to see me there with his mom challenging them to a game, he didn't show it. We really would be able to stay friends after all — a glad realization.

Halfway through the game, I wondered if maybe I had called our friendship too soon. Competitiveness ran like a marathon sprinter through the family. The boys didn't like that Caroline and I were up three points.

"How did you miss that layup?" Blake demanded of his father. Sweat beaded up on their faces. I ran my arm over my forehead to mop up my own mess and to keep it from running down into my eyes. "And you!" Blake fixed me with a stink-eye glare.

"You never told me you played! I feel like our whole relationship was a lie!"

I didn't remind him that it kind of was. Instead, I took advantage of his distraction to take a shot, but it bounced off the rim. Caroline recovered the ball and made a granny-shot right through the hoop. I gave her a knuckle bump as Allen recovered the ball.

But Allen stopped the game when Lucas called out, "Mom, Dad! I brought a special guest!"

Allen passed the ball to Blake, and Caroline joined him to greet the little girl.

Blake eyed me. "This doesn't mean you won," he said.

"If that makes you feel better," I replied.

"I'm kind of surprised to see you here this morning. Knowing how you hate dramatic exits and all." He lifted his eyebrows, clearly referencing the exit I'd made the last time I'd been here. "I'm glad you didn't leave. I think my mom likes you, and I'd hate to have to explain all this on her birthday. Thanks."

"No problem." I hadn't meant to stay, but he was right. I could help him save face at a family event. We were friends, after all. We meandered to where everyone else stood with Lucas's niece.

April hid behind Lucas's legs as Caroline squatted down to be at the little girl's level. April didn't speak, but her big eyes inspected the woman carefully.

"You remember me, don't you?" Caroline asked.

No response.

"What about me?" Blake said. And without allowing her to answer, he reached out and swept the girl up into the sky.

I blinked in surprise that he hadn't given her adjustment time, but if I felt surprised, Stephanie was downright upset.

"You can't just do that without her permission!" Stephanie insisted.

"What?" Blake said. "I can't hear you over little-girl laughter!"

And he was right. April laughed. She flung her arms out while he spun her around and called her a helicopter.

"Blake comes with me sometimes when I go to visit," Lucas said. He said it to Stephanie, but it felt like he meant the words for me. "Denise is afraid of him and acts better when he's around. April loves her uncle Blake. You've got yourself a winner there, Em."

I forced a smile. "He's all right, isn't he?" I approached the whirling helicopter girl and smiled at her. She tried to keep her line of sight on me as Blake spun her around. "Stop, Blake! Stop!" April called.

Blake slowed and then stopped, settling her on the ground. He continued spinning in exaggerated circles until he fell to the lawn. April laughed, but her attention was only on his antics for a moment before she turned back to me. "I'm wearing your lipstick!" she announced and pointed at her mouth. "Luc said it was a party."

I squatted down as Caroline stood up. "It is a party, and that lipstick looks amazing on you!"

"Does it?"

I nodded. "Of course. But you, my lovely girl, don't need lipstick to be amazing." I tapped her nose. She giggled and tapped my nose back.

"She's doing remarkably well for a child who just lost her mother," Caroline murmured.

"There wasn't much to lose there, though, was there?" Stephanie said with a spite that seemed to startle everyone. Lucas heard and shot a look at April to see if she had. If the little girl had, she didn't respond in any way.

Blake jumped up, brushed the grass from his jeans, and offered to show April the playhouse.

"Are you coming?" April asked me.

"Absolutely." I gave a pointed look to Lucas, unsure of how to proceed. He gave me a slight nod and a smile.

Blake and I walked with April between us, and when we were far enough away, Blake started laughing.

"What's funny?" April asked.

He widened his eyes at me and then said to her, "Nothing. Not really. Just surprised at how hard Luc's new girl is working."

"But she's supposed to be. Isn't she the —" I cut off and gave Blake a meaningful look over April's head and spelled out "C-A-S-E-W-O-R-K-E-R?"

"Yeah, well, that's not the job she's working hard at."

"I see." He meant she was working hard at catching the guy.

"But she's doing it all wrong. Insulting Denise will not endear her to him. He's loyal to a fault."

At the playhouse, we played a game where April was the queen, Blake was her knight, and I was the dragon.

Blake laughed when she made me the dragon. But April defended her choice by saying, "No one ever says dragon man; they always say dragon lady."

Blake laughed harder and promised he would never argue with such logic again. I socked him in the shoulder, but he kept laughing. The fun we had in playing together cemented the fact that Blake and I made great friends, but not great anything else.

On the way back to the house, I said, "I am glad to see you so happy, April."

"I get to see my mom today!"

Blake and I both halted, stared at each other, then stared back down at April. "What?" Blake asked, trying to keep the alarm out of his voice. Denise was supposed to be in jail. Blake obviously did not want her crashing his mother's birthday party.

"Luc is going to take me home today. He said I needed clothes. That means I get to see my mom today."

"Oh, honey," I said. I dropped to my knees in front of her and put my hands on her shoulders. "Your mom isn't home. Lucas is taking you to get clothes because you're going to stay with him for a while."

Her eyes, which had been wide and bright, narrowed and glossed over with concern. "But I have to see her." She turned to Blake. "You have a fast car. You could drive wherever she is."

I finally understood what Caroline meant when she said the child was so happy considering she had just lost her mom. She was happy because she thought they would be reunited again.

Caroline saw and understood far more than Stephanie did.

Blake tousled April's hair. "Let's find out where she is first. We might not be able to do that."

She took his *might not* as a *probably could* and returned to being happy. Blake looked at me and mouthed the word "Boom," spreading out his fingers in a mock explosion.

Lucas indeed had a ticking time bomb on his hands. We'd have to warn him so he and his social worker girlfriend could figure out how to handle the situation.

By the time we returned to the house, Lucas and Stephanie were tugging tablecloths into place and settling the flower arrangements that must have just arrived.

"Nice that you steal my niece to get out of work." Lucas tossed a tablecloth to Blake, who caught it.

Blake tugged Lucas by the arm and nodded to the other side of the tables. "Help me with the tablecloth."

The brothers went to the far end of the patio, their words a faint buzz in the late summer breeze.

I popped one of the flowers off of a centerpiece and twined the stem into the clip in April's hair. Lucas glanced my direction and then called Stephanie over.

Once there, Stephanie crossed her arms, taking on a defensive stance I knew so well. She then rolled her eyes and burst out with something that sounded like disbelief.

"She's mad," April said to me.

"Mm-hm." No reason to argue with the kid when she was right.

"She's always mad when she comes to my house. She yells at Mom a lot. And once, she dragged me to the car and made me sit in the backseat for hours."

I doubted April really had to sit for hours, but I didn't doubt it felt like hours to her. April viewed Stephanie as the enemy, which was something that had never occurred to me. I assumed all children loved the social workers who came and plucked them from the depravity and abuse they experienced in their homes every day. Showed how little I knew about how things worked.

"*I'll* talk to her!" Lucas said loudly. His declaration did not make Stephanie happy, but she gave a short nod of agreement.

While the rest of us pitched in and helped get things ready for the party, Lucas took April into the house. When they returned, she wasn't nearly as happy as she had been, but she held tight to Lucas's hand and wasn't crying.

Caroline and Allen watched the entire scene play out from beginning to sad little end, but they didn't interfere, merely observed. Caroline finally looked away when Lucas distracted April with more flowers. "That's a pretty flower in your hair," he told her.

"The dragon lady gave it to me," she said.

She said it loud enough that everyone heard. Blake laughed. I sighed, and everyone else looked confused.

"Who's the dragon lady?" Lucas asked.

She pointed at me, and Blake laughed harder. "You know, that is never not going to be funny," he said.

Stephanie gave a half smile and then pretended to be smiling at something on the table and not my new nickname.

"Why are you calling Emma a dragon lady?" Lucas asked.

"She was the dragon when we played castle. She was an awesome dragon. And she said her hoard isn't gold."

"Really? What was her hoard?"

"Cotton candy."

Lucas rolled his eyes at me. "That doesn't sound very healthy for the CMO of Kinetics to hoard cotton candy."

"What?" I defended. "I'm not eating it.

I'm just hoarding it. It's very healthy, plus it's way softer than a bed of lumpy gold."

Lucas undid the flower bouquet meant for the table he was working on. "Well, if I was a dragon, I'd hoard flowers." He twined several more stems through April's hair until she had a wreath of them. He held up a sliver vase so she could see her reflection in it.

He was sweet with her, careful in a way no one else in her life likely was. It pinged my heart to see him distracting her from her mom being gone. Memories of the ways my father distracted me in those first few weeks after Mom disappeared flooded my mind until I had to force them back so no one would see my eyes leaking out the flood of my heart.

The caterers arrived, and only then did I remember my suitcase still sat in the middle of the kitchen floor where I'd abandoned it for basketball. I hurried to fetch it and dragged it back to the room designated as mine for the weekend.

I showered and changed into that summer dress that showed off my legs. When I exited my room with a wrapped gift for Caroline in hand, I almost ran straight into Lucas.

We made awkward "excuse me" noises at each other until I finally asked, "Do you need help getting April ready?"

"No. Stephanie's taking care of it. Thank you, though."

I jiggled my head in what might have been a nod.

"You didn't need to bring a present," he said in reference to the package in my hands.

I glanced at the box wrapped in silver paper and topped with a navy-blue bow. "It's not much. Just a token of my appreciation."

"You've been working so hard, I can't believe you had time."

"We make time for the important things."

The conversation hit a lull, neither of us really having anything to say and yet feeling obligated to say something.

"So, you and Blake could do happy family advertisements," Lucas said. "You make a nice-looking couple."

I jiggled my head some more and moved past him to get to the stairs and away from the conversation. If he thought I'd return the compliment for him and Stephanie, he was wrong.

He let me go.

By the time I hit the bottom step, the kitchen was a bustle of energetic catering activity and guests were already in the backyard enjoying finger sandwiches and cakes. A DJ must have arrived because music filled the air. The whole event was festive and fun and elegant.

Caroline tossed her head back and laughed at something Blake said. They stood with several people I didn't know, but if I was staying for the party, I might as well meet some of the guests. I joined them and handed the gift to Caroline.

"Oh, you didn't need to bring a gift. Making it to fifty-five isn't exactly award-worthy."

"Then consider it a token of my appreciation for all your help yesterday."

She settled the package on the table where she could more easily tear the paper from the box as she spoke to the nearby guests. "Emma Pierce is a name you should all remember. This is a woman with a good mind in her head. She's running a foundation for Kinetics that has the potential to change lives in the best way possible. She's absolutely my new hero."

With that, she lifted the top off the box and gasped. "It's perfect," she declared and pulled out a framed picture.

The picture was of their family — a snapshot likely done with a phone by someone in their backyard. Caroline stood between her two boys, an arm around each of them. Allen stood behind her and also had an arm around each of the brothers. The smiles were big, the eyes filled with happiness. Lucas had it on his desk, and I'd borrowed it for a few minutes to scan it and put it back. I'd enlarged the picture and redesigned it so it looked like a meme, complete with a quote which Caroline read out loud, " 'I have no notion of loving people by halves; it is not my nature.' " She looked up at me and grinned. "*Northanger Abbey.* Jane Austen."

"You didn't," Lucas said from behind me.

I turned and tilted my head to the side. "I did."

"Why are you giving my mom Jane Austen quotes?"

Caroline scoffed. "Why shouldn't she? I love Jane. That woman was the greatest feminist who ever lived. She was years before her time. She did more for the cause of womanhood than even Virginia Woolf."

Some of the people from the party laughed. Many others applauded.

"You tell them, Caroline!" someone called.

"Feminist? She taught women that they had to get a husband to be happy." Lucas looked so scandalized I thought he might never forgive me for bringing Jane into his home.

But Caroline wasn't having any of it. "No, society taught them that, and there's nothing wrong with wanting to be in a healthy, functioning, loving relationship. What Jane taught women was that it was okay for them to read, for them to think, for them to not play the coquettish little games other women played. She taught them to be moral and smart and that their opinions mattered. And she did all that under the form of basic entertainment where the men would have no idea that a subversive revolution was happening right under their noses, where even the women had no idea that their minds were being enlarged and their prospects expanded. I had a professor tell me that Jane Austen took the pen out of the hand of man and proved it fit into the curve of a woman's fingers as well. She opened the door for women to write their own stories and to not be afraid to own the task. Yes, she was a feminist. And don't you dare bad-mouth her on my birthday."

"Sorry, Mom." Lucas managed to show some humility to her, but he rolled his eyes at me.

Caroline officially joined the ranks as one of my favorite women in the world.

Caroline thanked me, hugged me, thanked me again, and made me feel like I'd given her the best gift ever.

Lucas was called away when Stephanie and April arrived on the scene. Stephanie kept trying to hold April's hand, but the girl avoided Stephanie's hand as if she was playing dodgeball. Lucas took April's hand instead, which April allowed without argument or complaint. I watched as he took April onto the dance floor and let her put her feet on his shoes so he could dance her around.

"Want to dance?" Blake asked, startling me.

"Sure. Yes."

We joined Lucas and April and several others who were already moving to the music. And the afternoon passed that way: dancing, laughing, eating, and watching.

Watching at least on my part. At one point in the party, Lucas danced with Stephanie, reminding me how he had danced with me, how he had placed my hand against his chest, how his heart had pulsed a steady rhythm into my palm, how the heat between us had felt searing, how I'd almost kissed him.

I gasped with that memory and had to look away.

Because Lucas was with Stephanie, for one thing. And even if he wasn't, Lucas was not the sort of guy who would date a woman his brother had dated. All of his urgings for me to go back to Blake, all those myriad compliments on Blake's character and stories of Blake being the hero, those were the billboards in my life telling me the way things were. Lucas would only ever allow himself to see me as someone for his brother. Even if he felt the attraction between us, he would never act on it, and I would never ask him to.

Blake and I were dancing to a slow song when he tensed. I turned my head to see what it was that turned him into a statue and saw a woman entering the patio and being greeted by Allen. "Who's that?" I asked.

His eyes were filled with a mixture of guilt and also longing. He didn't answer, but I figured it out. "Trish?" When he nodded, I smiled. "You should introduce us."

His eyes snapped from me to Trish and back to me. "Are you kidding?"

"No. I'll be nice. I promise. And then I think you should ask her to dance."

He was shaking his head before I even finished the sentence. "That's a terrible idea." But then he said, "How do I look?"

I checked out his freshly shaved jawline, smooth and strong, and his brown hair, perfectly molded the way he liked it. Lucas's hair always seemed to be tousled by the middle of the day because he had a nervous habit of running his hands through it when he was thinking.

"You look perfect, like always. Come on." I stepped out of his arms and let him follow me to where Allen and Caroline were talking with their newest guest.

Caroline smiled at me and said, "Trish, we'd like to introduce you to Blake's —"

"Friend," I interrupted before she could toss the word *girl* in front of it. "Blake's friend." I shook her hand. "I'm Emma Pierce. I also work with Blake's brother, Lucas."

"It's so nice to meet you." She had a good handshake, the kind that was respectable in the business world. "My name's Trish Waters. I'm so sorry I'm late."

I tossed a playful look to Blake and said, "It's so nice to meet you, Trish. And don't worry about being late. It's *no big deal.* You're just in time to try the fish." I winked at Blake, who looked like he might either throw up or throttle me.

"Thank you!" she said. "I love seafood."

I smiled wider when I heard Allen mumble, "I don't remember ordering seafood."

That was my cue to leave. I turned my smile to Blake's parents. "Thank you for having me. It's been a fabulous day. I haven't had family interaction for a long time." My throat started to burn and close off. Seriously? I was going to cry now? I swallowed hard and continued, "Anyway, I think I'm going to take off. I have a lot of things that need my attention."

"How are you going to get home?" Caroline asked.

I waved away her concern. "Calling a driver is easy. No worries."

Blake pointed Trish to the food tables and whispered he'd join her in a second. He fished his key ring out of his pocket. "Don't call a driver. You can take my car. I'll pick it up from you later."

"You're letting me take the Audi?" I looked back at Trish. "It must be love."

"Don't tease," he said.

"I'm not teasing. I like her. And I'm not teasing about that, either."

"What's going on?" Caroline asked.

I gave her another quick hug. "Blake and I are just too good of friends to be in a real relationship. Besides, there's a special someone he actually blushes for when he looks at her." It was a low blow to rat him out for blushing, but it was true. His face looked like he had a sunburn.

Caroline smiled. "I assumed as much between you two, but that doesn't mean you have to leave."

I couldn't help it. I sketched a glance to Lucas talking with Stephanie, and to April, whose eyes had grown darker and sadder as the afternoon progressed. "I really do need to leave," I said.

April looked up at that exact moment and saw me watching her. She tugged on Lucas's untucked shirttail, said something, and pointed in my direction.

Panic overcame me, and I said to Caroline. "I really, really have to go." Whatever April wanted, she would have to want it from someone else because I couldn't be where Lucas was any longer.

Caroline put her hand on my arm, detaining me for those precious moments where I could have escaped. "Well, it looks like someone wants to say good-bye first." She finally let go of my arm, but when I turned to escape, Lucas blocked my way entirely.

"Hey, Emma, we kind of need a favor."

By *we,* he meant him and Stephanie since Stephanie was right on his heels.

Caroline gave me a sneaky grin as she slinked off to the table where Trish was looking for fictional fish. Lucas's mom was entirely too smart for her own good. And for mine.

"Favor?" I snapped.

"Will you come with us?" The favor came from April, not from Lucas or Stephanie.

I blinked and looked down into the eyes of a little girl who was asking something of me that I did not want to give. Going anywhere with them in a car . . . to sit in the backseat and possibly see Stephanie reach her arm over Lucas's seat and run her fingers through his hair while he drove was more than any one human could ever stand. Wars were fought with less provocation.

"I'm actually leaving." I jingled Blake's keys as proof. "Sorry, sweetheart." My chest tightened as I apologized to her, this girl who had lost her mom and who had no dad to tell her stories at night or make up games to take her mind off the bad things in the world.

When her eyes darkened with that familiar disappointment, I gave myself an internal kick. "Go where?" I asked, giving in slightly.

Lucas answered. "We need to go back to Denise's apartment to get April's clothes and toys she had to leave behind when — when they took her to the temporary home.

Denise was crazy late on rent and chances are good that everything will get thrown out if we leave it there much longer. April will be better if she has things that are familiar to her. I don't want her to lose anything else."

His eyes were pleading for me to just go with it, and while I could totally get behind what he was doing, I had no idea why any of it included me.

"April refuses to go unless you're coming, too," Stephanie filled in, not looking any happier about the plan than I felt. "She wants to show you the city from her room window."

I remembered how far Denise's apartment had been from the Hampton's house. It wasn't nearby at all. And going with them meant I would have to come back here and try to leave all over again. I felt emotionally scoured and not up to a round two of good-byes.

"I'll come, but I have to take my own car," I said.

"Can I go in your car?" April perked up at the idea.

"No, honey," Stephanie said. "The law says you can only go in cars that have been legally authorized to take wards of the state."

You could almost see prison-cell bars in Stephanie's words. I didn't blame April for not being happy.

"But I'll follow right behind you the whole time," I said, trying to smooth over the big "no" from the state.

With that settled, I ended up in the garage glancing over the gauges of Blake's Audi so I knew where important things were, like lights and wipers and radio dials. Then I backed out in preparation to follow Lucas.

The state rules make sense, I thought while easing through the Hampton gates. So why did it bug me so bad when Stephanie announced them to April?

Maybe it wasn't the announcement so much as it was that she took Lucas's hand for support while she made that announcement.

Could you shoot the messenger not for the message but simply because you really didn't like the messenger?

"You're not being fair," I chastised myself. "If you met her without the Lucas attachment, you'd probably like her."

This was the sort of self-talk that accompanied me on the entire trek to Denise's ghetto apartment building. I parked the car, got out, locked the door, saluted the baggy-pants gang on the street, feeling more confident that they wouldn't attack the car this time than I had last time, and waited for Lucas to unbuckle April and carry her to me.

I wanted to ask how Stephanie got a key to the apartment, but didn't. It wasn't my business, and I didn't want to talk to her. As soon as Lucas put April down, she bounced over to me, grabbed my hand, and said, "C'mon! C'mon! The dragon lady has to see everything."

Lucas chuckled at the nickname. April dragged me up the dirty stairs, past piles of litter in the corners of the landings, not seeming to notice the smell of body odor and urine soaked into the fibers of the frayed carpet that had worn to flooring underneath. April didn't seem bothered by the juxtaposition of the house she'd just been in and this place she called home. She was blind to all of it.

In her hallway, she patted her palm against the door in a knocking pattern as if she anticipated someone might actually answer, as if she hoped it would be her mom.

I froze in the hallway, watching her tiny palm tap-tapping the door, and tried to blink away the memory of me tap-tapping a different door in a different time and place. An echo of the voice that might have been mine when I was five called out to that door in my past. "Mom? Mom? Are you in there?"

My eyes burned. Why was I here in this place that opened up wounds and let them bleed out all over the floor?

"Emma?" A voice called me back from my past self, reminding me that this door didn't lead to my mom's bedroom. The hand tapping wasn't mine. "It's in here, Emma."

Stephanie unlocked the door and swung it open. An unpleasant smell from the apartment swept into the hallway. Denise had been arrested while there had been perishables on the kitchen counter.

April took my hand and led me through the land mines of clothes and empty pizza boxes and beer cans and into a room that wasn't much cleaner. The difference was in the type of clutter and dirt. This was a little girl's clutter. Pink clothes, various collections of rocks, feathers, seashells, and bits and pieces of debris likely located on the street and brought up to be counted as treasure.

"Wow," I said. "I hoarded cotton candy, but you hoard actual treasure! Look at those shells!"

She showed me each one while Stephanie and Lucas decided what to take and what not to take. Then April showed me the view from her window and told me how I could fly up here and visit her since I was a dragon and had wings and everything.

They filled garbage bags since no luggage could be found in the apartment. Lucas hauled the bags to the door as they were filled. Stephanie tried to get April to tell her what she most wanted from the room.

The whole scene broke my heart. Every garbage bag Lucas set by the door reminded me of the day Dad had taken garbage bags out of his bedroom and dumped them on the curb for some Boy Scout troop to pick up and haul away to Goodwill. Stephanie's voice explained the rules of the state. And I knew she meant well and that the rules were important to keep everyone safe, but it all sounded like lectures. Too much. It was all too much, and I didn't know if I shouted it out loud or only in my head when I said, "Enough!"

Stephanie fell silent.

Lucas came in to see what had happened.

I must have said it out loud.

I squatted down to be at April's level. "It looks like you guys have everything, and I've got to go, sweetie. I don't think I'm feeling too well. I loved getting to see you again, and . . . I have something for you." I reached in my purse and found another lip gloss. "This one has a little pink in it because some days a girl just needs pink, right?"

April nodded as if I'd imparted a great truth.

"You be good for your uncle." I didn't allow myself to glance at Lucas. "He knows all about the things you're going through, and he'll help make it all better. He might even be able to slay dragons better than Sir Blake. I'll see you later, okay?"

"When?" she asked as I straightened.

"When?"

"When will you see me later?"

I pursed my lips. Making a promise I couldn't keep was not okay. People couldn't be in and out of children's lives like that. It wasn't fair.

I finally met Lucas's gaze. He stood silent, not helping to fix anything or smooth anything over. "Lucas works with me," I finally said. "In my office. There's a company picnic next weekend at the beach. I bet if you're really good, and if he doesn't already have plans, he'll bring you. But if he has plans already, we have to respect that. We can't make promises for other people to keep because that's not fair." This whole apartment was a testament to how not fair it really was.

Lucas nodded. "We'll be there."

"Well," Stephanie said, stepping forward, "he might have to be involved in court proceedings. So let's try to keep calendars open and flexible by not making promises we can't keep, shall we?"

"Right. Sure," I said. "Then I guess it's good-bye, Queen April."

She nodded but didn't cry. How was she not crying when I wanted to so much?

"Good-bye, Lucas."

Not waiting to hear his reply, I left, abandoning the apartment with a fervor I imagined my mother felt when she left our house. I had to get away.

I never wanted to come back.

CHAPTER EIGHTEEN

"Till this moment, I never knew myself."
— JANE AUSTEN, *Pride and Prejudice*

I sat in my car for a moment, practicing the deep breathing the yoga instructor at the office advised. Since it didn't seem to help, I pulled out onto the road.

"Let's try to keep calendars open and flexible by not making promises we can't keep, shall we?" I said to the windshield, mocking Stephanie's voice.

"How can he like her?" I yelled to the traffic that didn't seem to care. I'd been driving almost twenty minutes before my phone rang.

It was probably Jared. Dear, sweet Jared, who liked to call on weekends and get me to do work-related tasks even though I was at home.

Please, Jared, I thought as I answered the phone without looking at it. *Give me some-*

thing else to do and think about.

"Hello?" I said.

"Do you have April?" The panic on the other end was like ice water in my veins.

"What do you mean do I have April? I left her with you. What's going on, Lucas?"

The moment of silence said he was processing the news, that he really believed I had her, and now he didn't know what to do. "She's gone."

"Gone where?"

"She disappeared about the same time you left. I thought she was with the next-door neighbor lady who came out to show April her new kittens. But the lady said she hasn't seen her since then."

"That was like a half hour ago!" I yelled.

"I know! Don't shout at me! I know!" He yelled back.

"Have you called the police?"

"No. Not yet. I thought we could find her without getting the police involved."

"You need to call the police, Lucas. This isn't the time to be protecting your precious Hampton name. This is the time you put her needs first."

"That's what I'm trying to do! This has nothing to do with protecting the Hampton family. This is about protecting her! I don't want to create a circus for nothing, especially since she's already been through so much. If I call the police and they decide I'm negligent —"

"So you're trying to protect yourself?" I cut him off at the same time I cut off a driver on the freeway as I jerked the car into the exit lane.

"No! I'm trying to protect *her*! Look, Emma, I know I don't mean anything in your life. But I need help. I don't know where else to look. I don't know what else to do. She was here, right next to me, when we stopped to look at the kittens. Then I started hauling down the bags of her stuff, and the next second April was —"

A truck must have rambled by him on his end because his last word was swallowed by a rushing roar of noise. He didn't have to repeat it. I knew that word intimately.

Gone.

"Stephanie says if I call the police, they might think I can't take care of April and they might take her away and put her with people like she was the last few days, people who won't understand why she cries so much, or won't know that she needs her orange octopus to go to sleep, or won't know that she doesn't act out because she's bad but because it's the only way she knows how to get attention."

"I'm sorry. Let's figure this out."

He was obviously still searching while I peppered him with questions. Where was Stephanie in all this? Why hadn't Stephanie been watching? I shouldn't have done it, but I used the moment to unload all my dislike of the woman.

He told me all the places he'd looked. I gave him a few ideas on where else he should try. After we'd exhausted every possibility we could think of, he groaned in defeat.

"I'm sorry, Lucas," I said softly as I put the car into park and stepped out of it. "I know what she means to you. I'm sorry I sometimes get judgmental and irrational. I didn't mean to be accusatory about the whole police thing."

"You're right, though," he said after a moment. "Her safety has to come first. Never mind. You're right. I'd rather have her safe even if she's safe with someone who isn't me. I'm sorry I wasted your time. I'll call the police. I can't do this alone."

I hung up on him.

"That's why I came as fast as I could," I said loudly enough to be sure he heard me.

His head shot up, and his pale blue eyes seemed almost gray as they widened in surprise. His cheeks were wet, and his eyes were rimmed red in his ashen, worried face. He stuffed his phone in his pocket and reached out to me. I closed the distance between us and gave him a quick embrace before pulling back and taking control of the situation.

"Ten minutes," I said. "I'm giving us ten more minutes to search this place before we call the police. I don't care what your stupid girlfriend says."

He agreed immediately. We entered the building together, went to the floor where Denise's apartment was located, and began knocking on doors.

"You already checked her apartment, right?"

He shook his head. "There's no need. We'd already locked it by that point, and it's still locked. She couldn't get in without a key."

I nodded my understanding as the cat lady from next door answered our knock. Our hope was that April had gone back into the apartment full of soft little fur balls. Lucas had already been there, already explained how April was missing, how he hoped maybe she'd slipped inside.

The neighbor opened the door wider to allow us entrance again.

I held back and looked down the hall to

where I had first seen April and Denise. Instead of following him in, I said, "I'm going to keep checking out here, knock on a few doors. Maybe she has friends on this floor."

He agreed and hurried into the apartment, anxious and hopeful that maybe April really had slipped inside between now and the time he'd checked before. But I didn't think so. When my mother left my father and me, the only thing in the world I wanted was to be close to her. Neighbor friends were entirely unimportant.

I quickened my pace, as anxious as Lucas to find her, to hold her, to verify her safety with my own eyes. I wondered for the millionth time since Lucas had called me what Stephanie was actually doing instead of helping. At Denise's door, I tried the handle.

Locked, just as Lucas had said. What had I really expected? That it would fall open and I would be the one to save the day? In desperate futility, I jiggled it harder, accidentally dropping Blake's car keys. When I bent to pick them up, a hot breeze from the one-inch gap under the door swept over the back of my hand.

A breeze that could never have come from anything except a window opened full and wide.

A window left open when the police took Denise away?

Unlikely.

Even a lousy slumlord like the one who obviously owned this building would never leave a way for squatters to get inside. He would have been through the place as soon as he saw Denise hauled off in handcuffs.

And I hadn't remembered the hot wind from the outside blowing in when we'd come in the first time. The apartment had smelled bad because it had been closed up.

I put my palm on the door, holding it there for several seconds while I wrestled with my own inner demons, and then I tapped. Not hard, not loud, just a patter of my palm against the wood.

"April, baby. I know you're in there. I just want . . ." What? What did I want? "I just remembered I forgot to hug you good-bye."

The words felt like they were ripped out of somewhere deep in my soul and dragged out my throat. They were the words my mother never came back to say, the ones I wanted so desperately to hear.

"I just remembered I forgot to hug you good-bye."

I swallowed the sob that wanted to follow the words up my throat and focused on the child of the present, not the one from the past. "Can you let me in and give you a hug? I promise to be a good dragon lady and count your shells and rocks for you so you can keep track of your hoard." The lock clicked, sending a vibration through the wood and into my palm.

She'd unlocked the door.

I turned the handle and let myself in.

She stood in the middle of the messy room as if she had unlocked the door and then backed away, as if she thought a real dragon might come through her door instead of just me. I went to my knees and held out my arms.

She didn't run to me or anything dramatic. But she took a step forward. Then she took another one. Each step came slowly, after much deliberation on her part. Finally she was close enough that I wrapped my arms around her and tucked her into my lap.

"You. Are. One. Amazing. Kid," I said into her hair. "How did you get in here?"

"My bedroom window," she whispered.

I squeezed her, so relieved to have her in my arms, so relieved something bad hadn't happened. "How did you know you could get in that way?"

"The lock's broken. It's always been broken, which scared me sometimes since bad guys could come in if they knew, but it was good, too, because Mom accidentally locked me out a lot."

Her words reminded me of things I had forgotten. "My mom accidentally locked me out sometimes, too."

I didn't let her go as I pulled out my phone and texted Lucas five words. "I've got her. Her apartment."

Lucas burst in on us almost at the same instant I sent the message. "April!" He cried real tears, his nose and eyes a leaky disaster. I loosened my arms to let her go, but she stayed in my lap. Lucas, not deterred by any of it, fell to his knees and wrapped his arms around both of us.

After a moment, he let us go and texted Stephanie. His phone buzzed with a flurry of incoming messages, but I didn't know what they said. I didn't ask, and he didn't volunteer the information. But whatever it was she said in return did not make him happy.

When Stephanie showed up at the apartment, she glared at me. "So you did have her."

Lucas stepped between the two of us, which was a good thing since it would have been a shame for April to have to watch me get hauled to jail for assaulting someone.

He grabbed Stephanie by the arm and dragged her into the hall. They talked in low voices, but there was no doubt that Stephanie held me accountable for the entire adventure.

Realizing I couldn't stay on the floor forever, holding and rocking the tiny kindred spirit in my lap, I kissed the top of her head and said, "Well, I really do have to go now. Thank you for letting me hug you."

"Will you try to see me again?" she asked.

"Yes. I'll try." And I meant to keep that promise. Blake was still my friend. Lucas did still work with me. I would try.

"Okay." She stood up and waited for me to do the same, which was harder for me since she'd cut off the blood circulation in my legs, and we went to the hallway.

"It's my job to protect her," Stephanie said.

Lucas surveyed Stephanie carefully. "Well, you didn't do your job any better than anyone else here. And it isn't your job. Maybe it is sometimes, but not today. Today, she is in my custody, my care. It's my job to protect her."

That didn't sound like the beginnings of a promising relationship.

I passed April's hand to Lucas and mouthed, "Good-bye." I didn't look at

Stephanie. And with that, I left the apartment building.

The long drive home was good for me. It cleaned out my head in a healthy kind of way. I thought of Blake insisting that his having Trish over for a fish fry was not some manifestation of my mother's abandonment.

I'd been mad at him.

But he was right.

Everything was a manifestation of that abandonment in some way or another. And admitting it and dealing with it was better than bottling it up and leaving that door closed.

By the time I pulled Blake's car into my garage, I felt cleansed. Things were going to be okay. I didn't get the guy, and, yeah, that kind of sucked, but there were worse things. My life wasn't terrible. I did have love in my life, and I could give love in my life.

I could also choose who got my love and who didn't. I unfriended Debbie on Facebook, immediately after untagging myself from the picture she'd stolen from my phone to post.

Though Silvia was out of town, I called her, just in case wherever she was happened to be terribly boring. She answered, said she was visiting her Aunt Bridget, who collected Beanie Babies and still believed they were valuable, and assured me that my emergency was important. She kept using words like "emergency" and "urgent" and "I really have to go." So likely her aunt was listening, and Silvia was using me to get out of whatever it was they were doing.

"I'll be there in an hour," she said.

She made it in forty minutes.

She filled me in on her new job, which sounded like she had some working up the ladder to do, and I filled her in on my relationship status, which also sounded like I had some working up the ladder to do. We also made cheesecake. Because cheesecake.

"What if it's a genetic defect?" I asked after confessing I wasn't at all heartbroken over breaking up with Blake. "I mean I just handed him off to the next girl as if he was an old Frisbee. What if I'm not capable of staying committed to other humans?"

"Just because your mom is an expert leaver doesn't mean you are destined, or genetically coded, to abandon your own future family. You are not her. She is not you. You choose your own way." She fixed me with her "do not argue with me, young lady" stare. There was something about a glass eye that made such an expression far more intimidating. We'd had this discussion on several occasions before, and she'd always talked me off the ledge.

"Besides," she reminded me, "you haven't mentioned anything about Lucas. I'm pretty sure we'll find evidence of your human commitment with that discussion."

So we discussed it. When the raspberry-drizzled lemon cheesecake was nearly gone, Silvia said, "The only thing I am getting out of all this conversation is a lot of blah-blah-blah, Emma Pierce loves Lucas Hampton. Then some more blah-blah-blah and some more Emma Pierce loves Lucas Hampton. In all of this blah-blah-blah, you've given me Stephanie, who is too clinical and competent at her job to be real competition for you, and Blake, who gave you the most amicable breakup ever. I wouldn't be surprised if you guys continued to send Valentine's Day cards to each other. Really. You two are kind of disgusting. I expected a better brawl out of you than that."

I shrugged. Our disgustingness could not be denied.

"Do you know what Jane would do —"

"I don't care what Jane would do," I interrupted loudly enough that I startled myself. "All of this is her fault anyway! She handed us men like Darcy and Knightley, who are so perfect that no other man can possibly compare to them. She filled us with all these false expectations, and we end up disappointed time and time again because men in real life aren't like the guys Jane has indoctrinated us into believing actually exist. And the women Jane wrote about don't exist either. I'm not a Miss Bennett or Miss Woodhouse. I'm a broken, motherless human! My mistakes aren't endearing. They aren't clever. They aren't going to get me the guy. And let's be honest — they aren't all that endearing with her characters either."

"If you criticize Lizzy, our friendship is over," she said, stopping me before I went to the obvious target.

So I shifted to the next obvious, the target that I'd taken so much pride in being like. "Emma Woodhouse is a prejudicial gossip," I started and hated myself for saying such a thing out loud. "She thinks she's the Sherlock Holmes of polite society, but she sees everything *wrong.* She sees people as they seem, not as they really are. *Seeming* and *being* are not the same thing. Emma's an idiot. And I'm just like her, Silvia. I see people as they seem, not as they are, and that's what's landed me in this mess of my life. Only, unlike Emma Woodhouse, this person" — I jabbed a thumb at myself —

"this Emma Pierce doesn't get to win in the end. Jane has sent me on a fool's errand by making me believe that love works. It doesn't."

Silvia watched me as I ranted. Her eye followed me as I jumped up from the table and paced in tiny circles and spouted all the reasons Jane was bad for me. I ticked the reasons off on my fingers until I ran out of fingers. Silvia took a few bites of her cheesecake as if I'd become the entertainment.

"Seriously, Sil. None of her characters exist in the real world." I swallowed the disappointment hard. None of them existed. No Darcy would love me. No Knightley would forgive the flaws in my character.

Silvia took another bite of her cheesecake while I panted off the excess adrenaline. Disappointment scratched down my throat, raw from ranting.

"You're wrong," she said calmly. "The women Jane wrote about totally exist. I've met my fair share of Lydia Bennetts, Fanny Dashwoods, and Caroline Bingleys, and I've met my share of George Wickhams and Frank Churchills, too. Austen did a pretty good job of describing people accurately."

She had me there. "Yeah. All the crummy ones. What about the good ones?"

Silvia smiled, which was all she had to do

to prove her point. My sweet Silvia. She was one of the good ones, the Elinor Dashwood, the Jane Bennett. The good girls existed. Good guys existed, too. I was just angry because the one good guy I wanted didn't want me back.

"But Jane Austen died an old maid," I said, not willing to let go of my angst. "So what does she know? Nothing. That's what! I thought I could break up with her and still watch her movies and read her books, but I can't take the brainwashing anymore. If she hadn't been filling my head with romantic myths, I would likely have a better head on my shoulders. I wouldn't be in this mess."

"Romance is not a myth." Silvia frowned and amended her statement with, "Sure, it feels like a myth, but it isn't."

"Prove it," I said.

"What do I have to prove? You — *you* can prove it."

"How am I supposed to prove anything?"

"If you think romance is a myth, then you can prove it by telling Lucas how you feel and seeing what happens."

I considered all the ways that conversation could be the worst thing to ever happen to me. I shook my head. "I don't think I want to prove it."

"Exactly!" Silvia jumped up from the table and took my place of pacing and gesticulating wildly with her arms. "Because deep in your heart you know Jane is right. Romance is fabulous, and it's worth it! All the crap we go through, all the worry and wondering — it's all worth it if we can find that one person who makes us happy, that one person we can go to and cry with when life is bad and laugh with when life is good. That is what life is all about. It's about relationships and making them work. It's about sharing our lives with someone else so we can have private jokes and people who have to put up with us even when we're disasters."

"But!" She whirled on me, almost hitting me in the face with the cheesecake fork she hadn't put down when she'd decided to run for president of the Jane Austen fan club. "If we don't take our own lives in our own hands, we lose. This is the power of Jane, Emma. This is the truth. This is where it all gets real. Cinderella is great and all, but fairy godmothers are all talk and no action. If Jane teaches us anything, it's that we have the right to choose our own loves in life. We don't have to settle for Mr. Collins if we don't want to. And!" She fixed me with the penetrating stare of her one eye. "If you find that one love and choose not to choose it, then you aren't worthy of the Austen happy ending."

She sat down.

I stared at her. Then I laughed. The moment certainly didn't call for laughter, but I couldn't help it. "She was right," I said.

"Who was right?"

"Caroline Hampton. She said that Jane's books empowered women, and she was right. Jane Austen really was the first feminist."

"So, will you do it? Will you tell Lucas the truth and let whatever happens happen?"

I scooted my chair back and stood. "No."

Chapter Nineteen

"It is not every man's fate to marry the woman who loves him best."
— JANE AUSTEN, *Emma*

"What?" She pushed out of her chair again and rounded the table to impede my movement to the kitchen. "No? How can you say no? After that great speech I just gave, you're not going to do this?"

"No, I'm not. Lucas loves his brother. Seriously. The hero worship is borderline unhealthy. Lucas would never reach for anything his brother might want."

"But you've already said Blake doesn't want you. So what's the problem? Why can't you do this bridge jump?"

She had to put it that way, didn't she?

"Okay, you know what?" I said. "Fine. I'll do it. I'll make a fool of myself. Jump off the bridge. But you remember this the next time you're afraid to try something new."

"I always remember the bridge when I'm afraid to try something new," she said.

I stopped and stared at her, then pulled her into a hug. "I know. But if I do this, you owe me a favor."

She pulled out of the hug and looked at me with suspicion. "What favor?"

"If he rejects me, you have to give up one of your old eyeballs so I can stick it in his drink at work during a tactical meeting."

She busted up laughing. We pinky-promised on it.

When Monday rolled around, my nerves were frayed. My stomach lurched and pitched in its own personal typhoon. I showed up to work early and hid in my office, waiting for the moment Lucas would arrive and I could spring the good news on him. I'd practiced it in the mirror all day Sunday.

"Hi, Lucas. How's April? You know I would be a better mother to her than that Stephanie psycho, right?" That one made me sound vindictive and petty. No one liked a bitter woman.

"Lucas . . . I love you. Love you. Love you. Love you." Too desperate and a little on the obsessive side.

"Hi. So, that whole thing with your brother is off the table, and he has given his permission for you to marry me. I've already designed our save-the-date cards and invitations." Technically, Blake never gave his permission for anything, and setting a wedding date right off the bat might be moving too fast.

"Hi, Lucas. In vain have I struggled. It will not do. My feelings will not be repressed. You must allow me to tell you how ardently I admire and love you." Clearly, practiced declarations were ridiculous.

I gave up and decided to wing it.

When my office door opened, my head snapped up, my mind freezing with the thought that it was showtime and I still had no idea what to say.

But it was just Debbie. She looked downright ticked. "Did you seriously unfriend me on Facebook?" she demanded.

My brain thawed. This was a conversation I was up to having. "Did you seriously unfriend me in real life?"

The talk after that didn't go much better than it began. She yelled at me, though I didn't yell back. I reminded her that professionals used social media in professional ways, not to create scandalous gossip in the workplace. She threatened to submit a complaint to HR. I countered that threat with the fact that there was only one person whose personal life had been smeared online, which meant that only one person in my office had a legitimate HR claim. I reminded her that the one person wasn't her.

Only then did she apologize. I didn't fire her. I didn't even submit a claim to HR. However, we both left the experience wiser. I would never trust her again, and she would hopefully be more sensible in the future. She did promise to take the picture down.

The day went on.

Lucas never showed up to work.

He never showed up on Tuesday either. During my high-and-low conversation with Jared, he said that Lucas would be working from the road as he had lots to do for the Kinetics family that he simply couldn't accomplish in the office.

Lucas didn't show up Wednesday, Thursday, or Friday.

On Friday, I felt emotionally beaten. He wasn't coming back. He had no intention of letting me say the things I'd practiced badly but felt deeply. I wanted to cry, but the glass door made me visible to anyone in the hall. So I did something I swore to never do.

I closed the blinds and let myself feel everything.

I cried myself empty, mopped up my face,

then opened the blinds again.

Saturday was the day of the annual company picnic. Stephanie had already said Lucas would be tied up in court proceedings on Saturday, so I gave up the idea of seeing him. The thought was actually a relief.

I thought of Elizabeth Bennett declaring, "Thank heaven! I am going to-morrow where I shall find a man who has not one agreeable quality, who has neither manner nor sense to recommend him. Stupid men are the only ones worth knowing, after all." I could not help but agree with her.

Fine. If Lucas wouldn't talk to me, I would throw myself back into work and help Jared build Rome.

The day was cold, not surprising for the early October season, but I joined in the surfing competition anyway, lost to Karl, changed into warm clothes, wrapped myself in the big, fuzzy blanket I kept in my trunk, and settled by the fire.

"You don't look very happy to be here."

I stiffened at the voice.

Lucas.

A week late.

"Of course I'm happy. I have a blanket," I said.

"A blanket is happiness?"

I didn't turn to that voice, didn't want to

see those eyes. Hang Jane Austen's feminism and women taking control of their own love lives. That idea had cost me a week's worth of misery. I stared into the flames dancing over the coals. "There's a reason we describe happiness as 'warm and fuzzy' and not 'cold and sharp.' Blankets and warmth are, in fact, happiness."

"Aren't you going to say hi to me?"

I did turn at that voice. "April!" I opened up my blanket and let her crawl onto my lap so I could wrap her up in a warm, fuzzy hug.

Lucas watched us. "Nice to see you can be warm and fuzzy and not cold and sharp when you want to be."

"Did you really come here to insult me?"

He settled on the ground next to me. I was grateful everyone else was playing volleyball so no one had to witness this moment where he insulted me. Especially since everyone at work had probably also seen the Facebook picture.

"No. I came because we promised April we would."

I rested my chin on her head as she poked the fire with the marshmallow stick someone had abandoned next to me. "Thank you," I said quietly. "I really wanted to see her."

"She really wanted to see you, too. I also

came because Blake said I needed to talk to you."

My insides coiled. What did that even mean?

Lucas looked away. "April, honey, didn't you say you wanted to build a sand castle?"

She inhaled sharply as if she'd forgotten and her whole life might have been ruined if he hadn't reminded her. She scrambled out of my lap and found a bucket and shovel that they must have dropped somewhere behind me.

We both watched as April began building a castle.

"You're late to the picnic," I observed to Lucas after several long moments of not saying anything.

"We visited my parents last night and stayed over. She likes the playhouse. It took a while to get this far north. Traffic." He smiled. "But no exploding cars."

I didn't smile.

"I'm sorry things didn't work out with Blake. I really thought the two of you were . . ." He didn't finish whatever it was he thought we were. He took a deep breath. Swallowed it. Then took another one. He started again. "Blake said that maybe —"

"I love you." The interruption came as

much as a surprise to me as it probably did to him.

Whatever he'd been about to say died on his lips as his brow furrowed with the effort of trying to make sense of my declaration.

I nodded. Bridge jump and then some. "I love you. It's pretty simple, nothing fancy, just the honest, open truth for a change."

His face went through a series of emotional responses before he shook his head and said, "No. You don't."

"You don't get to consult me on my own feelings, Lucas." I felt angry. Angry that the three words were met with such disbelief, such apathy.

"You can't love me. I'm the homeless shelter Hampton. I'm not . . . Emma, you can't have really thought about this. You've met my sister. You know I have April to take care of. You know where I've come from and the baggage that comes with me. You're an educated woman. If I was a company, you wouldn't invest in me. You'd invest in something without all the mess, something like Blake."

The blanket fell from my shoulders as I twisted so I could look at him, *really* look at him. "Are you kidding me?" I jumped to my feet, dropping the blanket entirely and kicking it away from the fire to keep it from going up in flames. "If Blake really talked to you, then you know he's not an option. We are great friends. We're only ever going to be great friends. Don't give me the whole 'I'm not like Blake, so I'm not lovable' garbage because I'm really not up to it. I'm furious with you right now; do you know that?"

He stood, too, and cast several looks back to the volleyball game and the grills to see if anyone was listening. Jeremy was listening. Lucas pinned him with a look that made him turn back to the game. After he shot another look at April, he lowered his voice and leaned down to where she was trying to get the sand to stack but where it kept crumbling. "Hey, baby girl, if we go down the beach that way, the sand is wet and stickier. Want to try it somewhere else?"

She jumped up immediately, clearly trusting Lucas's knowledge of sand castle architecture.

I sighed. Were Lucas and I fighting? I felt like we were fighting. I was so mad. And so hurt. I wanted to punch him hard. I also wanted to run away and hide. I also wanted to reach out and have him hold me and never let me go.

He walked me farther down the beach, away from all the people, back toward where the cliffs met the water, where we were no longer in view.

"This is perfect!" April gushed and went to work.

With her occupied, he turned back to me and whispered, "Why are you furious?" He looked mad to find out that I was mad.

"How can you even ask that?" I demanded. "You want to talk baggage? Is that an insult to me? Do you want to play 'Who has the most baggage' game with me? Because I nearly had a total emotional breakdown the day April disappeared. I don't know how she did it, but that kid wriggled her way into my heart in a huge way, and walking away from her so that clinical, cold, unfit social worker could pretend to play Mom with her just about killed me.

"And have you even met your brother? He comes with plenty of his own messes. And can you really believe I would pick him over you because of where you both started? I *am* educated. And what I know is that no investor only focuses on where a stock began. They look at everything. Where it began, how much it's risen, and its trajectory.

"I don't devalue myself because of where I started. So what if my mom ditched me

419

and my dad? That's her, not me. And I don't devalue you because of where you started. I'm looking at how much you've risen. The fact that you've taken on a child and that you aren't backing down from that commitment and responsibility is incredibly attractive. I'm looking at your trajectory, and I see it only climbing from here. I would invest in you every time."

"But Blake —"

"Every. Time. Without hesitation, without contemplation. Every time, Lucas. And if you decide you don't really want me or care about me in the same way and this whole weird brother-comparison thing is just your nice way of letting me down easy, then fine. You can keep avoiding me by *'working from home.'* " I did air quotes.

He caught my hands.

When I tried to struggle to free myself from his grasp, he pulled my hands against his chest, his heart thumping a racing rhythm through his shirt and into my knuckles.

"You have to understand," he said. "He's my brother."

"You have to understand: *I don't care.* If you don't love me, I'll leave." The words were harder to say when his heartbeat raced under my hand. I pushed my fingers out of

Lucas's grasp so they rested flat on his chest. "But I won't leave and go to Blake," I whispered. "I'm not an object that can be passed back and forth between you like an old skateboard. I get a say in who I'm with. And if it isn't you because you don't want it, great. Fine. But you didn't have to come here and ruin a work party for me. You could've been like every other idiot male out there and broken my heart by leaving me a text message."

He shook his head and appeared agitated, enough that his answer felt blatantly obvious to me.

Lucas didn't want me.

I sucked in a breath but felt like no oxygen came with it.

I moved to pull away but before I could, he'd used my momentum to tug me back to him, and suddenly his lips were pressed against mine. Warm. So warm. His kiss was gentle, inquisitive, as if verifying my acceptance of him. All my anger fled and became something far stronger.

His heartbeat pulsed harder under my palm, finally catching up to the speed of my own. I slipped one hand around his waist and kissed him back, not gentle, not inquisitive, just a release of all the emotion I'd kept bottled up for him and from him.

For this moment.

I pressed into him, tightening my hold on him, every place where our bodies connected feeling like fire. With my obvious acceptance of him, his lips pressed more firmly on mine, deepening the kiss into something that felt lasting. Something that felt true. My eyes were closed, but I saw more clearly than I ever had before. He layered kiss after kiss over my lips, each heated one a new promise. We were going to be okay. Like that pinky promise I made to him on the plane. Everything was going to be okay.

He cupped my face in his hand, his fingers threading in my hair, his thumb on my cheek where it brushed away a tear. Was I crying? Why was I crying?

His lips moved from my mouth to my eyes where he pressed a kiss to each eyelid and then down my cheeks, erasing my tears and leaving a trail of fire wherever his lips made contact with my skin.

"I *had* to come in person to tell you I love you," he said, resting his forehead on my temple, his breath warm on my face, his lips brushing against my earlobe. "I already told you. I hate leaving messages."

I smiled at his joke. "I was so sure you didn't," I whispered, still afraid he might disappear. "Love me, I mean. You gave no indication of how you felt."

"I couldn't." Then he gave me a half-smile, straightened his shoulders, and cleared his throat. "I cannot make speeches, Emma. If I loved you less, I might be able to talk about it more."

"You just quoted Jane Austen to me." I stared up at him in wonder.

"It seemed appropriate." He shrugged.

If I didn't love him before, I was smitten to smithereens, now. I pushed up on my tiptoes to show my appreciation with a kiss meant to knock him out of his shoes.

April interrupted us. "Did you see my castle?"

We both turned to look and found a two-story castle she'd built on the craggy rocks instead of on the sand. "It's perfect," I said.

"Are you going to marry my dragon?" she asked Lucas.

He smiled. "Well, I'm definitely going to date her."

"He told me he liked dragons best," she told me.

Lucas kissed me again to prove it. April laughed.

EPILOGUE

"It's such a happiness when good people get together."
— JANE AUSTEN, *Emma*

"I cannot believe I let you talk me into this," Lucas called out from my living room, where he waited to take me to the Jane Austen ball Silvia and I scored tickets to.

I laughed and pinned a disobedient curl back into the ribbon in my hair. "You'll change your mind when all the other ladies swoon over you in your breeches and coat."

"I feel like an idiot," he said.

"But you look amazing." I'd rounded the corner and felt my legs buckle at the sight of him. Colin Firth in a wet shirt was nothing compared to my own Mr. Hampton.

Lucas turned, and if the way his jaw dropped and he stood speechless was any indication, he thought the same of me in my Regency gown as I thought of him in his costume. "If you wore that dress to work every day, I'd tell Jared I changed my mind, stay on with the company for another six months, and never leave your side. And we'd be using the blinds in your office to our advantage."

Lucas's six-month contract with Kinetics was up. Jared wasn't delighted to hear that his consultant would not stay on for a lengthened contract, but Lucas and I felt our engagement to be married presented a conflict of interest in the workplace. Jared fretted at first, but when the meditation sky room in our newest location in Boston became an attraction that brought yogis from all over the world and his empire promised to grow stronger than ever, he praised himself for being clever enough to bring together such like-minded individuals.

"You're saying you like my dress?" I asked Lucas. "May I remind you that you once described the Regency period as barbarism dressed up as elegance and sophistication. Like vampires."

"You say vampires like they're a bad thing." He crossed the room to me and pressed his lips to my throat, tracing kisses down my neck.

I shivered and had to pull away before we

got carried away. "Silvia's waiting for us with her date."

"She can wait all night as far as I'm concerned. I'm still not sure I forgive her for the eyeball-in-my-drink prank at Halloween."

"You better forgive her since she's the best babysitter on the planet. Besides, the only other people April's willing to go with are your parents and Blake and Trish. And your parents are out of town a lot, and Blake and Trish need time to be a cute engaged couple, too."

Lucas dropped another kiss on my collarbone as he grunted an agreement. The truth was that Lucas and Silvia hit it off immediately.

He appreciated how much April thrived with all of us in her life. He had received permanent custody of April since her mother ended up in prison for distribution. The beginning was met with a lot of bad days as April tried to make sense of her world, but those bad days were met with love and patience, and they became fewer until they didn't exist at all. It helped that I was there for both of them to help smooth things over. It helped that we had the support of family and friends to make it easier. On the occasions where we visited Denise in prison and saw how hard it was for her to overcome her struggles, I considered the struggles my mom might have had. Through April's mom, I was able to consider forgiving my own. Forgive and move on.

"Okay, fine," Lucas said as he pressed another kiss just under my ear.

"Fine?"

"Barbarism isn't so bad when you dress it up like this."

The kissing indeed made us late to the ball, but it meant Lucas finally approved of my decision to make up with Jane Austen. Jane hadn't lied to me. She even warned me about where deception could come from when she wrote in *Pride and Prejudice,* "It is very often nothing but our own vanity that deceives us."

I had lied to myself.

But no more. I should have known I could never stay mad at Jane, *my* Jane, when she'd had my back from the beginning. When she'd been so right about everything all along.

ACKNOWLEDGMENTS

Is it weird to admit I own a Regency gown and have daydreamed about traveling back in time to meet a particular author and have lunch with her? Probably. So I'm not admitting anything, and no, you cannot go look in my closet.

The most obvious person to mention in the acknowledgments of a book like this is the one who inspired it: Jane Austen. From the moment my cousin introduced me to *Pride and Prejudice* all those years ago until now, I have been a fan. All of her books have filled me with joy and left me wishing she had lived longer and written more. Without Jane, I don't think I would understand love, much less understand how to write about it. I owe Jane a huge debt.

I also owe a huge debt to living authors. For their love, support, and friendship throughout my career, thank you to Heather Moore, Josi Kilpack, Jeff and Jen Savage, and James Dashner. I keep writing because you guys believe I can.

It was a fateful day at a writing conference when I was approached by the editor of a much sought-after publisher. When she asked me to go for a walk with her, I had no idea we'd have a whole book to show for it a year later. Thank you, Heidi Taylor, for being so awesomely you and for inviting me to join the ranks of something so exciting. Thank you, Lisa Mangum, for pulling me out of the slush pile all those years ago and for remaining my friend ever since. You're an amazing editor. I am honored to know you.

And thank you, Sara Crowe, for all that you do for me as my agent and for sticking with me as my friend. I so appreciate you.

And, as always, an infinite amount of gratitude goes to my Mr. Wright. Thank you for being my balance and for helping me raise the three most amazing kids I've ever known. I love you even more than I love Darcy.

ABOUT THE AUTHOR

Julie Wright wrote her first book when she was fifteen and has since written twenty-three novels. Her novel *Cross My Heart* won the 2010 Whitney Award for best romance, and her novels *Eyes Like Mine* and *Death Thieves* were both Whitney Award finalists. She won the Crown Heart Award for *The Fortune Café*. She has one husband, three kids, one dog, and a varying amount of fish, frogs, and salamanders (depending on attrition). She loves writing, reading, traveling, speaking at schools, hiking, playing with her kids, and watching her husband make dinner.